Shi

MW01235272

The CleanUp

Woman

Much love,

Alisha Yvonne
06/06/09

ALISHA YVONNE

Ebony Literary Grace

The CleanUp Woman

ALISHA YVONNE

Ebony Literary Grace
PO Box 18080
Memphis, TN 38181-0080

ISBN 10: 0-9746367-1-1
ISBN 13: 978-0-9746367-1-9

Library of Congress Control Number: 2009901872

First Printing: May 2009

Printed in the United States of America

10 9 8 7 6 5 4 3 2 1

This is a work of fiction. Any references or similarities to actual events, real people, living, or dead, or to real locals are intended to give the novel a sense of reality. Any similarity in other names, characters, places, and incidents is entirely coincidental.

For

Corry, Barry, Ronnie, Julia, Nicole, Al, Keith

Acknowledgments

To GOD, I give all the Glory!

To some of the most wonderful people in the world—My parents—Charles and Rhonda Brown & Donald and Bobbie Smith: GOD couldn't have given me a better set of parents. Thanks for all you do.

To Grandma (Lillie M. Garrison): My prayer warrior is what you are. Thanks for supporting me even though I haven't written a book I'm willing to let you read. ☺ It's coming, Grandma.

To Donna L. Brown, Gregory Savage, Bryant Smith and Ronald Byrd (Siblings): Boo Boo, Rock, Li'l Big Bro, and Mr. B. LOL Thanks for your love and for all the copies of this book you're going to hustle. ☺

To Keith Lee Johnson (Author of the Little Black Girl Lost series): Thanks for your continued support, advice, prayer and friendship. It's truly a blessing to have a friend like you.

To Kay Sikes: Thanks for always being available on a moment's notice. Your editorial skills are greatly appreciated. Lunch is on me—as soon as I get some money. LOL

Thank you: Some special family and friends—(Daughters) Ebony and Imani, all family and friends, Author Pat Tucker, Author Jihad, and all the book clubs and readers who support me.

To Anyone I may have forgotten: Please charge it to my head and not my heart. I appreciate everyone who has been a part of my success and endeavors.

Prologue

*I*t was our anniversary. Dim lighting, floating candles and the soft scent of two-dozen red roses, which sat on our table, set the ambiance in the restaurant. Any other woman might've been thrilled about having dinner at Ruth's Chris Steak House in Memphis with her husband, but my wife, Glenda, sat with her mouth poked, picking over her food. She clearly spoiled the mood, which pissed me off.

"Roses, dinner, a new Lexus, and I still can't make you happy," I fussed.

She raked her pasta with her fork, never lifting a bite to her mouth. "Money doesn't buy happiness, Colby Patterson."

"You can call me Cole as you always have. Don't wait until you're mad to say my whole name. Anyway, it seems as if I can't do anything to warrant your happiness these days."

"You could give your family more of your time. I could use some help when it comes to the kids and household chores."

I looked at her as if she had lost her mind. "Are you kidding me? Help around the house how? Have you counted the hours I put in at work?"

"You say you're working. I don't know that you are?"

I threw my napkin onto the table. "Then you obviously haven't paid attention to our bank account because the digits in there suggest I am," I said through tight lips.

"Yeah, and the many blocked calls to the house and my cell says you aren't."

I sighed. "That's your guilty conscience talking because you know you haven't been putting out like a wife should. I don't have to put up with you rationing sex to me when you feel like it, but I do—so lucky you." I took out my wallet. "Look. Let's go. You're obviously not going to enjoy this night no matter what. I'm ready to leave." I flagged our waitress over and let her know we were done.

"I haven't finished eating, Cole."

"We'll get a to-go box. I'm not staying here a minute longer. All you're going to do is sulk and complain about what I don't do in the marriage. What about what I do right? Do you have any idea how many women wish they could be you and have a husband like me?"

"I'm almost willing to let them have you."

She broke my face with that comment. "Be careful what you say, Glenda," I responded, pointing at her. "You should really be careful because I have no doubt that if I wanted to replace you, I could."

"And you should be careful also, Cole. You know God can put you in a predicament to have to eat your words." She rose from the table.

I paid for dinner and left a tip with cash. Glenda marched to the car ahead of me then stood on the passenger side, holding out the keys to me. "You drive. I'm not in the mood."

She knew she had me frustrated, but I avoided further argument. "Fine," I said, taking the keys.

If she had bought me a car for our anniversary, nothing could've made me mad enough not to drive it. I drove straight to my in-laws house to pick up the kids. Glenda didn't talk on the way, and I didn't try to force her.

Once we arrived, I let her go inside to get the children while I sat in the car. Three minutes later, I looked up and saw the Carters standing on their porch, stating goodbyes to my wife and children. Glenda helped our little ones in the car then closed the car door. Just before getting into the front seat, her cell began to ring. She glanced at the small screen on top of the flip then sucked her teeth.

Glenda closed her door then rolled her eyes at me before speaking into the phone. "Hello," she answered. There must've been complete silence on the other end because she answered again. "Hello?" she screamed. I could tell by the way she peered into my eyes that she still didn't get a response.

I shrugged then drove off. "What?" I asked, glancing over at her.

"You know what," she snapped. "It was *her* again."

"Please, honey. It's ten-thirty, and it's still our anniversary."

"And?" she snapped, rolling her neck.

"And . . . do you not agree that we need to give our best toward a great ending to this night?" Glenda kept silent. "Okay then, honey," I stated calmly. "Let's consider altering the mood somehow when we get home."

Glenda's cell rang again. When her face turned sour, I could tell it was another call as before. They usually came with a message stating: blocked call. Glenda placed the phone in her lap then picked it up again, seemingly contemplating whether to answer. She decided against it, throwing her cell into her purse. For the next several minutes, she sat pouting and sighing loudly. After another forceful huff from her, I couldn't take any more.

"Do you have to do that? The kids are trying to sleep back there," I said, fussing.

She turned around to glance at them. I peeked at the children through the rearview mirror. Our three-year-old son, Gavin, had propped his head on the side of his car seat. Shawna, our six-year-old daughter, sat on the right side, snuggled next to her brother.

"Is Shawna wearing a seatbelt?" I asked.

Glenda turned her attention to me then frowned. "You know sometimes I think I hate you, Cole."

"Really?" My eyebrows rose.

"Yes, really."

"Just because I want our daughter to wear her seatbelt?"

"Don't play stupid, Cole. What did you do to *her*—break up with her one week before our anniversary? The calls didn't start coming until then."

"I don't know who's making those calls, Glenda. If I did, I'd ask them to stop because they're driving you insane."

"I'm not the one who's insane. You are, Cole," Glenda yelled. "I can't believe I fell for your pampering. Anniversary—ha. I should've known more calls would be coming in. You knew it, too, didn't you?"

"Oh, like I don't always plan to celebrate our anniversary." I sucked my teeth. "Why do you always have to start with me while the children are in the car?"

"Because I need to know, Cole," Glenda cried. She tucked a few strands of curls behind each ear, clearing them from the moisture of her tears. "I'm sick of you brushing me off about this. Who is she? And why is she saying she knows you?" Glenda's beige skin was flushed with pain, and her voice trembled. "This is the third time she's called my cell tonight."

I kept my hands on the steering wheel as I shook my head. "I'm getting sick of this. All you do is complain and play the blame game. I can't believe you'd question me like this in front of our children," I said through clenched teeth.

"And I can't believe you'd break our marriage vows. I've been nothing but good to you over the years, Cole." She cried some more then took a deep breath. "You can't even look at me, can you?"

"I'm driving. What do you want me to do? Remove my hands off the wheel, take my eyes off the road, and risk having an accident? For Christ's sake, Glenda. For the last time, the kids are in the car. You wanna argue . . . then let's wait until we put them to bed."

I looked up just in time to realize I needed to make an abrupt stop for the red light. The car jerked. Glenda clutched her chest and began sighing as if she was relieved I had managed to brake. I shook my head.

"I guess since I just scared you, perhaps you'll be quiet until we get home now," I said with heat rising from my tone.

"And I suppose you don't want your kids to hear you're an adulterer."

A car pulled up next to us at the red light. I looked past Glenda and noticed two men staring at us. I nodded at them, and they nodded back. "Will you be quiet, Glenda?" I turned to face the windshield.

"No, you adulterer," she yelled, waking the kids. "You have a family at home. We love you, Cole," she said with tears streaming down her face. "You didn't need to cheat on me."

"Would you stop saying that," I screamed, ignoring the staring men in next lane over.

"No," she yelled back. "You're a cheater."

"Stop that . . . stop it . . . I mean it, Glenda."

She yelled, seemingly with all the strength in her lungs. "Make me!"

BANG . . . BANG . . . BANG . . . BANG . . . BANG

A spray of bullets rang out, redecorating the Lexus I had purchased for Glenda with large holes and shattering the front passenger window simultaneously. I heard tires screeching as the car next to us sped away. I put the car in park then called out to my wife as her bloody body lay limp while the seatbelt restrained her from falling forward.

"Glenda," I said, turning her face to me. "Glenda!" Her eyes were closed, and she wasn't breathing. I looked in the backseat at

6

the children. Gavin was screaming hysterically. Shawna seemed to be in shock. She stared at me with wide eyes. "Shawna, are you okay?" She nodded then began to cry.

I scrambled to find my cell phone. It had fallen between my seat and the armrest. After getting my hand stuck several times, I was finally able to pull it up. I frantically dialed 911.

"Help me," I cried just after the operator answered. "I think my wife is dead."

"Calm down, sir, and tell me where you are," a woman replied.

"I'm sitting at Hackscross and Winchester Road." It was hard to hear myself talk as I tried to yell over Gavin's screams.

"Sir, you say you think your wife is dead?"

"Yes. Hurry. Two men pulled beside me at a red light then opened fire on us."

"Are you hurt, sir?"

"No . . . no . . . at least I don't think so," I said, panting.

"Can you identify the shooters?" she asked.

"No. I've never seen them before. They did a drive-by—like it was some type of gang initiation or something."

"I hear small children. How many are there, and is your wife the only one hurt?"

"Two children. I don't know if they're hurt. Just hurry. Please . . . oh God, please don't let her be dead," I cried. "Glenda . . . baby, please. Glenda, you're right. I need you, baby. Please don't be dead." I dropped my cell as I shook her lifeless body. When she didn't respond, I took her seatbelt off, pulled her into my arms, and then rocked her like I would a small child. Blood covered the entire front seat and my clothing.

"Sir?" I could hear the operator call to me. "Sir, are you there?"

I left my cell on the floor of the car. I held on to Glenda, swaying and whispering sweet nothings into her ear like I did before we got married nine years before, but Glenda heard nothing. I knew she was gone. I threw my head back and let a steady flow of hot tears roll down the sides of my face.

God, I need my wife. Don't take her from me. I need my wife.

Six days later . . .

"Aaaaaahhh, Father, no, whyyyyy?" Glenda's mother, Thelma Carter, screamed as the choir sang "Soon and Very Soon" while the funeral-home workers removed the flowers to open Glenda's coffin for the last viewing.

A church usher ran to Mrs. Carter's side to fan her and offer Kleenex. Mr. Carter cried as he watched his wife kick and scream for help from above. I imagine for the two of them, this was the worse kind of pain they'd ever experienced—it certainly was for me.

The choir crooned, "No more dying there . . ."

"Aaaaaahhh," Mrs. Carter screamed again.

I clung to my children who cried into my lap, refusing to look up at all that was going on around them. People lined up to view Glenda's body one last time. There wasn't a dry eye for as far as the line stretched. Gavin held the sides of his face, plugging his ears. I began to feel sorry my children were even there to endure such a sad occasion, but it was their mother's funeral. I sort of thought we all were supposed to be there.

All of the local news stations were there filming for the evening report. Glenda's murderers still hadn't been found, and with me coming out of the situation without a scratch, the first thing everyone thought was that I had something to do with it.

I watched as one by one, Glenda's friends leaned over into the coffin to kiss her good-bye. One of them stood out the most because although everyone wore off-white per the family's request, she wore all black. She seemed to be taking Glenda's death very hard. The ushers had to come get her because it appeared she was trying to get into the coffin, but we all soon realized she was only whispering into her ear. *Poor woman,* I thought. *Her thoughts are better said in prayer because Glenda can't hear her.*

The woman turned around and broke down to her knees. Her large hat covered her face as she bowed, hindering me from determining which of Glenda's acquaintances she was. The ushers helped carry her down the aisle, and then every friend after her broke down just the same.

"Aaaaaahhh," Mrs. Carter screamed once again.

Gavin began to cry uncontrollably in my lap. "C'mon, son. Let's get out of here."

I grabbed my children's hands then led them out of the church. I had driven my car because Glenda's family wouldn't let me ride in the funeral car. They said there was enough room for the children, but not for me. My kids didn't want me to leave their sight, so I declined the Carters' offer. My children rode with me.

I drove over to the Carters' home in Germantown—where the repast would be held—then parked to wait for the arrival of the family limo. Some of Glenda's last words lingered in my mind, haunting me day and night. I never wanted her out of my life, but based on the things I'd said to her, I'm not sure she understood my true feelings before she died. Had I known our anniversary night would've been our final hours together, we wouldn't have spent them arguing. I didn't cherish my wife as I could have, and God made me pay for it.

My very good friend and co-worker, Nick Murphy pulled up behind my car. I asked the kids to remain seated while I step outside to speak with Nick.

"Colby, man, I saw you leave the funeral. Are you alright?" he asked as he approached.

I shook my head and answered tearfully. "No. To be honest, I don't know if I'll ever be alright."

Nick handed me his handkerchief. "I can imagine your wife's funeral is very hard to swallow."

"I loved that woman, man," I said, wiping my eyes. "I still do. We didn't have nearly enough time together, and on top of that, we spent our last moments arguing. I just want her to know how sorry I am. I loved her. I would've died for her."

"I'm sure Glenda is up there," he said, pointing, "watching and nodding because she understands that. This might be cold to say, but perhaps there's a lesson in this."

I gave him a strange eye. "Glenda said something eerily similar over dinner. I said something cruel to her, and she responded that God could make me eat my words."

"I don't think Glenda had to die so you'll be sorry for what you said, man. We don't know all the reasons right now, but we do know that He makes everything work for our good."

I knew Nick's words were true, but I still wanted my wife. I regretted having taken her to dinner, and I even wondered if things would've been different had we chosen to eat in another part of town, or perhaps left the restaurant a little sooner. I turned to look at the children in the car. Their faces were just as sad as mine. More tears fell as I began to hurt for them and for me.

The limo pulled in front of the Carters' home about thirty-minutes later. Nick went to lock his car while I helped the children out of mine. We walked across the street to greet their grandparents.

Mrs. Carter stepped out of the limo, looking at me as if she wished I were dead. "What do you want?" she shrieked.

I was taken aback. I knew she was hurt about Glenda, but so was I. I offered a hand as she stepped up on the curb. "Let me help you, Ma—"

"Don't you touch me," she screamed, jerking her hand from me. "What do you want? Haven't you done enough?"

I was confused. I knew she wouldn't allow me to help plan the funeral, but I thought it was only because of a mother-daughter thing she was feeling. I didn't know she had such ill feelings toward me. "Ma—" I started.

"Don't you 'Ma' me," she said through tight lips. "My child tried to tell me." I looked at Mr. Carter as he dipped his eyebrows, seemingly just as angry as his wife. "She said you were up to no good is what she said."

"Ma, I—"

"Save it, Colby." She gave me the halt hand. "I know about the phone calls, the arguments between you and Glenda, and then some. All I can say is I hope you didn't have my child killed." She began to cry again. Mr. Carter put his arms around her.

I looked at my children who stood silently with pain on their faces. "She was your daughter, but she was my wife—the mother of my children. I never—" I attempted to finish but was cut off.

"Shut up! Shut . . . UP. She's gone, and God forgive me, but I wish you were gone, too," Mrs. Carter spat at me.

I looked down at the kids again. "How could you say that in front of my children?" I was devastated by my mother-in-law's words.

She spoke between teardrops. "I'm sorry . . . but that's just how I feel." She pointed at Shawna and Gavin. "Bring these babies around to see me, but you and I have nothing else to talk about. You hear me?"

Mr. Carter intervened. "C'mon, baby, we're drawing a crowd," he said to his wife, pulling her by her arm. He turned toward me as she walked away. "Why don't you leave the kids and just go?"

The children began to cling to my legs. "No," Shawna cried. "I wanna go with my daddy."

"This whole scene is too much for them right now," I answered sadly. "I'll bring them over some other time."

I took the kids by their hands then walked back to my car. Not only was the scene too much for the children, but I had begun to feel sick myself. My wife was gone, and everyone felt it was my fault, including my own brothers in Nashville, Tennessee. My parents were deceased so I felt I had no one to turn to. *Could time really heal this wound?* I wondered.

I sat on my bed, wearing nothing except a towel just after having
a shower. I had pulled out the old Richmond, Virginia, newspaper clippings of when my parents died in the fire four years
before—a night I'll never forget. The whole incident caused me a
yearlong stay in the psychiatric ward. I had been partying and
drinking after my parents' death, and people said I had lost my
mind. I didn't feel my behavior was extreme. Sure, I was torn,
but at the same time, I knew it was the smoke that had killed my
parents and not the fire. I was comforted by the fact that they
didn't suffer much. Still, everyone said I was insane, so to keep
the peace, I went along with what they felt was best for me.
Besides, a year of lockdown wasn't going to be like eternity.

I kept every article featuring the tragedy inside a small photo
album, including pictures of my parents and the house we lived in
during my high school years. The headline in the *Richmond
Times* read: OWNERS OF JOLLEY NIGHTS SPORTS BAR KILLED IN
HOUSE FIRE.

My momma, Della Jolley, had thought it would be cute to
name me Karma after her deceased mother. My father, Melvin,

didn't care either way. From what I hear, he had hoped I was a boy since I wasn't really his child. Momma was already pregnant with me when he met her, and according to her, he felt like he would get better attached to a boy. Although he made me call him Melvin instead of Daddy, he seemed fond of me and became the only dad I knew.

I took out a younger picture of Momma to look at it more closely. There was an extreme likeness between us when she was my age. We had the same soft, black, shoulder-length hair; the same medium-brown skin tone, and the same big, bold eyes with long eyelashes. Mom didn't take care of herself after her twenties though. I don't ever remember her looking as fine as the figure I saw in the picture. They say like mother, like daughter, but at twenty-one, I rocked a size-six frame, and I planned on keeping it that way.

Melvin must've really taken Momma down, stressed her out over the years. I couldn't be positive he was abusive because Momma never talked about how things were going between them. All I knew was that he was strict on me and Momma kissed his ass. She and I were not to go against anything he believed in or wanted.

I couldn't take staying in Richmond after the fire. I didn't feel loved by my extended family and friends, and it seemed as if no one actually wanted me there. I moved to Memphis shortly after my release from the psychiatric ward, hoping to get a new start on life since I didn't know a soul in town.

Staring into the eyes of my mother's photo, I began to speak to her. "I'm sorry you had to go, Momma, but I've realized that dying is just a part of life. Well, the part that ends life, that is. Although it didn't seem like it, I loved you and Melvin very much." I sighed. "Despite what Melvin use to say, I wasn't the only hard-headed teen in town. I'm sure that if you're looking down on me, you understand that now."

I kissed the picture then slid it back into the photo album. Tears came to my eyes as I put the album back on the top shelf of my closet. Princess, my French poodle, came over and stood on her hind legs, trying to get my attention.

"Good morning. Are you hungry?" I asked her. "C'mon. Let's go fill your bowl."

I led her into the kitchen then prepared her plate and drinking bowl. I looked at the clock on the wall and realized I needed to get moving if I was going to see that handsome, hunk of chocolate I'd been spying on. His name was Colby Patterson, and he was gorgeous. He had no idea I'd been watching him. I could count on him to have his business meetings twice a week at Swig's on Peabody Place downtown during lunch hours.

I planned to be at Swig's also, handing out my business flyers. I'd been there several times before, chilling, waiting, watching, and hoping up on an idea of how to begin living my new life with Colby. I came up with the idea of the flyers during my last visit. I couldn't wait to finally be able to speak with him. After all, we'd made love many times before in my mind. Thinking of him always made me want to touch myself, make myself cream over and over again. Sure, he was older, but that's what I found to be so sexy about him. I was positive he'd find me sexy, too. He certainly wouldn't be my first romance with a mature man. Colby Patterson didn't know it, but he was bound to be mine. I headed to the shower, thinking, *Oh, if I have anything to do with it—well, I have everything to do with it—I, Karma Jolley, am finally about to have my way.*

I sipped my tea then closed my eyes, settling my nerves as I sat at one of the tables on the patio of Swig's. My lunch guests hadn't arrived, and thank goodness they weren't on time because I was frantic while trying to get there myself. Routinely, I would arrive to business meetings before the guests, but on this day, Shawna had been acting out in school, so I was called into an immediate parent-teacher conference right at lunchtime.

It had only been six months since Glenda's death, and Shawna was having a tough time coping and adapting to her counseling sessions. Not to mention, the fact that I was hardly around for two and a half months while the district attorneys tried to build a case against me, leaving my in-laws to care for the children. At first, it seemed as though I would be tried and found guilty of Glenda's murder by any means necessary. The prosecutors were good during the preliminary hearings. I began to fear spending the rest of my life behind bars for something I didn't do, but then they finally ceased the hearings since there wasn't enough evidence to begin a trial. I became available to care for my kids fulltime again.

My daughter had become very mean, and loud noises disturbed her, causing her to have weird behavior I'd never seen before. I got the call from her school just before my break. The teacher began a schoolmate's birthday party during lunchtime. That's when a little boy accidentally burst a balloon near Shawna. She reacted by repeatedly beating the boy over the head with her spelling book. This was her third occurrence in a month. I was told to report to her school immediately or else she'd be expelled. *Therapy doesn't seem to be helping her,* I thought, staring at the building across the street.

"Hey, Colby. How's it going?" Sean Martin, the CEO of Best Tronics, yelled, snapping me out of my trance. He extended his hand into my face.

I shook his hand. "Not bad, Sean. The weather couldn't be more perfect for a September noonday in the M-town."

He took a seat across from me then grabbed a napkin to wipe his bronze-colored forehead. If it wasn't for the reddish tones in his complexion, our skin color would be exact. My skin was a little bit more chocolate than his.

"Speak for yourself, my brotha," he said. "I'm about to melt. Excuse me while I remove my jacket and loosen my tie."

I laughed. "No problem. Do what you must to be comfortable because I've got a deal and a half to work out with you. You don't want to snooze on this one. By the way, how're things over at Best Tronics anyway?"

"Man, I have to tell you, business is ideal right now. I don't ever remember having a September with numbers so high."

"High numbers are a good thing." I nodded.

"True. So true."

"Say . . . where's Janine? If Ms. Chief Financial Officer isn't here, this deal is going to go a lot smoother than I had anticipated. It doesn't take as much to win you over. Is Janine not joining us today?" I asked, looking around.

"She is, but you know women. I headed straight to meet you, and she went into the restroom first. Mark my words: she'll be out here in a minute with a ton of lip gloss on. She wasn't wearing any before we got out of the car." Sean winked.

"I don't know why she's getting all beautified. I didn't bring pretty boy James with me today. I'm the only one conducting this meeting with you two."

"Dude, she doesn't want James. You're the only one she has an eye for." He made his eyebrows dance then laughed.

I shook my head. "Naw . . . not me."

"Yes, you. I don't mean any harm, but you're the eligible one, remember?"

Suddenly I felt awkward. "Yeah, right. Sorry, Sean, but I'm already forty years old. I just don't think I can be into women older than me. Besides, she's not a sista." I sipped my tea.

He leaned in to me. "Oh, yeah? Then try telling her that. Janine is the blackest white woman I know," he whispered.

"I still can't. Almost doesn't get it for me. I'm raising African-American children. The next woman I put on my arm, if there's another—"

"If?" he asked, cutting me off. "What? Are you into men now?"

"Ha, ha . . . very funny, man. No, I'm not into men. I see you wanna have jokes, but you're not funny." I winced. "I'm just not ready to date yet, and as I was trying to say, when there's another woman, she's gonna look like my mother."

"Eew, you're sick," he teased.

"You know what I mean."

"Sure I do, but I think you're shallow to be caught up on color. Janine's a nice woman."

"Then why aren't you dating her?" Sean was silent. "Un-huh . . . just like I thought—no real reason."

"I don't have an excuse, but that doesn't mean I wouldn't introduce her to one of my friends."

"Whatever. You wanna get started with this meeting? Listen. That conversation is over?"

Before he could answer, Janine joined us at the table. I suppose Sean had worked closely with her long enough to know her well. Her lips were so shiny, the glare from the sun beaming on them damn near blinded me. Just my luck, I didn't bring my sunglasses from the car. The waitress came over and saved my day. I had an excuse not to look into Janine's face for a minute.

"I see your guests have arrived," she said, looking at me. She turned to Janine and Sean. "What can I get you two to drink?"

"I'll have a Coke, please," Sean answered.

"Tea will be fine for me," Janine replied.

"Gotcha. And I'll be right back with a refill for you," the waitress responded, looking at me before she left our table.

"So are we eating, or are we here to just talk business?" Sean asked.

"Sean, my man," I answered. "I'm surprised at you. Don't I always feed you at these meetings?"

"You do. I'm just wondering why we couldn't order lunch at the same time with our sodas."

"Sounds like someone's hungry," Janine said.

"Don't get me started on you, ma'am," he said. "Aren't you the one who kept hounding me about what time we were going to lunch?" He laughed.

Janine blushed then rolled her eyes. "Anyway . . . Colby, tell us about what you've done with the new software."

That was the cue to do my thing. I opened my laptop then gave them both a handout. "What I'm about to show you is the answer to your e-business development. Your consumers will not only be impressed, but as a thanks to you for making their shopping lives easier, they'll be loyal for a lifetime."

"Alright, now that's what I want to hear," Sean said.

Our lunch meeting went well over two hours, but my mission was accomplished. Sean and I shook hands then Janine offered me a hug, which I gladly accepted. Sean was right. Janine was a nice woman. Though she was in her mid-forties and divorced, I was sure that because of her personality, she'd find another love someday—he just wouldn't be me.

They left me sitting alone, finalizing a few notes. The waitress came over again to see if I needed anything. I declined then asked for the check. She agreed as she walked away. Only a few seconds later, I thought I felt her presence standing over me again.

"Well, that was quick—" I started then stopped after looking up to notice it wasn't the waitress who stood before me. A strikingly beautiful young woman standing about five-seven held a bright yellow piece of paper out. "Oh, hello. I thought you were someone else," I managed to say.

"Hello to you, too," she said with her arm extended.

I accepted her delivery. "What do we have here?"

The flyer had a picture of a maid in the top left corner. The bold font in the middle of the paper said: the jolley cleanup woman. I began to skim the remaining contents, but slowed down when I spotted words of interests. The ad went on to state: ALLOW ME TO ALLEVIATE ALL OF YOUR PERSONAL HOUSEHOLD NEEDS. The bullet points noted: CHILD CARE SERVICES, HOUSE SITTING, and LAUNDRY. I began to smile when I noticed the last notation: NO TASK IS TOO BIG OR TOO SMALL FOR KARMA JOLLEY, YOUR CLEANUP WOMAN. I nodded as I sat the paper down then looked up at her.

"Wow. This is nice to know, Ms. Jolley. I like how you've tied your last name in with your chosen occupation."

"An errand girl/housekeeper isn't exactly my chosen occupation. It's more like a forced one. Nevertheless, I manage to enjoy the work."

I was confused. "What do you mean forced?"

"I'm trying to put myself through school, but I don't have the finances. Housekeeping and nanny services bring in decent money . . . nothing like the cash from stripping in a night club, but decent."

"Is stripping something you've had to resort to?" I stopped myself. "Oh, excuse me. Don't answer that question. I was just being nosy."

She pasted an innocent smile on her face. "That's okay. The answer is not yet. I don't want to take off my clothes for money, but my friends who do say they can't quit. They say the money is right on time." She lowered her eyes to the ground.

Karma seemed to have a lot on her mind. "Please . . . have a seat," I offered. "And by the way, I'm Colby Patterson."

"Thank you, Mr. Patterson."

"Cole is fine."

"Oh . . . well, thanks, Cole." She sat across from me, but her attention was still drawn to the pavement.

I went into my pants pocket. "A penny for your thoughts," I said, sliding the copper piece in front of her.

She looked up at me and smiled. "Whoa." She laughed. "What do I need to give you for a nickel?"

"Five of your innermost thoughts."

"I thought it was supposed to be a nickel for a kiss."

"Hmm . . . cute. Tempting and cute, Ms. Jolley."

"Yes, and so are you."

I expected her to give the ground her attention again, but she shocked me by sharing a gaze with me. She stared at me with large, ebony eyes, enhanced with long, black lashes—the sexiest pair of eyes I'd ever seen. We must've been trying to figure each other out because we were silent for several seconds. She stood then pushed in her chair. Although her sundress was loose, I couldn't help but notice how the fabric hit her curves nicely in all the right places, and its aqua color complemented her medium skin tone very well.

"Are you leaving already?" I asked. "You just sat down."

She fanned a stack of flyers in the air. "Yes. I need to get moving if I'm going to finish handing these out before dark. I'd love to be back in Whitehaven before five this evening."

"Whitehaven? Do you live out there?"

"Yes. Why?"

"So do I. I mean, well, I live in Southaven, which is practically down the road if you live near I-55 South."

"Okay." She nodded and smiled. "Then I really expect you to take me up on at least one of my listed services. You're practically around the corner. And besides, you should look at it like we're turning each other a favor."

I folded the flyer then put it into my pocket. I stood to shake her hand. "I'll keep the offer in mind, Ms. Jolley—"

"Karma."

"Okay, Karma. Thanks for stopping by my table, and if I can think of anyone else who could benefit from using your services, I'll be sure to pass your information on."

"Great. Enjoy the rest of your day."

I stood, watching her make an entrance into the restaurant from the patio and then out the door. *The Jolley CleanUp Woman,* I thought. *She seems young, but I bet she's pretty responsible.*

When I got off work, I was running late to the child care center, and traffic was backed up for miles. "Oh, c'mon," I screamed out loud, blowing my horn. It wasn't like I could change anything by honking, but I didn't know what else to do. An hour later, I made it to the center. The director was not pleased with me. She met me just as I stepped into the door.

"Mr. Patterson, our staff loves your children, but we have lives outside of this child care center that we'd love to go home to before seven every evening. We have rules and guidelines, and it doesn't appear that you're trying to adhere to them."

"I'm trying, Ms. Potts. I really am. Sometimes my boss just doesn't understand that I can't stay over."

"Then you've left me with no other option but to terminate our services for you. Follow me into my office."

"No . . . no . . . no, Ms. Potts," I said, pulling on her arm. "Don't do that. The kids like it here. You can't kick them out."

I turned and noticed them coming down the hall with one of the teachers, so I began to whisper. "Please . . . I'm going to figure out something that'll work for all of us. I promise."

The children came and stood next to me. Ms. Potts looked at them then back at me. "Alright, but no more chances after today, Mr. Patterson. I mean it."

"Thank you. I'll be on time tomorrow. You'll see."

I put the kids into the car, but before I pulled off, I made a call to my boss to find out if he anticipated a late meeting the next day. To my dismay, his answer was yes. I drove home feeling burdened. *Glenda, now I know how you felt,* I thought. *Now I wish I had been more cooperative with transporting the kids back and forth. How did you do it for so long?*

As soon as the kids took off their shoes in the middle of the living room floor, they ran into the kitchen where I sat reading the mail. Their baby-like voices yelped for food.

"Daddy, we're hungry," Shawna said. "When are you gonna cook?"

Cook, I thought. I hadn't intended on cooking because I needed to work on the paperwork for the Best Tronics software deal. I meant to stop for take-out, but with the stress of the matter about the child care center, I forgot. I took off my suit jacket and placed it across a dining chair. Karma's bright yellow flyer peeked out of the pocket at me, causing a lightbulb to go off in my head.

I pulled out a large apple then cut it into slices for the children to snack on until I could get them something to eat. I gave them bowls then called Pizza Hut for delivery. I was told there would be more than an hour wait, which was frustrating, but I had no other choice.

I sat down at the table then opened Karma's flyer. After reading it again, I felt a sense of relief. I picked up my phone to make a much-needed call. *This woman must be God-sent,* I thought.

Karma 4

I'd only been in my apartment ten minutes when my cell rang. I started to let the voice mail answer it so I could fix me something to eat, but my instincts told me to take the call.

"Hello," I answered.

"Hello. May I speak to Karma?" a sexy male voice replied.

"This is Karma."

"Hi, Karma. This is Cole. Did I catch you busy?"

I cupped my mouth, unable to speak for a moment. "Um, could you hold on a second, Cole?"

"Sure," he replied.

I set the phone down on the couch then danced around the living room for a minute. *Yes . . . he called me,* I thought. *He really called me.* It was a pleasure to have a brief chat with the ever-so-fine Colby Patterson at Swig's, but to have him actually call me sent chills up my spine. I tipped back over to the phone. After a couple of sessions of breathing in and out, I returned to the line.

"Hello, Cole. Are you still there?"

"Yes, Karma. I'm here."

Damn, I love the way he said my name. "Great. I take it you've thought about utilizing my services."

"Indeed I have. As a matter of fact, I was wondering how soon we could draw up a contract."

I tried to remain calm, but I truly wanted to scream with excitement. "That depends, Cole. How soon would you need my services?"

"Tomorrow," he said with a little chuckle.

"Wow. I guess my timing at Swig's today couldn't have been better, huh?"

"Absolutely. I'm in sort of a bind trying to juggle the kids, work, and home. My wife is deceased, and now I've learned there just aren't enough hours in a day. I could really use your help."

"Oh, I'm so sorry to hear about your wife. I'll be glad to help. What do you say if I draw up a contract when we get off the phone, and then I'll meet you with it tonight?"

"That'll be great. In fact, since I'm going to need you to pick the children up from their aftercare program at the child care center tomorrow, you should come over to meet them."

"I'd like that. Let me get started then I'll call you back for directions. Is the number on the ID fine?"

"Yes, it's my home number. I'll be here."

"Okay, Cole. Thanks for calling, and I'll talk to you in a bit."

I hung up the phone then did the Michael Jackson moonwalk. In just a while, I would be in the home of one of the finest brothers I'd seen in Memphis since relocating three years before. I had made him feel I was in a hurry to handle business when I jumped up from the table at the restaurant, but the truth was he made me nervous. His mocha-colored skin was calling out to me. I kept having flashes of me licking his neck—probably not the norm for most women who'd just sat down for the first time with someone they'd never met.

After mastering Michael Jackson's famous moonwalk around my living room, I did the cha-cha all the way to the bedroom. I forgot about being hungry. I needed to shower then change if I was going to see Cole in an hour or so. I stood in the doorframe of my bedroom and gasped. *The contract,* I thought. *He's expecting a contract.* I'd never been a maid or nanny before and had never even met one. I ran into the second bedroom, which I'd made into an office, and then turned on the computer. The Internet always had answers.

After finding a makeshift contract from a housekeeping company online, I tweaked it to fit the services I felt Cole would need. I had no idea what to charge him, so I left blanks in many places to be negotiated. I printed it then placed it into a folder. Feeling more confident, I skipped to the shower.

In thirty minutes, I was dressed and out the door. I plugged in my earpiece then called Cole on the way. He talked me through the directions to his house, which I thought was really sweet. He could've easily just let me write them down, but he refused to hang up with me until I was in his driveway.

Since the temperature had cooled down, I put on a pair of chocolate-colored fitted slacks and a long-sleeved, v-neck cream-colored blouse. It stopped at my waist, so my hips and ass were still accentuated. The chocolate three-inch sling backs added the right touch of sex appeal to the ensemble. I couldn't wait to see if I could catch Cole's attention.

I stepped out of the car then walked to the door. He opened it before I could knock. We both spread huge smiles across our faces.

"Hi, Karma," he said, reaching for my hand.

I was a bit disappointed it was a handshake rather than a hug, but at least I was at his door. "Hi, Cole. Thanks for seeing me tonight."

"No, thank you. Come on in," he said, stepping back and opening the door wider for my entrance.

I turned around and saw him waving at someone. "Someone out there?" I asked.

"Oh, that's just my nosy neighbor, Ms. Willis. She's a widow and lives alone. I think she's so nosy because she's lonely, but don't get me wrong, she's a very sweet lady."

"Oh. Well, if you hire me, I suppose I'll get to meet her."

"Yes. Let's get going with this interview. I'm just going crazy trying to organize my life."

"Well, that's why I'm here."

Cole led me into the living room. "Have a seat." He motioned toward the couch.

His home was elegant—quite like a woman's taste rather than a man's. As I glanced around the living room, I noticed it bore a chic vintage interior design. The couch, loveseat and armchair had a floral pattern and looked fairly new with the exception of deliberate markings on the assembly wood pieces. I could tell the smudges and scratches were done in an effort to give an illusion of distressed or used items. *What man is into floral pieces?* I asked myself. Then I remembered: he did have a wife once. I sat on the couch, and he sat close by in the armchair.

I didn't see or hear the children anywhere. "Where're your kids?"

"Gavin, my three-year-old, is in his room watching cartoons, and Shawna has homework, so she's in her room studying. She turned seven over the summer, and she just started second grade this fall."

"Is she excited about being a second-grader?"

He sighed. "Shawna is going through a difficult time right now. She loved her mother very much, and life without Glenda just isn't the same for any of us."

"Do you mind if I ask how she died?"

He dropped his head. "She was murdered this past spring. Some young creeps did a drive-by on us on the night of our anniversary as we sat in the car at a red light." He huffed, shook his head, and then continued. "We'd been arguing about something stupid, and I wish I could erase the whole night because she needed to know how much I loved her. Apparently, I wasn't doing enough to show her what she meant to me, and it was driving her crazy. The kids and I miss her so much." His voice cracked.

"Oh, I understand. I can empathize with all of you. I lost both of my parents to a fire when I was only seventeen."

"Oh, gosh. I'm sure that was hard for you."

"Yes . . . very," I said, looking at the floor. "I had been out late with friends when I returned home to what seemed like hundreds of flashing red-and-blue lights on my street. I took a closer look and discovered it was my home. I was devastated. I spent my senior year of high school in foster care because I had no other family to turn to."

"That's sad, Karma. How are you today?"

"I'm better. It's still tough to think about at times, but I'm much better than I was four years ago."

"How old are you?" he asked.

Damn. Here we go, I thought. I was afraid Colby would think I was too young for the job. "I'm twenty-one, but I'm experienced—with housekeeping and errands, that is."

He looked down at the folder in my lap. "So what do you have there?"

"Oh, this is the contract." I handed it to him. "Take a minute to read it then let me know if we should add or change anything."

I was so nervous about what he'd think of the contract that I began to wring my hands. Once he finished reading, he put it back into the folder then looked at my hands. "Are you okay?" he asked.

"Yes. Why do you ask?"

"You seem nervous."

"I am. I really need this job, Cole. How does everything look in the contract?"

"Fine."

"Oh, good," I said, relaxing a bit.

"The only problem is you left out your résumé and references."

Damn-it, I thought, but almost said out loud. "Oh . . . well . . . um, I, um . . . can get those to you," I responded, trying not to panic.

His eyes were so serious-looking, and they made me even more nervous. I just knew he was about to dismiss me, but then he said, "Don't worry about it. As you said earlier in so many words, we kinda need each other. You can bring your résumé and references to me whenever you get a chance to get them together."

Whew! "Thank you so much, Cole. I will." *Now breathe.*

"Let's talk about salary so we can fill in some of these blanks."

Cole and I spent the next thirty minutes discussing details of chores, assignments, and such. We agreed on my salary then he signed the contract. I felt like jumping up and shouting, but I didn't want him to detect I'd never had as much responsibility. I just shook his hand and promised to always aim to please.

He went upstairs to get the children so I could meet them. Once the kids came down, they sat quietly on the couch with me as I told them a little about myself. I was nervous about how they'd warm up to me. After all, they'd recently lost their mother. Though they seemed well behaved, I worried things would change if they felt I was trying to take their mother's place. I let them know upfront that I would only be there as a friend of the family who helped each of them with homework, chores, and whatever ways they would need me.

Shawna seemed to be a sweet, caring child. She spoke up for her brother whenever he was too shy to answer or didn't know how to respond to me. They both had a strong resemblance to Cole. I could tell Gavin was going to be the spitting image of his father when he got older.

Once I finished talking to the children, I asked if they had questions for me, but they still didn't have much to say. Shawna did most of the talking.

"So you live all by yourself?" she asked.

"Yes, Shawna. Well, I have my pooch, Princess. She's my three-year-old French poodle. I've had her ever since she was a week old."

Shawna's eyes lit up. "Really? What color is she?"

"White," I responded.

"Will you bring her over to play with us sometime?"

Cole detected the excitement in Shawna's voice. "Yes, Karma," he said. "Why don't you bring Princess over when you come? I'm sure she'd take a liking to both of the kids."

"Oh, I'd love to. Princess loves to follow me. And don't worry, she's house broken."

Since there were no more questions, I took this as a good sign that the children were cool with my presence. I was proud that I remembered to mention Princess because the thought of having a poodle around seemed to have brightened the kids' hearts. *Winning them over from this point should prove easy,* I thought.

Three months later . . .

I wanted to ask Karma for her references, but I also felt maybe I should leave well enough alone. It was December, and she'd done more than enough to prove she was a jewel. She cooked and cleaned, washed and ironed clothes, picked the kids up from aftercare, helped Shawna with homework, and then some. Basically, Karma went above and beyond the call of duty. At times, I felt I underpaid her, but she continued to decline an increase in salary. She'd always remind me we were scratching each other's backs—or so to speak.

The kids were in love with her poodle, Princess. I purchased several dog toys and a bed for Princess once she began staying over with the children. Karma didn't seem to mind the nights she went home without her poodle. I even began to enjoy having Princess around.

Nick was tickled to know I had a young woman in my home, taking care of the kids and me. He was a forty-two-year-old divorcee, and let him tell it, he'd been in celibacy since his wife left him nearly two years before. I never liked being a judge, but in keeping it real, a lie was nothing for Nick to tell.

After a long day at work, I locked my office to go home. Nick called out to me.

"Colby Patterson, whatcha know good?" he said.

"Not much, Nick." I turned and was startled by him. He stood only inches from me. I pushed him away. "Get off me, man." Nick laughed as I frowned. "You always playing when it's time to go home."

"My bad man. You can't take a joke?"

I walked off. Nick followed. "Yeah, I can, except when you look like you're about to kiss me."

Nick laughed again. "A'ight . . . a'ight. I'll let you have that one. Just wanted to trip you out . . . make you laugh for a change. You stay so stressed. Like right now. W'sup? I thought that new honey you hired is making life easier for you."

We exited the building and walked out into cold night. "She is," I said, fastening my coat. "I still got other things on my plate that she can't handle though—like this job. I'm just glad she's at my place fixing dinner right now."

"See what I'm saying," Nick practically yelled as he panted, trying to inhale the freezing air. Clouds of smoke flowed from his mouth and nostrils as he spoke. "That's what's up. I've got to figure out where I'm picking up dinner tonight. Everybody ain't got it made in the shade like you."

"What do you mean? I ain't got it made in the shade either. Hell, I pay for Karma's services."

"Yeah, but I wish I could afford somebody like Karma. Sure would make my life better. Anyway, what does she charge?"

I picked up my step, heading toward my car. "Now ya dippin' in my business, man."

He laughed as he followed close behind. "Speaking of dip-pin' . . . you hit that yet?"

"Say what?" I asked over my shoulder.

"C'mon, man. I haven't met her, but from what you say, she sounds like a tender young thang. I know you get lonely, don't you?"

"Man, Karma is too young. She's fine—I'll give her that—but she's only twenty-one years old. What's an old man like me to do with her?"

"Colby, you're forty, right?"

"Forty-one next month. Karma's still got milk on her breath compared to me. When I look at her, I see somebody's baby."

"Man, any woman you meet is gon' be somebody's child. I know you miss Glenda, but you can't neglect yourself forever."

When I stopped at my car, Nick paused, too. "You're a fine one to talk, Mr. Celibacy," I told him. "But I can admit it: Part of me doesn't look too closely at Karma because I haven't let go of Glenda."

"Just what I figured," he said, patting me on the back.

"But at the same time, Nick, I've never been into young girls. Besides, Karma and I couldn't have anything meaningful at this point. She seems like family—one of my children, in fact."

"You make it sound like incest. Ain't no blood ties to you, man, and you never know . . . she might be willing to give you some."

I frowned. "The thought of laying Karma down just doesn't excite me. I've always had emotions to go along with sex. Believe it or not, Nick, I've loved every woman I've ever put Mandingo in."

Nick cringed. "You named your dick, man?"

I laughed. "So what? My mouth isn't foul like yours."

"Still . . . you named it." He shuttered then fanned at me. "Never mind. Continue."

"Yeah. Like I was saying: I'm positive that when I finally move on, it'll be with someone more on my level. I'm more attracted to maturity and intelligence than anything. Karma may have those aspects, but the bottom line is she's twenty-one."

Nick turned to walk away, shaking his head, and then stepped back to me with an afterthought. "Well . . . when will she be twenty-two?"

"Hmph." I let out a chuckle. "Is that supposed to make a difference?"

"Not in my mind . . . just wondering if it did in yours." He laughed. "Hey, I know I'm celibate, but not for long. I'm getting old. It's time I get a tenderoni in my life."

I clicked the button on my key ring, disarming the alarm to my Infinity M45. "I guess that's good for you," I said, opening the door. I reached inside and cranked it up.

I glanced up in time to see a fox approaching. Audrie Davis, a tall, delicious-looking, chocolate business associate, spoke just as she made it to her car. She had parked next to me.

"Have a good evening, Audrie," I said just before she got in.

"You do the same, Cole." She winked then closed her door. She started her car, and then sat as it warmed up.

"Dayum, she fine," Nick said, watching as she adjusted her radio. "Whatcha think about her, Cole? She wants you, man. And guess what . . . she's mature, intelligent . . . oh, and don't let me leave out fine. I wish she would wink at me like that."

"She did wink at you." I laughed.

"Un-un. You know that woman's had a crush on you ever since she started with the company three months ago. Just tell me you ain't gon' hit it, so I can make my move." I jumped in my car and snuggled into the heated leather seat before pulling off, leaving Nick standing in the parking lot. He continued to yell. "You gon' hit it? Huh?"

I looked in my rearview mirror. Nick's lean frame stood with arms opened wide like he'd been left hanging. I laughed nearly ten minutes.

By the time I made it to I-55 South, rain hammered my windshield. Traffic was backed up for miles. Visibility was nearly zero, so everyone moved at a pace of five miles per hour. Half an hour later, I wasn't even close to getting home. Given the time and the weather, it seemed Karma would have to spend the night as she'd done before. I called home.

"Patterson residence," Karma answered, although I'm not sure why, considering the phone had a caller ID.

"How's it going, Karma?"

"Good. Shawna and I just finished studying, and now I'm running Gavin's bath water."

"Hey, I'm sorry for being so late. I didn't get off until seven, and now this darn traffic is backed up because of the rain. I'm guessing I should make it home about eight-fifteen."

"That's fine, Cole. It's not like I have a ton of other things to do. I brought my books with me, so I'll just study some more."

"Well, with this rain coming down as hard as it is, I was thinking you should probably spend the night. You were the last person to sleep in the guest room, so the sheets should still be clean."

"No problem. Dinner is warming in the oven, but if you're looking for a beer, you might need to stop at a store. I noticed this evening you were all out."

"Okay. I'll see you in a bit."

I hung up the phone then gave the road my full attention. Upon making it to my exit, I thought about that beer Karma mentioned and decided to stop at a corner store. I found myself thumbing through a few car magazines and the December *Ebony*. Harsh wind and rain pounded the windows and door of the store. I figured I'd be better off hanging out there until it slacked.

When I noticed it was past my children's bedtime, I purchased my beer and magazines, and then got out of there. I felt awful that I wouldn't get to see their smiling faces when I got home. I could only hope they weren't mad at me.

I was home ten minutes later. My stomach immediately went into growling mode when the whiff from the kitchen met me at the door. I walked farther into the dim living room, and then toward the aroma. I opened the oven to find a plate of steak, candied yams, green beans, and corn bread. *Who in the hell taught this little girl to cook like this?* I thought. I closed the oven door then set my beer in the refrigerator. I needed to shower and change.

Once at the top of the stairs, I noticed a mild rambling noise coming from my bedroom. It was obvious Karma was awake, but why she was in my room was a mystery to me. I pushed opened the cracked door and discovered her standing in the long mirror on the wall, posing in one of Glenda's dresses.

She turned toward me. "So," she said, holding her arms out, "what do you think?"

I was speechless. Not because of how stunning she looked, but how dare she try on my wife's clothes without asking me?

"What the hell are you doing?" I asked, unmasking anger. She looked surprised by my question. I walked closer to her and discovered several boxes lined around the walls of my room. "What . . . what is . . . Karma, what is all of this?"

"I'm cleaning out your room," she replied.

I opened one of the boxes and almost fainted when I saw Glenda's belongings crammed inside. "What are you doing with my wife's things? Not only are you wearing one of her dresses without asking me, but you had the nerve to pack up her things."

"I'm getting rid of them for you." Her face was meek and innocent.

"Why? Did I ask you to do that?" I asked through tight lips. I didn't want to wake the children. "Did it ever occur to you that I might not want to get rid of Glenda's things?"

Karma huffed and put her hands on her hips in an I-can't-believe-this-nigga kind of way. "So, after all of this work I've done, you want me to just put everything back?"

"That's right. I do. First, take off Glenda's dress then put everything back where you found it."

She shook her head then stepped closer. "But Cole, keeping Glenda's things couldn't possibly be healthy for you." Her hand rested on the back of my neck.

I grabbed her hand then flung it down. "Don't tell me what's healthy for me. If you want to see unhealthy, then don't unpack these boxes. You and I are going to have a problem if you don't." She took a step back then looked me up and down, sucking her teeth. "As a matter of fact," I continued, "it's no longer raining. After you've finished putting everything back, you should leave."

She was silent, gazing with a face of disbelief as I walked around her to get my pajamas out of my drawer. After rolling her eyes, she began unpacking the boxes. I headed into the bathroom as though she wasn't there. I jumped into the shower, damn near letting the water scald me from head to toe. My emotions over-whelmed me, but I knew it was time to stop counting my tear-drops every time I longed for my deceased wife. I stood under the showerhead to let the steady flow of water mix with my tears.

Maybe I was too harsh on Karma, I thought while lathering my body. Karma had been helpful in many ways. It didn't make sense that she would deliberately do something to piss me off. *Someone must've taught her some steps of dealing with grief,* I thought. *She only wanted to help me, but I chewed her out.*

I dried off then hurriedly put on my pajamas. I owed Karma an apology, but I wasn't so sure she'd accept it. The children were fond of her, and I didn't want them to lose another woman they loved. Karma had only unpacked three boxes when I walked into the bedroom. I'm sure she heard me coming into the room, but she didn't bother to look at me.

"Let me help you," I said.

"I've got it," she responded without turning to me.

"No, really. It's after nine, and it'll take you at least an hour to put all of this back."

She stopped and looked me in the eyes. "I said I've got it." Her eyes were tight and red as if she'd been crying.

I sat on my bed and watched her stomp about the room, putting item after item back into its rightful place. I felt terrible for the way I had talked to her.

"Karma, I'm sorry," I offered.

She kept her back to me. "Yeah, and me, too."

I didn't know how to take her response. "Are you being sarcastic?" I didn't get a reaction from her that time. "Karma, please accept my apology. I'm finding it difficult to let go of Glenda. I really didn't mean to take it out on you."

She kept scrambling about the room. I stood then walked over to her. She placed a dress on a hanger then hung it in the closet. I grabbed her hands just before she turned to walk away. She looked at me with sad eyes.

"You hurt my feelings, Cole."

"I've apologized, Karma. I don't know what else to do. I'm hurting, too, and I don't know how to deal with my pain. I appreciate all you do to help me, but I just don't want you forcing me to forget Glenda. That's not going to happen."

"You should never forget Glenda. She was the mother of your kids, but staring at her things every day isn't going to help your pain either."

I shook my head then let her hands go. "I hear you, but again . . . I'm just not ready." I began taking things out of the boxes and putting them up. Karma came over and stopped me.

"Cole," she called, placing her hand on top of mine as I set a bottle of perfume on the dresser, "I've got it." We stared at each other for a minute. "Go eat your dinner. I've got this."

I nodded then left the room, heading to the kitchen. After settling at the table with my plate, I said grace then stuck a forkful of sweet potatoes in my mouth. The buttery sweet flavor was like a taste of heaven on my tongue. It didn't take me long to gobble everything on my plate. Once I finished, I sat, drinking my beer and reading the *Ebony* I'd purchased. I knew I should be heading to bed, but I just wasn't sleepy.

Karma came downstairs and joined me in the kitchen about thirty minutes later. "I'm done, so I'm heading out now."

I looked at the clock on the wall then shook my head. "You don't need to leave now. It's too late."

"I have to go to class in the morning. I need a change of clothes. I'll be fine," she said, walking away.

"Karma," I called. She stepped back to the table. "Please. I don't apologize or beg often," I said, looking into her eyes. "Please stay. You can get up and go home in the morning."

She nodded. "I'll need to use the shower in your room so I won't wake the kids."

"That's fine. I'll be down here a minute anyway."

"And I need to borrow one of your T-shirts."

"No problem," I responded.

She walked out. I sat thinking of how it was a shame Karma wasn't closer to my age. She seemed to have all the necessary skills to make a good wife, and Lawd knows she was fine. I couldn't imagine that a young woman with a body like hers wouldn't be good in bed. The more I thought of her, the more curious I became. I started to get horny—a feeling hard to ignore.

When I got upstairs, Karma had taken her shower and was in the guest room. The door was cracked, so I pushed it open to peek in. Karma sat in front of the vanity mirror, brushing her shoulder-length hair. She turned around in the chair to look at me. I didn't say anything, but neither did she. She stood in place while I was in the entrance of the room. Her eyes said she knew what I wanted. She further confirmed she'd read my mind when she lowered her eyes to the rise in my midsection. Embarrassed, I walked away without saying a word.

I went into my room and turned out the light. Frustrated would be an understatement for what I felt. I pounced down on the bed then lay flat on my back with my hands behind my head. I wanted to get under the covers and go to sleep, but with the head between my legs throbbing, sleeping was out of the question.

ALISHA YVONNE

My attention drew to the door as it slowly opened. Karma soon appeared in the doorway, staring. I waited for her to say something, but she never did. Instead, she stepped inside, closed the door, and then started toward me. I couldn't move. I felt nervous that one of the children would wake up and see her in my room half-naked. Just as she climbed on the bed, I tried to sit up, but it was too late. She had straddled me and began rotating her hips in slow, sensual motions.

My hands met her bare ass when I reached under her shirt. She licked her lips and massaged her breasts while gazing into my eyes. *Mmm,* I thought. My flesh desperately needed to meet hers.

Karma leaned over and placed a wet, soft peck on my lips, and then on my neck. *Oh, God, I haven't felt like this since Glenda last touched me,* I thought. *Glenda!* Like a reflex, I threw Karma off me. Thank goodness she landed on the edge of the bed.

"I'm sorry, Karma," I said, pulling her into the middle of the bed. "I didn't mean to toss you like that."

I'd clearly startled her. She held her chest, staring at me a few seconds before she spoke. "What happened?" she asked. "I thought you wanted me."

"I do . . . I mean, I did. I mean . . . Karma, I can't. Not like this. This bed belonged to my wife. I mean, it was ours, but I don't see me sharing it with another woman."

"Then let's go into the guest room," she pleaded, stroking my face.

"No, Karma. We aren't—"

"I've got condoms," she said, cutting me off.

"That's not—"

"Daddy," I heard Shawna call.

My eyes grew large. I mouthed to Karma to get down on the floor. She hesitated, staring at me with a how-dare-you look. When Shawna's voice grew closer, I gave Karma pleading eyes. She soon obliged.

41

"Daddy, are you in here?" Shawna asked.

"Yes, sweetheart," I said, meeting her at the door. "What's wrong?"

"I can't sleep."

"Really? You haven't been to sleep at all?"

"Yes, sir, but I keep waking up after having bad dreams. I miss Mommy."

I felt terrible. I barely knew how to comfort myself, let alone my little one. Plus, there on the floor, lay a woman who had just tried to be intimate with me, but she wasn't Glenda. I hugged Shawna because it was all I could do at the moment to console her.

"How about I go sit in your room with you until you fall back to sleep?"

"Yes, sir," she whined.

"Okay. Let's go," I said to Shawna.

I looked over in the direction where Karma hid and thought, *The operative word is go. That's your cue to get the hell out of my room.*

The alarm on my cell was set to go off at five-forty-five in the morning. Considering how I didn't doze until sometime after midnight, I figured I'd probably sleep right through the buzzer. However, not only was I awake on time, but I had been awake since three o'clock. Cole had ruffled my feathers. I knew he wanted me—even before having seen that *thang* about to burst out of his silk pajamas—he clearly wanted me. He'd put too much effort over the past months toward trying *not* to notice me.

I remained patient because I felt time would prove me right. I knew it would come—the moment I'd get the eye that said it was okay for me to make the first move. What I don't understand is why he recanted. We vibed. It was about to be on. And it would've been good, too. I imagined not only would he show me what he's working with on our first time, but it would've also been makeup sex because of the way he treated me about packing Glenda's things. Damn, why did he have to stop?

Around six A.M., I heard Cole go into the kids' room. Five minutes later, he was out of their room and back into his. I got out of bed to see what he was doing. His door was cracked, so I spied on him. I saw him kneeling beside his bed, apparently praying. After he got up, I knocked on the door.

He turned to notice me. "Come in," he said, sitting on his bed.

"Morning," I responded with hesitation. I didn't know what kind of mood he was in, and the last thing I wanted to do was make him think of firing me.

"Morning," he shot back.

"My turn to apologize now." I stood with my hands behind my back because I was nervous. "I'm sorry I came on to you last night. I honestly thought we were both feeling the same thing. It won't happen again."

He was quiet for nearly a minute before he spoke. He looked everywhere except at me. "I'm not blaming you for anything. We're both human . . . got needs . . . and last night was an attempt to satisfy them." He paused. "I do have to say that I'm glad to hear we can get past what happened. You're a bright young woman with a good future ahead of you. Your focus should be on studying so you can graduate. Don't let any man, not even me, get in the way of that. Okay?" He looked up at me.

"Okay," I said, full of hurt and anger. "I'll go fix breakfast."

I went into the bathroom and washed my face then put on my clothes from the day before. I was tired, but I headed downstairs to make breakfast anyway. No matter how I tried, I couldn't get past being upset with Cole for dissin' me. He wanted me. I knew he did. And he knew I wanted him, but he came at me with some "don't let any man, not even me, get in the way" bullshit. I could see the bigger picture—Glenda Patterson still ran my house from the grave.

Glenda was gone, and Cole needed to get past her absence. The Patterson family home was mine. I lived there. I took care of the household *and* Cole. All he needed was for me to show him a little more tender loving care—that's all that was missing— but he seemed to be running from it as if Glenda was going to walk in and catch us. How ridiculous would that be?

I had spent many days going to the bookstores, looking for cookbooks with recipes of the foods Cole said he liked to eat. While he thought I was enrolled at Lemoyne Owen College, studying computer science, I was actually at Karma Jolley's College of Learning How to Cook Good Food Quick In Order to Keep Your Man—in other words, my apartment. I knew I needed to be in school, but winning Cole's heart was more important to me than anything else. I purchased textbooks off some of the students at Lemoyne Owen so Cole would think I was studying.

Cole came into the kitchen, interrupting my thoughts. "Where's my can opener?" he asked, opening and closing drawers.

"It's in the drawer next to the dishwasher," I responded.

"Why is it over there?" He went to the drawer and opened it. "Oh, I see you've rearranged the whole drawer."

"Yes. Is there a problem?"

He hesitated then answered. "No. I'm just use to the way Glenda had things arranged."

There was that name again, pissing me off. I remained calm. "Well, really, Cole . . . it wouldn't be a problem for me to put things back the way they were. I just thought with me being the one who cooks and deals with things in here the most, I should fix them so they would be more convenient for me."

He opened a can of coffee then turned to me. "You're right, Karma. I can get use to the change."

Good, I thought. "Thanks, Cole. I appreciate that." I started out of the kitchen. "You're going to be okay with getting the kids off to school?"

"Yes, I'll be fine."

"Okay. I really need to get going if I'm going to get changed for school. Princess has enough food, so I may not be back here until after I pick the children up."

"That's fine. I'll see you later. Have a good day."

"You, too, Cole."

I went about my business and stayed away from Cole's house for most of the morning. I straightened up my place a bit then went to an ATM to get some cash so I could get my hair done. My beautician was booked, but when I informed her what her tip would be for helping a sista out, she managed to squeeze me in.

I got my hair set with rollers so it would fall into a nice, shoulder-length body wrap. I felt that perhaps if I looked older, Cole wouldn't bring up my age again. I left there with my hair, nails, and feet hooked up. *Let me see him turn me away now,* I thought. *He won't be able to resist.*

When I headed back over to Cole's house, it was one o'clock in the afternoon. Although I had told him I wouldn't be there until late, I really couldn't stay away. I wanted to be at his house more than my own place.

I opened the door to a happy, jumping poodle. Princess obviously missed me. "Hey, girl," I said, bending to pick her up. She began licking me, and I almost dropped her. I hurriedly put her back down on the floor. "Are you crazy?" I sneered at her. "Save that licking shit for the kids. You know I don't play that."

I rolled my eyes at Princess then walked off into the den. She followed. I sat on the couch then turned on the television. It was a fifty-two-inch flat screen that sat on top of a platform. The surround sound along with the big screen gave the room a theater aura.

As I sat watching *Family Feud,* the doodads which decorated the thin shelf just above the television drew my attention. The ceramics were cute, but I could hardly stomach that damn Glenda grinning at me. An eight-by-ten silver frame housed a portrait of her sitting in a chair with a floral background. Something evil came all over me.

I went upstairs to the children's room then opened the closet. The aluminum bat was still sitting in the corner where I had placed it while cleaning up. I grabbed it then went back downstairs. Upon walking into the living room, I charged Glenda's picture, swinging a massive blow that sent it hurling across the room with glass flying everywhere.

Then I turned around and noticed her crooked grin on a four-teen-by-sixteen that hung over the couch. I drew back then smashed the bat into the frame. Glass covered the couch and floor. Heaving, I ripped the lopsided frame from the wall then slammed it to the floor. Glenda needed to see the bat coming at her head-on. I smashed the bat several times into her face, wrinkling the photo and causing many deep scratches on it.

After catching my breath, I decided to go on a rampage. I searched the house, high and low, looking for any sign of pictures of Glenda. After about half an hour, Glenda's smile no longer existed in many places in the house. I tore up all the photos that were an image of her with my man. I calmed down again, and then thought, *Shit, how do I explain this mess?*

I walked into the children's room and found one last five-by-seven of Glenda with the kids sitting on her lap. I took the picture then headed back downstairs. Since the children would be out of school in a couple of hours, an idea came to mind that I should go to the childcare center early to get them. Their early arrival would be crucial for explaining what happened with the shattered pieces of glass and torn pictures. I put it all in a large garbage bag.

As I hurried out the door, I saw the nosy old neighbor Cole had told me about, peeping out her window. Ms. Willis was her name. I waved at her, and she waved back. She lived across the street, so I wasn't worried that she'd heard the ruckus at Cole's house. I smiled and waved once more after pulling out of the driveway.

The kids were surprised to see me before five o'clock. I told them I wanted to get them home so they could get in an extra hour or two of TV time as a reward for being so good the day before. They were extremely excited considering *Fat Albert,* one of their favorite cartoons, was about to come on.

Shawna ran upstairs to her room immediately upon entering the house. Gavin wanted to take off behind her, but I stopped him.

"Would you like a snack, Gavin?" I asked.

"Yes, ma'am," he responded politely.

I walked him into the kitchen then opened the cabinet to get some crackers. "Have a seat at the table, Gavin."

I watched him climb into a chair. He noticed the picture of him, his sister, and his mom. Just as I had expected, he got on his knees in the chair for more reach, then stretched his hand out for the picture. I walked over to assist him—or so he thought. I deliberately caused the frame to fall to the floor as soon as his hands were on it. "Uh," he gasped, clutching the sides of his face.

I gasped, too. "Gavin, look what you did. You broke it. Do you know your father is going to be angry with you?"

He began to cry. I put my arms around him. "Shhh . . . it's okay. I'll talk to Daddy for you. He won't be mad." Gavin nodded then calmed down. I fixed him a few cheese crackers then sent him on his way. "Here you go, Gavin. Now go upstairs and get changed so you can watch TV with your sister."

I walked over to the phone then dialed Cole. "Hey, you," he said just after answering.

"Hey to you, too. You seem to be in a pretty good mood. Where are you?"

"Um, actually I'm not far from home. I was given an early leave because of a deal I pulled off today. Yeah, I'm feeling damned good. What's up?"

"The kids are here. I went to get them early. I figured they need a break from the center every now and then."

"Okay. Sounds good. What are they up to?"

"Well, I was in the kitchen taking things out for dinner when I heard a little disturbance."

"Disturbance?" he screamed.

"Calm down, Cole. Everything is fine. We'll talk about it when you get here. I need to get dinner going."

"Are the kids okay?"

"They're fine, Cole. There's nothing to panic about. It's just that I have something to show you."

I probably should've waited to tell Cole there was a slight problem because it was tough getting him off the phone. I guess he broke all the speed limits, too, because he was home within ten minutes of our phone conversation.

I was in the kitchen making macaroni when Cole walked in. "Cole, please tell me you didn't do a hundred miles per hour in order to get here so fast," I said as he walked in.

He shook his head. "No. I told you I was almost home," he snapped.

His attitude caused me to do a double take. "My . . . how quickly our good mood has changed."

He sat at the table. "Well, when you tell me something like a disturbance has gone on in my home, I'm subject to worry."

I wiped my hands on the dish towel then grabbed the garbage bag filled with the broken pictures. I set the bag on the floor next to the table then pulled down the shattered five-by-seven off the top of the refrigerator. I sat it down in front of Cole.

"This is the disturbance I was speaking of," I said.

His expression was far less upset than I had anticipated. "How did this happen?" he asked, trying to mend the frame.

"Gavin went ballistic this afternoon." I tried to sound torn. Cole seemed shocked. "This isn't the only picture he broke up." I slid the garbage bag closer to Cole. He opened it as I continued to talk. "After hearing what sounded like shattering glass, I went into the den and discovered him climbing on the couch with his aluminum bat. I couldn't stop him in time. The picture fell after he hit it. It missed him, but he beat it over and over."

Cole stood, frowning. "How did he . . . I mean, I know it doesn't weight much, but he usually needs my help holding that bat."

I shook my head. "Cole, I can't tell you where he got the strength from."

"Why would he do something like this?" Cole looked as if he was in deep thought then gasped. "Did he break the clock?"

"What clock?"

"The anniversary clock Glenda had inscribed for our anniversary?"

Damn, why didn't I remember the clock? "No, Cole. I think the clock is okay." I grabbed his hands. "Cole, please sit down. I spoke with Gavin, and I promised him I'd speak with you for him. The bottom line is he's frustrated that his mother has left him."

"But he's been to counseling. I was told he was getting better. He's never acted out like this." Cole turned around to call Gavin. "Gavin, get down here right now," he yelled.

"Cole, please," I begged. "He's just a little boy. He doesn't know how to handle his anger like an adult."

"Yeah, but all of my memories are destroyed because of him." He continued to yell. "Gavin, I want you down here now."

I panicked that Gavin would deny breaking all the pictures. "Cole, why don't you let me do the talking?"

"No. I've got this," he said, turning to notice Gavin looking pitiful as he walked into the kitchen. "Gavin, did you break this?" Cole asked, holding up the five-by-seven frame.

Gavin began to shed tears so rapidly, he couldn't speak. Cole let him off the hook by picking him up and embracing him. Gavin held on to his daddy's neck and cried long and hard.

I sneaked off to put the bag in the outdoor trash before Cole had a notion to see what he could salvage. When I returned to the kitchen, Gavin was gone and Cole was sitting at the table, looking like he was about to burst. I went over and stood in front of him then stroked his head. He stared up at me with watery eyes then pulled me down onto his lap.

"I miss her so much," he whispered. "I never thought that one I'd have to live my life without her." He continued to talk softly, squeezing my waist. "Counseling isn't enough. I don't know what to do."

"I know it's difficult," I said, pushing his head into my breasts. I could feel the warmth of his breath on my cleavage. "It took me a while to get use to my parents being gone, too." I stroked his head and neck. "Just know that you'll get better in time. I'm here to help you," I said slyly.

Cole gripped the small of my back as he held on to me. I kissed the top of his head, but it was the wrong thing to do. He seemed to have suddenly had a notion that what we were doing was wrong. He pushed me out of his lap then headed out of the kitchen. I followed him, but I stopped when he headed upstairs.

I stood smiling inside. *That bitch Glenda is almost out of my house.*

*D*inner was good as usual, but very little conversation went on at the table. Karma was probably pissed at me for rejecting her again. She had promised not to come on to me anymore. I didn't feel it was fair to put all the blame on her though. She caught me at a vulnerable moment. I don't know what I was thinking when I set her down on my lap. I needed to be comforted, and I couldn't resist having her close to me.

When she pushed my face into her breasts, I wanted to stay there forever. She smelled great, and her cleavage felt wonderful on my skin. She had the right touch as she stroked my head and neck. I could feel myself slipping deeper into her spell, and she knew it. I quickly got her off me then hurriedly left the scene before disaster happened.

Gavin seemed to be afraid to talk at dinner, and Shawna looked as if she had things on her mind. The whole dining room was filled with awkwardness. Karma decided to be the first to break the ice.

"Well," she said just after chewing her last bite, "who's up for playing a little family game?"

The children hardly looked up from their plates. "Karma, I don't think anyone is in the mood."

"I know, but you can't blame me for trying, right?"

I sipped my tea then answered. "No. And I appreciate your concern, too." I nodded and she nodded back.

"Daddy, I'm done. May I go upstairs to my room?" Shawna asked.

"You don't want any dessert?" I asked. "Karma bought a chocolate cake from Picadilly's."

"I knew I wouldn't have time to bake a cake, so Picadilly's was the next best option. Try it, Shawna," she said, sliding the cake plate toward her.

Karma picked up the cake cutter then took the top off the cake, but Shawna still wasn't having it.

"I wanna go to my room," she cried.

"Oh, sweetie, what's d'matter?" I asked.

"I'm tired. I wanna go to my room."

I looked at Karma. "It's okay," she said. "We'll save you some cake, Shawna." Shawna stood then slid her chair under the table. "I hope you feel better," Karma yelled to her.

I shook my head in dismay. "I need to get the proper help for these children."

Karma patted my hand. "It takes time, Cole. They'll come around as they get older."

Her words weren't comforting. I wanted results for all of us right then. Dealing with Glenda's death was more difficult than anything I had ever imagined. At times, I wished I had been killed, too. Not a day went by that I didn't think of Glenda. I tried to push on for the kids' sake because I knew that's what Glenda would've wanted.

Karma began slicing off the cake. As soon as she slid a piece to me on a saucer, I realized I didn't have a taste for it. "Karma, I think I'm going to pass, too."

She looked hurt. "But I thought double chocolate was your favorite. I just knew you'd be happy that I stopped to pick up one."

"I'm very happy about the cake, Karma. I'm just going through something right now." I stood then slid my chair under the table. "C'mon, son," I said to Gavin. He jumped down from his chair.

"Gavin's not eating cake either?"

"Maybe later," I said. "I need to spend some alone time with my children. We're going upstairs to my room to look at some old family videos and reminisce."

She stood, frowning. "Cole, you don't need to put those children through that."

"Through what? Remembering their mother during the happy times? That's exactly what they need." We were silent as we stared at each other. "C'mon, Gavin," I said, reaching for his hand.

"Fine," she shot at my back. "Don't worry about me. I know how to let myself out once I finish eating."

"Great. Have a good night," I retorted without looking back.

It was the middle of the night, or so it seemed, and I had just turned over in bed. I felt a presence over me. When I opened my eyes it was Karma standing in an all-white satin-and-lace teddy with a matching garter. Her hair was pulled back in a ponytail, making it easier for the diamond-studded earrings to bling in the dark. I batted my eyes, trying to focus, hoping that what I was seeing wasn't real. Every stitch Karma had on belonged to Glenda, even the earrings. I sat up in bed to ask her what she was doing.

"Karma, I thought you went home after dinner. What are—"

"Shh," she said, cutting me off. She climbed on top of me, forcing me back down on the bed. "I know you don't like it when I wear Glenda's things . . . but, I want to help you. I paid attention when you said you miss her, so I'm willing to let you use me." She kissed my neck. "Don't worry about the children. The door is locked. Pretend I'm Glenda." She kissed my lips. "Make love to me, Cole." She stuck her tongue into my mouth. "Make love to your wife."

She kissed me passionately—just like Glenda used to. She began to grind as she tongued me, causing my erection to meet her inner thigh. Her moans were soft and seducing. I'd known for a while that she wanted me, and given the current circumstances, I wanted her, too. I pulled her up by her shoulders then took one of her breasts out of the teddy to caress it with my mouth. Her breathing became heavier as I sucked and licked her with intensity. Before I knew it, I was helping her to unfasten the seat of the teddy.

"Take me, Cole," she said.

I looked into her eyes. I knew she wasn't Glenda though she was trying to play a mind game to get me to have sex with her, but in my horny state, it didn't matter who she was or what type of game she was playing. I wanted her. I had to have her.

I turned her over, feeling her body up and down. I traced her torso then her lower stomach. Once I was low enough to feel the softness of her lips, she spread her legs. I sat on my knees between her legs and watched her caress herself. She was beautiful—young, tender, and sexy as hell. She began another attempt to mess with my mind.

"That's right, baby. Here I am," she said, grinding. "Make love to Glend—"

I put my finger to her lips, shushing her. "Stop it, Karma. I know who you are."

She looked shocked, but she didn't let my revelation cease her mission. She reached into the teddy just underneath her breasts and pulled out a condom. After placing it on me, she began to massage one of her breasts as she rotated her hips and fingered herself.

"I need you." She licked her lips. "Don't leave me hanging, Cole."

"I hadn't planned to," I said, inserting myself into her.

Her warmth damn near made me lose my mind and my cool.
I stopped stroking her after only about a minute because I could
feel myself going there. As I lay panting, barely able to breathe,
Karma leaned over then rotated underneath me.

"Stop it. You're gonna make me—" I paused. She ignored
me. I tried to pull myself up, but I felt her hand grip me, forcing
me back into her. "Karma, you're gonna make me—" I tried to
warn her that I was about to explode, but she refused to stop.

I pounded her pelvis. Her moans became louder and louder,
so I kissed her to muffle the sounds. She squeezed my hips as I
went deeper into her canal. I tried to slow my roll again, but she
wouldn't let me.

"Karma, please. It's been a long time. You're . . . gonna . . .
make . . . me . . . aaaahhhh." And like that it was over.

I lay limp, and she lay underneath me, still grinding and
whispering in my ear. "Did you like that?" she asked. I didn't
answer. She kissed my earlobe. "Let me do it again. Let me
make you feel good again, baby."

I shook my head. "No," I said, pulling out of her, feeling
guilty.

I glanced down at the muscle whose brain had just overruled
the one in my skull. Not only did it lay weak and limp, but it was
also cold and naked. *Where's the damn condom?* I wondered. I
sat back in a panic, looking down at myself. The condom was
missing. I looked at Karma as she lay on her back with her legs
still apart.

She smiled. "What's wrong?"

"The condom. It's missing."

"Oh, we didn't need that," she said matter-of-factly. "I pulled
it off while you were trying to get up."

"What?" I yelled. "What the fu—"

"Daddy," Shawna called as she knocked on the door.
"Daddy, let me in."

My heart felt like it had fallen into my stomach. I began to hear an annoying, high-pitched laughter. When I turned to look at Karma, she was rolling all over the bed, tickled at the situation. The condom issue had already pissed me off, so the laughter was the icing on the cake. I drew back to slap her.

KNOCK, KNOCK, KNOCK, KNOCK.

I opened my eyes and rolled over, breathing heavily. "Daddy," Shawna called. "I can't sleep. Let me in."

I sat up in bed and looked around. It was a dream. I pulled the covers back and looked at myself. Other than my stiff erection and a little moisture in my briefs, everything seemed to be intact. I still had on my silk pajamas bottoms. *It was a damn dream. Whew!*

KNOCK, KNOCK, KNOCK, KNOCK.

"Daddy," Shawna whined again.

"Hold on, sweetie. I'm on my way." When I opened the door, Shawna hugged me. "Sorry, sweetie. I didn't know it was locked. Are you okay?"

"I can't sleep," she said.

"Another dream?"

"Yes."

"C'mon. I'll go sit in your room with you again."

We started out into the hall. As I passed the guest room, I peeked in. "Hold on, sweetie," I said to her as I checked out the room. Karma wasn't in there. She had gone home after dinner like I remembered.

I sat in the rocking chair next to Shawna's bed. When I glanced at the clock on her nightstand, I noticed it was only ten o'clock. The kids and I had been in bed since eight-thirty. We had a slice of cake just before lying down, which was probably the cause of our outrageous dreams. Gavin only had a taste, and it was a good thing that was all I gave him. Shawna could fall asleep quickly once I was in the room with her, but Gavin would be up for hours if his sleep was disturbed.

Once Shawna was back into dreamland, I retired to my room. I left the door ajar just in case she needed me again. I lay thinking for nearly an hour, and I still couldn't get back to sleep. I remembered my job was having a Family and Friends Day at Crystal Palace Skating Rink on the weekend, and I was going to need Karma's help—that was if I hadn't run her off. I looked at the clock then decided since the eleven o'clock hour hadn't hit, it would be okay to call her.

"Hello," she answered groggily.

I took a deep breath before speaking. "Hello, Karma. It's Cole. I can see you were asleep, so I'll rap to you in the morning."

"No, Cole, it's okay," she said, yawning. "We can talk. What's up?" I paused because I began contemplating an apology. "Cole? Are you there?"

I sucked up my hesitation. "I'm here, Karma. First of all, how are you?"

"I've seen been better nights, but I'm okay."

"I imagine I'm some of the cause for your not-so-good night, huh?"

She blew into the phone. "I don't take being snapped up and yelled at very well, so yes. My mood has been tampered with by you."

I sighed. "Just what I figured."

"What're you doing up?" she interrupted.

"Shawna woke up from another dream."

"Poor baby. Is she okay?"

"She's fine. She drifted back off not too long ago."

"Oh, good. I wish there was something I could do or say to help her, you know? And to help you and Gavin, too."

"You do enough, Karma. I think the children appreciate you just as much as I do, if not more."

"That's nice to hear. What else is on your mind? I'm not use to you calling me so late."

I paused again, but before she could call my name, I responded. "Karma, I'm sorry. I know you've heard that before. To tell the truth, you might have to hear it again. I'm just—"

She cut me off. "I know, Cole. I don't expect everyone to be able to cope with the loss of a loved one like I have. I just wish I knew how to make things better for you all. You know . . . make life fun for you again."

"Well, we can certainly try. My company is having Family and Friends Day at Crystal Palace Skating Rink on Third Street this weekend. If you don't mind accompanying us, we'd love to have you. Besides, the kids are going to be a handful for me. I think I can use your assistance."

She laughed. "Say no more. I'm there with bells on. Sounds like fun anyway. I know the children will have a great time."

"And just so you know, we enjoyed the cake. Sorry we didn't sit down to eat it with you."

"That's okay, Cole. I understand. The important thing for me is that you enjoyed it."

"Yes, we did. We started craving it just before bedtime. Hell, that's probably why Shawna and I had such weird dreams."

"Really? What were you dreaming about?" she asked.

I got choked on my words. "I . . . uh . . . uh . . . I . . . well, I just . . . well, you know how dreams can be. They start out making sense, and then they switch up on you . . . next thing you know, you're driving down the street in a race car naked with no brakes."

She laughed then I chuckled, too. "That sounds like a wild one. I think you better stay away from the chocolate cake for a minute, Cole. I'm scared to ask what else happened."

"Believe me . . . you don't wanna know." I laughed.

"Well, I guess I can finish off the cake tomorrow since you guys are affected by it."

"Oh, no you don't. I'll slice you a piece or two, but I'm hiding the rest. That's my cake."

"Ah, now why you gonna do me like that?" I could almost hear a smile in her tone.

"Un-un, my sista . . . you've got to get your own," I teased.

"But I bought that one."

"Mm-hmm, but like I said: you've got to get your own."

We both laughed and continued to tease each other for a while. I actually had fun chatting with her on the phone like two teenagers. Her voice sounded more enticing than it did in my dream, and I could imagine she had on something sexy just like in my dream.

By midnight, I had to get off the phone. I had begun to get sleepy again, but Karma wasn't trying to hear it. She fussed that I had awakened her, only to leave her hanging. She sounded so sweet and innocent. I promised to make it up to her another time then we hung up.

God, help me not to bang that little girl.

Karma 8

*I*t was Saturday, and it sure as hell didn't come quick enough.
As soon as Cole and I hung up the phone after he'd invited me on
the family outing, the countdown to Saturday began. I stayed
over the night before so we could all get up and leave together. I
think I was more excited than the children. Cole did me a favor
asking me to spend the day with them. I really felt like part of the
family.

I was dressed and downstairs before everyone. Cole and
Gavin came down shortly after me. I went to see what was taking
Shawna so long. "Hurry up, Shawna," I called up the stairs.

"Coming," she screamed back.

By ten in the morning, we were on our way to the skating
rink. Once there, everyone from Cole's company, including the
four of us, was wearing the company-ordered, long-sleeved, light-
blue shirts with their logo. I also wore my denim-colored,
spandex pants, which showed off my youthful, sexy figure. I
caught Cole taking a glimpse here and there once I took off my
coat. Poor Cole just didn't know how to play innocent. He

simply tried too hard not to look at me, and I'd catch him every time.

Once I got my skates on, I went over to assist the children with theirs. Cole sat on a bench about ten feet away, tying his laces. I looked up when I overheard him speaking to a fairly attractive, dark-skinned lady. She seemed to be flirting with him, and from what I gathered, he liked her advances. I was pissed as I continued to strain as I eavesdropped.

"Yes, they are growing up," he said to her while looking at the children. "You should go and speak to them. I'm sure they'll remember you from the last company event."

"I'll do that," she replied.

I kept an open ear while pretending not to be into their conversation. Soon after getting Gavin's second skate on, the woman stepped over to us. "Helloooo," she sang looking at all three of us. She sat next to me on the bench.

I was the only one who spoke back. "Hello," I responded, helping Gavin stand up.

"My . . . Shawna and Gavin . . . the two of you have grown since I last saw you some months ago."

They looked at each other as if they didn't know who she was and what she was talking about. The floor was made of wood, so the children walked over closer to their father, balancing on the wheels of their skates. Since this woman didn't have the courtesy to introduce herself, I made the first move. "I'm Karma Jolley," I said, extending my hand.

She took my hand and gave it a firm shake. "I'm Audrie Davis. I work with the children's father."

"Really?" I asked, trying to seem surprised. "He's never mentioned you before."

"Well, I've only been around six months now, so I'm still new to the company."

"I've only been around about three months myself, so that makes the two of us being new into Cole's life."

She looked as if she was confused by my response. "I'm sorry . . . I don't quite follow you. I thought you were someone I'd seen at the company before. Do you not work for Essential Software?"

"No, but maybe someday. I'm in school studying computer science." She nodded at my response, but her face still said she was baffled. "I was invited to this event by Cole. I mean, it's only right of him, considering the fact I'm practically family now."

She put on a smug grin. "So you're a friend of the family?"

I looked over at Cole and noticed him engaged in a conversation with a tall, slinky-looking gentleman. "No, actually, I'm Cole's girlfriend. We practically live together though. I'm there day and night, taking care of the house and the children." I giggled. "Oh," I said, holding up my finger, "and let me not forget about Cole. You know as his girlfriend, I make sure to take great care of him . . . if you know what I mean."

She stood, giving me a jealous eye. "Oh, I see," she said abruptly. "Well, I just came over to speak to the children, but since they're sort of preoccupied, I'll catch them later."

"Well, don't take it personal. They're just excited about skating. You should try speaking to them before we leave. They should be more receptive by then." I stood then went over to sit next to Cole.

I put my arm around him then whispered into his ear, trying to get under Audrie's skin. "The children are very excited," I said to him.

He looked at me with a huge grin on his face. "I know. Thanks for coming to help out with them," he said.

I turned back to see if Audrie was watching. She stood in the same spot where I left her. Her face looked as if she was saying all sorts of cuss words in her mind. I smirked then turned back to Cole and his male associate.

"Who's this handsome gentleman?" I asked.

"Did you hear that, Cole?" the man asked. "She called me handsome. I wish I had a collar to pop right now."

We all laughed. I looked at Audrie. She rolled her eyes then walked away. I turned back to the two men. "Well, you are handsome. My momma always taught me to speak the truth."

He seemed to blush. Cole sat looking at me as if he couldn't believe the nerve of me. "I guess I owe the two of you an appropriate introduction then." He put his hand on the man's shoulder. "Nick, this is Karma Jolley, my nanny and gracious family friend." I wanted to throw up on the "friend" part. He turned to me. "Karma, this is Nick Murphy, a coworker, friend, and confidante."

I shook his hand. "Nice to meet you, Nick."

Nick turned my hand over then kissed it. "Likewise, my dear."

Cole stood. "So, are we going to get this party started or not?"

I felt a little embarrassed because I hadn't skated since my middle school years. I stood in place as the men headed to exit the rest area. "Well, I'm going to help the children out to the floor."

Cole called the kids over then turned to me. "You don't have to do that. They've been skating hundreds of times. They might be able to teach me a thing or two." He chuckled.

"Uh . . . well, uh . . . I thought you needed me here to help them. What about Gavin? I'm sure he needs help, right?"

"Only when he needs something to eat or drink, but he'll be fine when he's out on the floor. Gavin thinks he's a big boy. Besides, Shawna's very protective of her brother in the rink. They skate as a pair. Now c'mon and enjoy yourself." I stood in place, feeling ashamed. When Cole noticed I hadn't moved, he turned back to me. "What's wrong, Karma?"

I began to mumble. "I forgot to mention I haven't skated in years. I'm afraid I'll fall."

He took a few steps closer to me. I could've sworn I saw disappointment in his eyes, but his response was subtle. "Did you ever learn how to roller skate?"

"Yes."

"Then you'll be fine. C'mon. I'll guide you."

I felt my heart flutter when he took my hand. "Okay," I answered, relieved.

I couldn't believe how patient Cole was with me. I was supposed to be more of a help to him and the children, but there it turned out they all were more of a help to me. After about fifteen minutes, the children had noticed their father assisting me around the rink, so they came over and joined the fun, too. I only slipped a few times, but thank goodness I never hit the ground. Besides, I could feel Audrie's evil glare from the sideline, piercing me while I was with Cole.

Cole swung me out into the middle of the rink then let me go. My heart fell, and I thought I was going to die. He laughed at me, teasing me from the sideline. *Relax, Karma,* I said to myself. *You can do this.* Once I was calm, I began to maneuver the skates on my own. Before I knew it, I was gliding like a pro. I looked over at Cole. Nick had joined him on the sideline to watch me. I playfully stuck my tongue out at them then laughed. They laughed back.

I felt pretty good about myself as I continued to sashay on the floor. After about ten minutes on my own, I looked around for Cole and noticed him heading toward the rest area. Audrie passed him as she started onto the floor, grabbing his hand in an effort to lead him to the rink with her. I couldn't read his lips, but I could see him shaking his head. She looked disappointed, but I was glad that for whatever reason, my man had turned her down. I was also pissed because I had just told her he was my man, so for her to ask him to skate with her despite my presence was like a slap in the face. She didn't know I was nothing to play with, but she was about to find out.

I circled the rink then eased up beside her while she struggled to stay on her feet. "Having problems, Audrie?" I asked.

She twisted her lips, looked off then back at me. She didn't seem to want to hold any type of conversation with me, but I didn't back away. I began to circle her, which apparently made her uneasy because she began to wobble in place. "Would you stop that?" she snapped.

"Why? Am I making you nervous?" I smiled, continuing to circle her.

"I'm trying to keep my balance here. I'm not a very good skater. I tried to get Cole to come out here and teach me—"

"I saw that," I interrupted. I stopped skating in order to face her. "How 'bout I teach you what I've learned."

She frowned. "But you only learned less than thirty minutes ago."

"Which should be the convincer of how easy it would be for me to teach you . . . so, c'mon."

I grabbed Audrie's hand before she could protest then began skating, pulling her along.

"No . . . stop. No," she yelled. I ignored her. Her objections were too late. "Stop it."

Where the strength or the will came from, I don't know, but I began to skate fast, and then even faster, pulling Audrie along for the ride. When I got sick of her yelling behind me, I let her go, but not before jerking her arm, 'causing her to fall—hard. I looked over my shoulder and noticed she landed on her stomach. I turned around, skating toward her. I cupped my hand over my mouth, pretending to be apologetic.

"Oh, Audrie . . . are you okay?" I asked, seconds after stopping my wheels inches from her face.

She didn't respond as I continued to offer fake apologies. Two guys came over to assist her on her feet. She caught a glimpse of me smirking just before the men helped her over to the rest area.

Shawna skated over to me, pulling Gavin along. They were ready for food and drinks. Cole met us just as we exited the floor. He handed me some money then the kids and I were on our way. While seating Shawna and Gavin down at a table, I saw Cole head over to chat with Audrie. She was near the benches, changing into her shoes.

When I saw Cole look up at me with scowl, I quickly turned away. I began to chat with the kids. I imagined Audrie was telling him what I had said about being his girlfriend and how I had made her look like a fool around the rink, but it didn't matter if she stepped to me with Cole face-to-face. I was going to deny everything until the end.

The children were just about finished eating when Cole walked up to the table with fire in his eyes. "I need to talk to you," he spat, glaring at me.

"Okay . . . I'm listening," I responded, sipping my soda.

"I need you to step over there for a minute," he said, pointing to a secluded area.

I looked over at the benches and saw Audrie eyeing us. "Cole, why don't you take a seat, so we can talk right—"

"Now, Karma," he barked, cutting me off.

I stood then started to walk off. I heard Cole telling the kids to sit tight until we returned. The tone in his voice let me know he was about to let me have it, so I attempted to change the mood before he could speak. "Cole, I can't adequately tell you how much of a good time the kids are having. They—"

"Who did you tell Audrie you are to me?" he interrupted.

I tilted my head, dipped my eyebrows, and created a perfect "O" with my mouth before saying, "Excuse me?"

"You heard me, Karma. What did you tell Audrie you meant to me?"

"What did I tell Audrie?" I repeated. "She asked me—"

"I didn't ask you what she asked you," he said sharply. "I asked what—"

"I told her I was a friend of the family. Why?"

"That's not what she told me you said."

"Well, I don't know what she told you, but—"

"Did you tell her we're romantically involved, Karma?" His eyes looked like he was ready to dismiss my ass with a quickness.

"No," I answered, sounding offended. "No. Why would I do that?"

"So, what? You're saying she made that up? Audrie just told me a lie, right?"

Cole's demeanor said he wouldn't believe me no matter what I said, but there was no way I was going to fess up. "Yes, she lied. Bring her over here if you don't believe me." I developed a harsh tone in my voice, hoping Cole would feel he'd offended me. "Go get her," I said, staring into his eyes while he said nothing. "I can't believe this . . ." I cut myself off to pace for a few seconds then ranted again. "All I . . . I only said the truth. I am a friend of the family, aren't I?" I looked at Cole for a response.

"Where did she get the idea that you and I are sleeping together?"

I shook my head. "Oh, my God, Cole . . . she just totally made that up. I don't know how she—" I said just before stopping to cup my mouth. I slapped my forehead. "Oh, no, Cole."

"What?"

"She must've taken something I said out of context. I told her how excited the children were about today, and that I, too, was like a big kid at heart this morning before we left. She asked if I met you all here, and I told her that I'd stayed over last night in order for us to all leave together this morning." I slapped my forehead again. "Oh gosh . . . I'm sorry, Cole. If you call her over here, I'll clear everything up."

He was a lot calmer than he'd been when we first stepped off in private. He turned to look in the direction where Audrie was. She still sat on the bench, but she had her coat on, chatting with Nick. He returned his attention to me. "No, it's alright."

"Cole, are you sure? I feel terrible this misunderstanding came about," I lied. "Please let me go over and talk to Audrie. I need to clarify things."

"No, just drop it. I'll straighten everything out when I'm back to work on Monday. I'll take her to lunch and explain then. Let's get the children. I'm ready to leave."

I glanced back into Audrie's direction. "Okay," I managed to say.

Audrie . . . have lunch with my man? Oh, hell, no.

*W*hen I got to work on Monday morning, I rarely made eye contact as I headed to my office. I knew my coworkers probably had begun talking about what went down at the rink with Audrie and Karma before I got there, especially the female associates. They all were known gossipers. I hated the fact that Audrie was involved period because she was a sweet woman. She didn't deserve the same intense looks I got from our peers or the whispering.

I gave Karma the remainder of the day off on Saturday. I even extended her break through Sunday. I was so disappointed in the behavior Audrie had accused Karma of, I just didn't know anything else to do except leave. I'd never known Audrie to be the type of woman who would lie, let alone about something as serious as a vicious attack. However, Karma spoke so innocently when I addressed Audrie's accusations that I really didn't know what to believe.

I'd been at work for nearly the entire morning when I realized no one had stepped into my office to even speak to me. The only people who mattered to me were Audrie and Nick, so I made up my mind to try to soothe things over. I called Nick first.

"What's going on, man?" I asked just after he answered his line.

"Just trying to get the budget laid out for the Bluff City Entertainment project," he responded.

"Oh, dude, do you realize if you get that contract, you're going to be paid?"

"Why do you think I've been working over every day for the last couple of weeks? My deadline is coming up in five days, but I just might finish early."

"Cool. Glad to hear it. What else is up?"

"Nothing much. What's on your mind?"

"Are you pissed at me?"

"About what?"

"About Audrie?"

"Colby, you're not making sense. Why would I be mad at you about Audrie?"

"Well, I know everyone knows about what happened between Audrie and Karma at the skating rink, and it just seems as if no one is talking to me. Usually you would've called my desk at least once by now."

"Man, first, let me say I've been busy today. Second, I don't know what the hell happened Saturday, but when I looked up, Karma had just let go of Audrie's hand and down on her face Audrie went."

"Karma said it was an accident, but Audrie didn't seem to think so."

"I'm not taking sides, but it didn't look like an accident to me either. If you ask me, Karma's got it bad for you."

I sighed. "Now what could give you that impression? She was only there to help keep an eye on the kids so I could enjoy myself, too. Plus, she's been around long enough for me to treat her like family."

"You might want to be careful with her though, Colby. Karma's cute, sexy, and all that good stuff, but I'm telling you . . . I think she could eventually be bad news for you unless you give her what she wants. And, play dumb if you want, but we both know what that is."

Karma had made advances at me before, so I knew exactly what Nick was saying. I refused to reply to his warning because I didn't feel like getting into that discussion. "Anyway, you heard from Audrie today?" I asked.

"Yeah, I saw her come in this morning, but she's been hemmed up with Wayne and Mary on a project ever since."

"I think I'm gon' give her a shout. I need for her to know how sorry I am."

"Do your thang, man. I'll rap to you later."

"A'ight. Cool."

After hanging up with Nick, I immediately dialed Audrie's desk. Since Nick had said she was tied up, I figured I could leave her a voice message. To my surprise, she answered the phone. "This is Audrie," she answered sweetly.

"Audrie," I replied, startled. "This is Cole. I wasn't expecting for you to pick up. I thought you'd be busy."

"Hi, Cole. I'm a little busy, but what's up?"

My nerves had begun to get the best of me, 'causing me to stutter. "Um, um, I, um, I was, um . . ." I paused and took a deep breath. "Audrie, I owe you an apology." There was an awkward silence between the two of us. I didn't know if she understood how I felt or not, so I began to ramble in an effort to show my sincerity. "Audrie, I'm just as embarrassed as you are . . . and that's why I left . . . I just didn't want—"

"It's okay, Cole," she said, cutting me off. "I'm fine."

"I don't want you to be mad at me, Audrie. Karma says it was an acci—"

"Yeah, well, okay. Anyway . . . I'm not mad at you, Cole."

"How about I make it up to you?"

"I'm listening."

"Lunch?"

"I can't."

"Dinner?"

"I can—"

"Please, Audrie," I interrupted. "Please. I'd love to have dinner with you this evening. Not just because I'm trying to apologize, but I'm also trying to get to know you on a personal level."

When I heard her take a breath to speak, I sensed a smile in her tone. "Cole, I was about to say I can do that."

"Whew! Girl, you know how to make a brotha sweat. Cool. What time do you think you'll be off this evening?"

"I'm thinking around six-thirty or seven."

"Then I'll make reservations at the Tower Room for seven."

"Tower Room? Cole, we don't have to—"

"I want to, Audrie. I'll be waiting for you in the lobby, okay?"

"Okay."

I felt so much better after hanging up. I called to make dinner reservations then attempted to continue with my day. I'd only been working for ten minutes when my cell phone rang. I looked at the caller ID and noticed the number was coming from my house.

"Hello, Karma. What's going on?"

"Hello, Cole. How's your day going?" she practically sang. She certainly seemed to be in a good mood.

"Not bad. What can I help you with?"

"I was just checking with you to see how your day was going."

"Thanks for checking in, but I'm fine, and I'm busy. I'll call you back," I said briefly. "By the way, I'll be delayed getting home. Can you stay over?"

"Sure. Not a problem. I'll see you later on."

I hung up without saying good-bye. I contemplated calling her back to be honest about why I would be late getting home, but

I decided against it. I wasn't over being angry with Karma, and I didn't feel like having more conversation with her right then. There was no way for me to determine what really happened between her and Audrie, but something was telling me Karma was less than ladylike in my absence.

Six-thirty sharp, I was in the lobby waiting for Audrie. She stayed cooped in her office all day, so I hadn't seen her yet. This made me even more anxious. I couldn't believe what I was feeling. The last time I'd felt nervous about being with a woman was when I was about to have my first date with my wife. *C'mon now, Cole. Shake it off. Glenda would want you to have a life. Don't start a guilt trip now.*

Audrie came down the hall looking like America's Next Top Model. She might as well have been on the runway because she certainly strutted her stuff as she headed toward me. She wore a white, off-the-shoulder mohair sweater with powder-blue leather slacks and white boots. She carried her floor-length, matching leather coat across her arm. When I smiled at her, she smiled back, easing the butterflies in my stomach.

"How are you doing, gorgeous?" I asked just as she came closer.

"Great," she said, leaning in to hug me.

I reached for her coat. "Very nice," I said, holding the coat up for her to put on.

"Thanks. It's amazing the things you can get when you shop online with Victoria's Secret, huh?"

"What? Vickie selling powder-blue leather coats, too?"

She laughed. "So the two of you are on first-name basis or what?"

I fixed her collar then stepped around in front of her. "I wish." I laughed. "I'd love the opportunity to meet the face behind Victoria's Secret. Launching a software development project with a company like that would be huge. I'd be paid. You know what I mean?"

"Definitely, but if you don't know already, online shopping with Victoria's Secret seems to work wonders for women. I don't see anything wrong with their e-business, so you might find it difficult landing that deal. 'Vickie,' as you call her, already has it going on."

I nodded and grabbed her hand. "I hear you. C'mon, let's go."

"Okay, but do you mind if I ride with you? I carpooled with Wayne this morning, so that leaves me kinda stranded."

"Girl, please. With me around, there's no such thing as you being stranded. Besides, aren't I the one who's paying for dinner?"

"Then I'm ready."

The ride to the Tower Room on Poplar Avenue wasn't very long, considering our workplace was less than ten miles from there. Most of our conversation came during dinner and over dessert. Audrie savored the cheesecake one bite at a time while I devoured the warm apple tart in just a few gulps.

By eight-thirty, we still weren't ready to leave. I could tell she enjoyed chatting with me just as much as I did with her. Every so often, she'd reach across the table and caress my hand—something I certainly didn't mind.

"So are we gonna close this place down or what?" she asked, smiling.

I looked around and noticed we were two of four people still in the restaurant. I looked at my watch. "Hmm. The restaurant closes around ten-thirty, I think, but I imagine the staff would like to clean up and go home. I better ask for the check."

I signaled for our waiter. He already had the check in his hand. Once our bill was paid, Audrie and I were on our way. She gave me directions to her apartment, which was only about fifteen minutes from where I lived. I was surprised to know she lived close to the Crystal Palace Skating Rink.

"I didn't know you live in Westwood," I said, driving. "You're just minutes away from me. I live in Southaven," I said.

75

"What . . . Mississippi?" she asked.

"Yeah. Not far, huh?"

"No. So maybe I should be carpooling with you, too, especially since you have to come past where I live to get to work. I pay my way. Ask Wayne."

"Oh, no need for that. I believe you. You seem to be pretty responsible."

We were silent for a moment. "You think it's going to snow tomorrow?"

"I don't know, but please, let's not talk it up. The kids only have this week left in school before Christmas break then it can snow all it wants. I hate when they have to do makeup days later. It cuts into their summer vacation."

"I remember those days."

I glanced over at her. She looked at me then we both laughed. "Okay," I said, cracking my side.

"What?" She couldn't stop giggling.

"You talk like it was yesterday," I said.

"And that's hilarious to you obviously."

"No . . . no . . . no," I said, trying to stop laughing. "No, Audrie. I don't mean any harm. On a serious note, I don't know how old you are, but it really doesn't matter. I know you're an adult, and you're beautiful. Inside and out."

Her chocolate skin seemed to blush. "Aw, Cole, that's sweet." She grinned from ear to ear. "You wanna know how old I am?"

I nodded. "It'll be nice to know."

"Thirty-six. Is that older than what you're use to? I know your girlfriend can't be older than twenty-one."

I rolled my eyes and sighed intensely. "Ah, here we go. I knew the night wouldn't slide without me having to explain things again."

"No, you don't have to explain, Cole."

"Yes, I do."

"No, you really don't. What you and that little girl do is none of my business."

I pointed to her apartment complex. "You live over here, right?"

"Yes, that first door right there," she answered, pointing. "You can pull into my guest parking spot over here."

The vacant spot was right next to her car. I parked then turned off the engine. I couldn't leave without clearing the air. "Look," I said, turning to her, "I know you said it was none of your business, but how about I make it your business." She looked at me, squinting, obviously confused. "I want to explain the situation with Karma because I like you," I continued. "The last thing I want you to think is that I'm a dirty old man. I'll be forty-one in a matter of weeks. I don't know if anyone in the office has bothered to tell you I tragically lost my wife several months ago. Since then, I haven't been looking to replace her. For the most part, I've felt it was too soon to date.

"The young woman, who for whatever reason told you she was my girlfriend, is only an assistant aka nanny or whatever people are calling help these days. I'm not sure what you think of me, but in the last few days, I've come to know you're someone I could spend time with. I think we should get to know each other. If you feel differently then let me know. I won't push the subject."

She smiled. "I didn't know you had begun to push." I smiled back. She opened the car door. "Your kids are probably wondering what happened to you tonight, so I'll let you get home to them." She must've seen the disappointment on my face because she paused to stare at me. "Unless, you'd like to come in for a minute or two. I've got some gourmet decaffeinated mocha coffee."

"Gourmet, huh?"

"Yeah, sir, and it's good, too."

"I bet it is. I'm sure my kids have been in bed ever since eight-thirty, so I'll come in for a bit."

We got out of the car then headed into her apartment. Just after turning on a lamp, she offered me a seat. "Let me take your coat," she said, as I took it off. "You can have a seat over on the couch. I'm going to change then get the coffee going."

"Sure," I said, heading to the couch.

I looked around the living room. It was clean and cozy-looking, mainly with earth tones. I noticed a beautiful crystal elephant, which looked to weigh at least two pounds, sitting on top of Audrie's coffee table. A deep-red table runner lined the coffee table, giving the appearance of the elephant walking on red carpet.

Audrie had gone to the back of the apartment and returned less than five minutes later wearing a pair of sweats and a T-shirt. "Sorry, Cole. I had to get out of that leather."

"No problem," I said, still scoping the elephant. "I gather you're a Delta."

"You gathered correctly."

The room was dimly lit by the lamp in the corner, but some-how her dark skin had a radiant glow. She turned to walk away, but I gently grabbed her arm. She looked down at my hand then into my eyes. I stood to meet her face-to-face. "Thanks for inviting me in tonight, Audrie . . . because I wasn't ready for the night to end."

She stepped closer to me, locking only our eyes at first and then our lips. I slid my hand around her waist, pulling her into me. She moaned as I gently sucked her bottom lip. When she opened her mouth to moan again, my tongue happily greeted hers for a sensual slow dance.

After several minutes of passionate kissing, Audrie pulled away. "I was supposed to be making coffee, remember?"

I chuckled. "That's okay. How about we sit and talk some more?" I said, pulling her to the couch.

She leaned over on my chest, and I wrapped my arms around her. "I can't believe you're here, Cole."

"To tell you the truth, neither can I. So, where do we go from here?"

She sat up to look at me. "Let's take things slow. We need to be friends before anything," she said, sliding her finger down my chin. "I'm divorced with no children, but you have little ones. There's no sense in rushing me into their lives right away. They still need time to heal. I'm patient, and I'll be here. I'm not going anywhere, okay?"

I smiled then took the same finger she'd used to trace my chin and kissed it. "Gotcha."

We cuddled on her couch and talked until one o'clock in the morning. I had to force myself to leave so we could both get some kind of sleep before going in to work.

When I got home, I opened the door carefully and shut it even quieter. I turned the alarm off in the nick of time then tipped into the living room to head up the stairs. Just before I stepped onto the first step, the lamp near my wing chair clicked on. I was startled by the sight of Karma, sitting in the chair, staring at me with a blank expression.

"Where were you?" she asked, unblinkingly.

"Excuse me?" I stopped in my tracks.

"Where were you?" she repeated, standing up to walk toward me. She had on one of Glenda's short nightgowns, and as she got closer, I could smell Glenda's Tommy Girl cologne. "Your children were asking for you, and your dinner sat in the oven so long, it dried out."

I popped my forehead. "Oh, Karma. It didn't even dawn on me that you'd save me dinner. I'm sorry, but I appreciate it anyway." I started upstairs then turned around. "Is that my wife's gown and cologne you're wearing?"

She gave me the and-so-what look. "I didn't have anything else to put on. You should've told me all of your T-shirts are in the dirty laundry. I would've washed clothes a day early."

I shook my head and threw my hand. "Okay . . . whatever." I started upstairs again.

"So, you aren't going to tell me *what* took you until—" she turned and glanced at the clock on the wall— "one-thirty in the morning to get home?"

I sighed. "Not what, Karma. Who. *Who* took me so long to get home."

Her mouth flew opened. "You mean to tell me you were with someone all this time? I was worried sick. I called you several times so you could say good night to the children, but you didn't even bother to answer," she snapped.

"I forgot my phone in the car, Karma. I'm sorry I made you worry, but I think you need to relax a little bit. Better yet, take a chill pill," I said sternly. "I'm done speaking about this tonight. Try again in the morning."

I left her standing at the foot of the stairs. I went into my room and looked through Glenda's clothes in the drawer to see if anything else was missing. I was disturbed to see Karma wearing Glenda's gown and smelling just like her. I had a notion to go ahead and get rid of everything Glenda owned. If my beloved couldn't benefit from those things anymore, neither would another woman.

Five minutes after I'd been in my room with the door shut, I heard Karma stomp up the stairs and into the guest room, slamming the door behind her. *She's gon' be a fuckin' problem,* I thought. *I can see that right now.*

*C*onsidering the fact that Cole didn't go to bed until nearly two in the morning, I knew he would sleep in late. It was after 6:00 A.M., so I got up to fix breakfast and get the children off to school. I was burning up mad about how Cole had disrespected me by coming in at an ungodly hour. He owed me more courtesy. I was the one at home with *his* children, cooking, cleaning, doing homework, and more. The more I thought about it, the more bothered I was.

After dropping the kids at school, I went back to the house to find Cole in the kitchen eating the breakfast I'd cooked. Although I was angry, I tried to remain calm. "I was going to wake you, but I kinda figured you had intended on sleeping late. That's how some people have it when they can work on their own schedule."

He nodded, still chewing his sausage. He took a sip of orange juice then spoke. "Sometimes I have it like that. When my boss hasn't called a mandatory meeting, then yes, I'm free to go in later. How are you feeling this morning?"

"I'm okay," I answered, taking a seat at the table.

I noticed his brown skin was smooth from an obvious shave. His hair was lined and so was his mustache. I ogled him long enough for him to look up, apparently confused about why I was staring.

"Why are you looking at me like that?"

"You shaved and lined up this morning, didn't you?"

"Yes. How nice of you to notice," he answered shortly. I kept staring. He looked at me again. "Now what?"

"You hurt my feelings, Cole."

"Again? What did I do now?"

"Nothing. Forget about it," I snapped. I got up to fix me a bowl of fruit. When I sat back down, Cole kept his eyes buried in his plate. I broke the silence. "I was just thinking how nice it must've been for you to be out on a first date in a while."

He nodded without looking up. "I must say, I enjoyed myself."

"Well, may I know who she is?"

He paused then took a deep breath. I waited patiently with my hand under my chin. "Audrie . . . from work," he said.

"Oh." Disappointment had to have reeked from my voice because he stopped chewing his food then looked at me.

"Something d'matter?"

I shook my head. "No. Nothing's wrong." He continued eating, and I got up to fix me some juice. "So tell me what you like about her," I said, leaning into the refrigerator.

"What's there not to like about her?"

I turned around. "She's all that, huh?"

"Truthfully, I think she is. She's in the same career field as me, divorced with no children, beautiful, kind-hearted, closer to my age—"

"Are you taking a stab at me?" I asked with much attitude. I sat down staring intently into his eyes.

"No, no, not at all," he said, looking at me. "I'm just saying she's just a few years younger than me."

"You really have an issue with our age difference, don't you? I wonder why it doesn't matter though that I'm capable of being your cleanup woman, handling your children, fixing your meals, washing your clothes, being your right-hand girl and everything else a good wife should be—but it's not okay for us to have a relationship."

"Why are we discussing this?" he yelled. "Huh? I could've sworn we had agreed we weren't going to be discussing the subject of you and me anymore."

"I'm just trying to understand, Cole. You know—" I started then stopped myself. "Never mind." I shook my head. "Forget it. I've never been one to beg a man to want me, and I'm not about to start now."

Cole huffed then pushed his plate away. "Karma, it's not you. I've always been attracted to women my age or older. I've never been into younger women. I don't know why, but that's just the way it is. You're a beautiful young girl, but that's all I see. I'm sorry."

I got up from the table. I wanted to flip out, but I feared being fired. I set my glass in the sink then started out of the kitchen. "You don't have to be sorry, Cole." *At least not yet,* I thought as I headed up the stairs.

I went into the guestroom to gather my things. "Karma, I'm out," Cole yelled up the stairs.

I didn't even bother to respond because I was still upset. I heard the front door close then I tipped downstairs to make sure he was gone. I peeked out the window and was glad to see his car wasn't in the driveway. I went into the laundry room to look for the shirt he wore the night before. Once I found it, I sniffed it. It smelled just like his Sean John cologne.

I hurried back upstairs with the shirt then stripped naked in the guest room. I stood in front of the mirror on the dresser, rubbing his shirt all over my body so I'd have his scent on me. The fabric felt wonderful to my skin. When I slid it down between my legs, I accidentally left a wet spot near the collar. It was too late to be concerned because my kitty was on fire. I propped my foot up on the dresser, exposing my recently shaved girlfriend in the mirror. The sight alone made me even hotter.

I sniffed the shirt while fondling myself. I went crazy, barely able to stand as I imagined Cole lapping me. "Oh, yes," I moaned out loud. "Yes, Cole. Like that, baby."

I could only handle a few minutes of masturbation before letting go. This was the quickest climax I'd ever experienced. I was out of breath as I leaned over the dresser, sucking in as much of Cole's cologne into my lungs as I could. The scent had me hypnotized. I had an urge to get off again, so I went to the bed, taking the shirt with me then spread eagle.

Two more orgasms came just as quick as the first one. Just as I finished the last one, I heard the front door opening downstairs. When I heard Cole's voice on his cell phone, I panicked. I went to the door to eavesdrop.

"I should be there in about an hour," he obviously said into his cell. "I just got in a hurry after waking up late and forgot the file. Don't worry. I'll be there. Talk to you later." I heard him drop his keys on the coffee table then start upstairs.

I closed my bedroom door and locked it.

"Karma," he called.

My heart dropped because I didn't want him to smell sex, which wasn't really sex in the air. "Hold on, Cole. I'm not dressed." I looked over on the bed and spotted his shirt. After ditching it in the closet, I put my top back on then headed to the door. I stood behind it then cracked it to stick my head out.

"Hey," he said with Princess bouncing at his feet. "What are you still doing here? Aren't you going to school today?"

"Uh," I started then paused to think. Just when I was about to tell him that I would be leaving for school in an hour, he finished my statement.

"Oh, I know. I forgot that your college schedule is different than the city and county schools. You're already on winter break, right?"

Damn, I almost messed up. "Right," I said. "No school for me until January."

"Okay. I came back home because I forgot something. I was worried when I saw your car still out there. I know you and I aren't seeing eye-to-eye right now, but the last thing I want to do is interfere with your schooling."

"I'm okay, Cole, and I know you care. School is out for a while, and I'm just taking advantage of some chill time. I'll be stepping out in a bit, but I'll be back later on."

He nodded then walked to his room. I closed the door then got dressed. When I heard the front door open then close, I felt it safe to come out of my room. I went into the closet to get the shirt then sprinted downstairs. Just as I was about to go into the laundry room, Cole came out of the kitchen, startling me.

"Cole, you scared me," I said, picking up the shirt I'd dropped. "I thought you were gone. I heard the door open and shut."

"I shut it after realizing I needed to go into the kitchen to get this piece of mail," he said, waving an envelope. "What are you doing with that?" He frowned, pointing to his shirt.

"I . . . uh . . . I was just . . . uh." I couldn't seem to think of anything quick enough. *Face it,* I thought, *you're caught with your juice all over this man's shirt.* "I . . . uh . . . I had gone in the laundry room to get the things that need to go to the cleaners, and uh . . . my uh . . . cell started ringing upstairs, so I uh . . . unknowingly took your shirt with me." *He is not going to believe that shit.*

"Oh, well, I've got one more shirt that needs to go to the cleaners. It's upstairs. Hold on while I get it," he said, darting past me.

Close call. "Okay, Cole."

He came back downstairs with the shirt then gave it to me. A minute later, he was out the door. I gathered the clothes for the cleaners then went on my way. "Princess, I'll see you later," I said, heading out the door.

To the cleaners was my first stop then it was off to my apartment. I needed to get on the Internet to do some research about that Audrie Davis. I was glad she told me her last name at the rink because it would prove helpful in finding out what I needed to know about her. As far as I was concerned, she was not going to have my man.

After only about three hours on the web, I found out Audrie Davis was born Audrie Mitchell until she married Rodney Davis in 1998, only to divorce him four years later. Audrie lived in Westwood and Rodney still lived in the East Memphis area where he and Audrie once owned a home. I had a wealth of information by the time I got offline, but I had planned to pace myself in order to create the perfect scheme.

When I get through, Cole will be angry enough at Audrie to never want to deal with her again.

"**O**h, my God, Cole, yes, baby . . . yes, right there, baby," Audrie whispered while I tapped her from the back as she bent over the desk in my office.

It was a Friday evening in January, one month after we had begun dating, but the sex had started only a week into our relationship. Despite having said we needed to take things slow, we couldn't seem to keep our hands to ourselves. I had pulled down all the blinds and locked the door. The adrenaline from the notion of possibly getting caught was a high all by itself. The workplace was mainly empty with the exception of a few associates like Nick who stuck around trying to finish last-minute details, so we knew there stood a chance of getting caught.

Audrie had worn a sexy red, form-fitting sweater dress with a pair of black knee-high boots. Her hair was pulled around to one side in a collar-length ponytail, but by the time I got a hold of her, it was all over her head. "Right there, Cole," she said, moaning, holding on to the desk.

"Is that the spot, baby?" I asked. "Tell me. Is that the spot?"

"Yes . . . mmm . . . oh, yes, baby."

The CleanUp Woman

I loved her sexy groans and moans when we made love. Just after bending her over, I had peeled her dress around her waist and discovered that not only were her legs bare, but so was her ass. She only had on a thong. I kneeled then licked her Hershey-colored ass, which by the way tasted like candy. She wore some type of sweet-scented lotion. Smelling and tasting it made me harder with every whiff.

Audrie and I spent as much time together as possible. I never realized love would hit me when it did because I felt getting involved with another woman only months after my wife's murder would be wrong. I felt my kids didn't deserve to see me dating, and that it was unfair to my beloved Glenda. Her murder hadn't been solved, which kept me looking guilty and provided no closure for our family. My in-laws still weren't speaking to me. Be it right or wrong, I felt if they didn't want anything to do with me, then they shouldn't have anything to do with my kids either.

Audrie rubbed herself and squeezed her muscles around me as I stroked her. I held tightly to her waist and thrust my pelvis into her with rapid strokes. "That's right, baby," she whispered. "Get it, baby. Hit it."

"Aaaaaahhhhh . . . ooooohhhhh . . . shiiiiittt." I huffed. It was hard trying not to be loud, considering how I had just released the best climax I'd had in our days of sex.

"Shhh, baby," she warned. "You're gonna get us caught." She began to slowly rotate her chocolate moon as I leaned over her back, wheezing in her ear.

"Un-un, baby. Stop that. You know he's sensitive," I said, referring to the descending erection between my legs.

"Well, get up then."

"I can't move," I said out of breath.

Audrie rested herself on the desk with her elbows. She kept sighing, seemingly impatient, and frankly, I couldn't blame her. She didn't get hers, and there I was weak and limp from getting mine. I pulled out of her then went into my desk drawer for some

88

Wet Ones. Audrie snatched them from me then began to fuss. "You know what—"

"Yes, I do know what," I interrupted. "That's why I'll meet you at your place at seven to finish. Okay?"

She smirked. "You better be over at seven on the dot, too."

"I will."

"I ain't playing with you, Cole. You've got me all horny and everything, so I don't expect for you to keep me waiting."

"I'll be there, baby." I gently kissed her lips then her neck. "You just be ready for me."

"A'ight," she said, rolling her eyes as she left the office.

My birthday was coming up on Saturday, and I had hoped Audrie would spend some time with me. She knew about it in advance, but she still hadn't responded to my request to have dinner. I alternated weekends between spending time with Audrie and the kids, so I assumed her hesitation was due to having already made plans for that day. However, with it being my birthday, I had hoped she'd cancel any other reservation to be with me.

Glenda and I would celebrate our birthdays together every year. I knew waking up without her on Saturday would be hard for me, unless Audrie was around to occupy my mind. I gathered my things then headed out but not before calling home. I asked Karma if she'd mind me staying out late. She didn't sound enthused, but she agreed then she passed the phone to the children so I could get their permission as well. Shawna said she and her brother were helping Karma bathe Princess, and from the cheer in her voice, I was the farthest thing from their minds.

I looked at my watch when I rang Audrie's doorbell. *Hmm, six-fifty-six.* She opened the door, smiling.

"Have you glanced at your clock?" I asked, standing in the doorway.

"No, but c'mon in," she replied, beckoning me.

"Un-un." I remained in the doorframe. "I still have four minutes to spare—"

"Get in here," Audrie snapped, snatching me into the apartment with a fist full of my collar and tie.

I playfully coughed as if she choked me. She let me go then we both laughed. She was wearing a pair of hot-pink Daisy Dukes and a white halter top. She closed the door behind me then started toward the bedroom. Her butt cheeks eyed me, daring me to follow her. "Girl, what have you got on?" I headed into the bedroom with her.

"I'm at home, and I wasn't expecting anyone over except my man." She turned around once in the bedroom, threw her hands around my neck, and kissed me, catching me off guard.

My eyes were closed as we kissed, but once I decided to take a peek, my attention was drawn to her dresser. "Rodney sent some more flowers I see," I said, breaking our embrace.

She looked back at the dresser. "Yeah, he did. C'mon, now. Let's not get into that argument again."

"Audrie . . . if the shoe were on the other foot, you'd understand where I'm coming from. He sends flowers to the office, to your home, and not only do you feel it's okay to accept them, but you even bring them into your bedroom—our bedroom."

"So, you're jealous?"

"Call it what you want, Audrie. I think it's time you tell your ex-husband you have a new man in your life. He's getting way out of hand with sending these flowers, and I think it's because you keep accepting them."

"I've explained that before. Many times I'm not around when they're delivered. What do you want me to do? Throw them away?" She put her arms back around my neck. "The flowers are innocent bystanders. I shouldn't take it out on them," she said teasingly. She placed a soft kiss on my lips then on my neck.

I wanted to play tough, but she made me smile inside. "Girl, you know that's my spot." I put my arms around her waist then slid my hands down to her behind. She kept kissing my neck. "You know that's my spot, girl. Mmph. You ain't right."

She laughed, but continued seducing me. After reaching between my legs and feeling my erection, she really began to have her way. She unbuckled my belt, unzipped my pants then slid them down to my ankles. She stood, staring into my eyes with her hands cupped behind her back as though she was innocent. "Still think I ain't right?"

My man was throbbing so bad, I had to massage it to ease the pressure. "Hell naw. You ain't right," I said, panting.

She dropped to her knees with her hands still behind her back and began to fondle me hands-free. She licked as though I was something delicious. I gripped her hair, accidentally forcing her to take more of me than she had intended. When I heard her gag, I stopped. "Sorry," I said.

"Cole, I can't do that, baby. It's too—"

"I know it's too much for you. Don't worry about it, baby. Get up on the bed."

She lay on her back and opened wide. I started down on her, but she stopped me, begging for her love handle. I reached for my jacket and took a condom out of the pocket. After placing it on, I dove deep into Audrie.

"Aaaaaahhhhh," she screamed. "Yes, baby."

Audrie began to wildly grind with me, but she didn't stay in the missionary position for long. Before I realized what happened, she had turned me over and began to ride me with the same vigor as she had when I was on top of her. She leaned over and whispered in my ear while rocking me. "It's yours, Cole," she said, blowing her warm breath into my ear. "Nobody else's. All yours. "

On that note, I gave it to her. Her rocking motion and my upward thrusts caused her to explode two times back to back. I damn near lost my mind each time she climaxed with me inside of her. The warmth of it all made it hard for me to hold back. I turned her over to take control. When she released her third orgasm, it was all over for me.. We let go together, and then as usual, I went limp.

"I know you don't like it when I put all my weight on you, but hold on for me," I said, panting. "I'll get up in a minute, baby."

Usually, she would fuss, but she was too spent to talk. Instead, she lay breathing just as heavy as me. I rolled off her and onto my back. After a few minutes, she climbed on top of me, resting her head on my shoulder. "I love you, Cole. I think you know that."

"Mm-hmm," I answered. My tone was sarcastic. "Although you continue to accept roses from a man you once shared a bed with despite how I feel about it . . . yeah . . . I know you love me."

"Now wait a minute, Cole—"

"What am I waiting for, Audrie?"

"Because . . . Cole, I've told you . . . he doesn't even call me. I don't know why he keeps sending the gifts and flowers. I don't bother reaching out to him either. I just think that if he sees I won't call him no matter what he sends, then he'll quit his efforts."

"Really now? Is that what you think?"

"Yeah, I do. I think he's looking for a reaction out of me, and I won't give it to him. He'll have to give up eventually."

I rolled over on my side, turning my back to her. "A'ight."

She pushed my shoulder. "A'ight? You know what? Just forget it. I keep trying to show you signs you're the only man for me, but you keep playing ignorant. Just forget it."

"I have," I said coldly, pulling the cover over my head.

Before I knew it, morning came, and I was awakened by blinding sunbeams in my eyes and Audrie's piercing voice, singing the chorus to Stevie Wonder's version of "Happy Birthday." I playfully buried my head under the pillow, squeezing against my ears. Audrie jumped in bed on top of me. We began fighting for the pillow while she continued to do what she thought was singing. I laughed so hard, I lost strength to hold the pillow. She snatched it out of my hands.

"What's so funny?" she asked just after cracking the last note. "Baby, you're beautiful, I swear you are . . . but you can't sing."

She playfully hit me several times with the pillow. "That's not funny, Cole. You've never said that to me before." "I thought you would've caught the hint when I turned up the car radio every time you started singing. It wasn't so you could hear the music. It was to drown you out." As I laughed, she beat me some more.

"My feelings are hurt. I'm not going to give you the breakfast I fixed."

"You fixed me breakfast to eat in bed?" I asked, making my eyebrows dance.

"Yep, but you're not going to get it unless you take back what you said about my singing."

"Okay," I said, sighing. I looked up at the ceiling. "Lord, forgive me for the lie I'm about to tell." She whopped me a good one with the pillow then jumped off the bed, pouting.

"I ain't playing with you no more, Cole."

I wanted to tell her I wasn't playing with her either, but her feelings were hurt enough. "Okay, baby. C'mere." She walked over and sat on the bed with her arms folded. I stroked her back. "I'm sorry for what I said about your singing. Who cares if you can sing or not? Certainly not me. You're good at so many other things that it doesn't matter to me that you sound like a toad."

She turned to look at me. I tried to keep a serious face, but she burst into laughter before me, causing me to laugh, too. "This isn't the first time someone's checked my singing. I'm just mad that it was you this time."

I slid closer to her and began kissing her back with soft pecks. "I said I'm sorry."

She stood. "Un-un, Cole. We're not getting ready to roll around in the haystack this morning. Your children are probably wondering where you are. You need to eat so you can go spend time with them." She placed the breakfast tray on my lap.

"Okay, but I *am* going to see you tonight, right?" I knew the answer, but I was hoping she'd had a change of heart. Audrie stood in the mirror, picking at her hair while ignoring my question. "It's a simple question, Audrie."

She turned around and huffed. "I'm sorry, Cole. I just—"

"Save it," I said, removing the breakfast tray from in front of me.

I got out of bed and got dressed. Audrie stood against her dresser watching my every move. My feelings were hurt. I didn't understand what was so important that she could deny celebrating my birthday with me. I didn't have words for her, so I grabbed my keys and walked out of her bedroom without saying anything. She called after me.

"Cole," she said, following me to the door. I stopped to look at her, but I still felt too hurt to speak. "Call me later tonight, baby, and we can talk about it."

I shook my head then sneered as I walked out on her. *She's got a hell of a lot of nerve.*

Eight o'clock in the morning and his ass still hasn't come home, I thought, piling the breakfast dishes into the dishwasher. When Cole called the night before to say he would be home late, I trusted him. Although he wanted me to believe his tardiness was due to work, I knew he would be hanging out with Audrie. What I hadn't counted on was the fact that he'd actually stay out all night with her. I had allowed the children to stay up an extra hour, thinking Cole would be in to bid them good night. His so-called private relationship with Audrie had totally changed him. I never meant to allow him to get so close to her. I needed to put my foot down—immediately.

The children continued to sit at the table, watching as I mixed the cake batter. Once I was done, I gave them the bowl so they could lick the excess batter, then I placed the mixture into the oven. Princess kept whimpering because she wanted to taste the bowl with the children.

"It's chocolate, stupid," I yelled to the dog. "You can't have any or you'll die."

"Yeah, it's chocolate, stupid," Gavin said, mimicking me.

"Hush," I fussed at him. "Nobody asked you for your two cents."

"I ain't got two cents—"

"Didn't I tell you to hush?" I gave him an intimidating stare then he lowered his eyes back into the bowl. "One hour to an hour and ten minutes," I read aloud from the cookbook.

"One hour? Aw, man," Shawna said, pouting. "That's a long time."

I set the cookbook on the table. "Not as long as it'll be when we get to taste the cake," I responded.

"Huh?" she said, wiping her hands on the damp dishrag I had placed on the table. She picked up the book.

"Huh? What did I tell you about that word?"

Shawna looked up at me. "You said not to say that to you."

I placed my hand on my hip. "Okay. Now what's the proper response?"

"Ma'am?"

"That's right. Don't ever let *huh* slip out of your mouth to me again. I'm not one of your little friends. You can't talk to me like that. You understand me?"

"Yes, ma'am," she said, placing her eyes back in the book.

"Now . . . to answer your question . . . we're not going to eat the cake until later this evening." Neither of them bothered to look up at me. "What are you trying to look for in that book?"

"I'm just reading it," Shawna answered.

"I know, but what are you looking for?"

"The picture of the cake looks like it has pieces of coconut in the icing."

"It does, but I'm not going to use coconut icing. Do you not like it?"

"I like it, but I don't know if Gavin can eat it. He's allergic to stuff like peanuts, but I forget what else. He'll start wheezing and gasping for air."

My jaw dropped. "Your father never told me that. What happens when Gavin can't catch his breath?"

"He has an EpiPen in each of the bathroom cabinets," she responded. "Plus, sometimes we take him to the doctor afterward."

I stared off in wonder. How could have Cole been so careless not to mention his son's allergies to me before? Shawna broke my daze.

"Are we eating the cake after dinner?" she asked, fumbling with the book.

"Yes. I already said later this evening."

"What's for dinner?" Gavin asked, licking his fingers.

I was getting agitated. I took the bowl from him and the book from Shawna. "Look. Get out of here. Both of you," I said, pointing toward the kitchen door. I threw the bowl into the sink. "You two are asking too many questions." The children got up from the table then headed out of the kitchen. Princess followed them. "And wash your hands before touching anything," I yelled behind them. I hid the cookbook behind the refrigerator so Cole wouldn't discover the secret of why I cooked so well.

By nine-twenty the cake had cooled and was ready for the icing. I mixed up the chocolate icing according to the recipe then smoothed it onto the cake. Just as I was finishing, Cole walked in.

"Good morning," he said.

"Morning," I answered shortly.

"Something smells great." He looked at the cake then smiled. "Is that for me?"

I looked up, rolled my eyes then continued icing the cake. "Maybe."

"What do you mean maybe? Who else in this house has a birthday today?"

I didn't bother to look up. "Who says this is a birthday cake?" I snapped.

"Oh, well, excuse me."

He went over to the stove then stood in front of it as if he was looking for something. I had cleaned it and put all the dishes away.

"I didn't bother fixing you breakfast because I didn't know when you'd be home."

He turned, shaking his head. "That's okay."

I rolled my eyes again. "Besides, I figured you'd probably eat breakfast wherever you laid your head last night."

He walked in front of me with his hands on his hips. "I said that's okay."

I placed the cake lid on top of the plate then set the container on the counter near the refrigerator. Cole stood silent, looking as if he'd lost his best friend.

"Is something d'matter, Cole? You look like you've got something on your mind?"

He sat at the table then sighed. "I'm okay. Where're the kids?"

"I think they're up in their rooms. We ate breakfast pretty early. I told them to leave the kitchen while I finished the cake." I sat at the table with him. "You sure there isn't anything on your mind."

"No," he said, unable to look at me. He kept his eyes fixed on the table. "I'm alright."

I got up then went over to the cabinet and opened the drawer with the envelope I'd placed in it the day before. I sat back at the table then passed it to Cole.

"Happy Birthday, Cole." He looked up at me. "It's from me and the kids."

He gasped. "Should I call them down here before I open it?"

"Well, you can, but it's not necessary."

His face glowed with anxiousness. He tore open the envelope, took out the gift card then read the note. He looked up at me after setting the card on the table.

"I don't know what to say. How did you know I like Ruth's Chris Steak House?"

I shrugged. "Oh, I just took a wild guess."

"Really?" he asked, tilting his head and twisting his mouth in a peculiar manner.

I smiled. "Yeah . . . a wild guess, plus calling Nick's office to find out what you like really helped me." We both laughed.

"Well, Nick certainly knows how to keep a secret. I had no clue he ever spoke to you." He smiled and shook his head. "Thanks, Karma." He picked up the note and read it again. "There's enough on this gift card to feed four."

"Hmm . . . I wonder who the other three people will be. I'm sure they'll be some people who are very special to you."

He nodded. "Absolutely. I'm going to call up my friends, Nick, Evan, and Lewis right now."

I gasped. "Un-un," I said, pouting.

Cole laughed. "No, I'm just teasing."

"You better be."

"Well, I'd love for you to accompany me and the kids to dinner this evening."

I pretended to be shocked. "Well . . . I'd love to, but what about Audrie?" I could've sworn I saw his face turn sour just before he looked off. "Don't you want to take Audrie with you?"

He turned his attention back to me. "Audrie has things to do, so she wouldn't be able to go."

"Oh, I'm so sorry to hear that," I lied. "In that case, I'd love to have dinner with you tonight."

He stood then started out of the kitchen. "Good, I'm heading upstairs to tell Shawna and Gavin. I'm sure my babies miss me."

"Yes, we do," I whispered.

"I'm sorry. Did you say something?" he said as he turned to look at me.

"Um . . . I was just saying they sure do miss you."

We all showed up to Ruth's Chris dressed in our best. I had fixed Shawna's hair into one spiraling ponytail centered on top of her head. She wore a red velvet dress with a black collar and matching buttons. Cole had helped Gavin get dressed. They both wore charcoal suits with white shirts and black ties. I wanted to wear black, too, but the only black dress I owned wasn't right for the evening, so I wore red instead. I had on a long-sleeved, crush velvet, form-fitting dress that had a deep V-cut in the back. We made a lovely family, and deep down, I could feel that Cole knew it.

Our reservation was for six o'clock, so we made it to the restaurant fifteen minutes in advance. The hostess seated us then the waitress took our beverage orders. Cole and I ordered a bottle of Merlot and the children ordered soft drinks. Shawna seemed just as happy as her father to be eating out for dinner.

"Daddy, this place is nice," she said.

"Yes, it is. I use to come here with your moth—" Cole stopped himself then looked away from our table.

"Are you okay?" I asked. He nodded, but didn't bother to turn to look at me. "Oh, Cole, I'm so sorry. I should've known when Nick said this was one of your favorite places that you and—" I looked at the children. "Well, you know what I'm saying. I should've known this was your spot."

He nodded then excused himself to the restroom. The truth was that I didn't care whether it used to be his spot with Glenda. The key phrase was *used to,* and Cole didn't need to feel like he couldn't do the things he once loved to do because Glenda wasn't around. I had two things I wanted to accomplish before the night was over. One was to show Cole he could have a wonderful family night with me and the kids, and the second thing was to make him wish he never cared about Audrie. Too bad that plan had to be set in motion on his birthday, but it was going down.

When Cole came back from the restroom, we placed our dinner orders. As we awaited our food, Cole and I laughed and chatted, enjoying each other's company. The children were coloring on their kids' menus and comparing each other's work.

All talking ceased once our food was served. The entrées were so good we didn't care to talk over dinner. Just as I stuck a forkful of corn in my mouth, I looked up toward the door and noticed the second part of my master plan walking in. Audrie and her ex-husband Rodney marched in behind the hostess. They were escorted over to a secluded table in the far left corner. I smiled inside. Things were going as planned.

I kept my eyes on Audrie as she sat chatting with Rodney. They both seemed confused as they each held out a letter I had sent to them, detailing that the other had some very important and confidential news to share. I also conveniently included a gift card in Rodney's envelope, so he wouldn't have an excuse not to make it on the night Audrie needed him to be at the restaurant.

We were all stuffed, which was a good thing because I wasn't ready to leave yet. There was more to happen with Audrie and Rodney before I would make Cole aware of their presence. I began to relax when I saw they had placed a drink order. Cole sat back in his seat, making me nervous all over again. I feared he'd say it was time to go.

"Don't we have cake waiting for us at home?" he asked.

"Yes, but sit back and chill a bit. I don't think the waiter is ready to kick us out of his section yet. We need to let our food settle before heading home."

Cole shrugged then rubbed his stomach. The children giggled at him. I chuckled a bit then intentionally struck an aggravating question to Cole.

"Your phone hasn't rang at all this evening. Have you heard from Audrie today?" He grimaced then sighed. "I mean, as your girlfriend, I would've been dying to share your birthday with you."

He got ready to respond then loud sighing rang out from Audrie and Rodney's direction. "Aaaahhh," the patrons said in unison as they applauded. The waiter had just dropped off a huge bouquet of red roses to Audrie. Cole turned to see what the commotion was about. The waiter stood in front of their table, blocking our view. Once he walked away, the roses shielded Audrie's face as she examined them.

"Wow," Cole said. "He must really love her."

"Yeah, I believe so. That's far more than a dozen of roses."

"Absolutely. I'm quite sure it's at least three dozen. They must've cost him a fortune."

Audrie set the roses on the floor. When she rose, Cole's eyes nearly popped out of his head. He slid back his chair then stood. "Where're you going?" I asked. He didn't respond. He stood silently staring. I glanced at Audrie's table. "Oh, my God. That's not Audrie, is it?" I asked just before cupping my mouth.

Cole walked away from our table without saying a word. He headed in Audrie's direction. I didn't want to miss what would be said, so I told the children to sit tight then followed him.

Audrie didn't bother to look up until Cole and I were standing over her. "Cole?" she asked, surprised. "What are you doing here?"

"Celebrating his birthday with his family," I answered for him. "Now try answering what you're doing here." I folded my arms across my chest.

"Cole . . . baby . . . it's not what it looks like," she said, stumbling over her words.

"Typical answer, Audrie," he finally responded. Cole's face seemed to display both pain and anger.

Audrie stood. "Cole, I—" she started, placing her hand on his shoulder.

He brushed her hand away. "Don't bother explaining. There's not an excuse in the world that would be acceptable in my book." He turned his attention to Rodney. "So this is the infamous Rodney, huh?" We all remained silent. Cole placed his hands in his pockets as he continued. "I'll tell you what, man. Give me back all the money I spent on her over these past months and you can have her."

"Cole—" Audrie snapped, taking her seat.

Cole silenced her by holding up his hand. Still looking at Rodney, he said, "Never mind. She ain't worth keeping. You should know: you once divorced the tramp."

The look on Audrie's face was priceless. I should've had my cell out to snap a picture of her chin damn near resting on the table. A few seconds of awkward silence went by, and then I grabbed Cole's hand.

"C'mon, sweetie," I said to him. "Let's not make a scene." I looked Audrie up and down then turned back to Cole. "We don't need anything to spoil our appetite for the delicious chocolate birthday cake I baked."

Cole and I calmly walked back over to the table where the children were playing tug-of-war with a napkin.

"It's mine," Gavin said.

"No. It's mine. Yours is on the floor," Shawna fussed.

Cole took the napkin from them then sat down. The children immediately hushed, apparently sensing something was wrong with their father. He put his hand on his forehead. I began to feel sorry for him.

"Cole, why don't you take the children to the car while I find the waiter to take care of the bill?"

Without saying a word, he handed me the gift card then offered tip money. I declined it then pulled out my own money. He walked away abruptly.

When I got to the car, Cole was sitting on the passenger side. He looked up and noticed me outside the car. He rolled down the window.

"Do you mind driving us home? I can feel a headache coming on," he said.

"No. I don't mind."

I went around to the driver's side then got in. I backed the car out of the parking space, and then looked back toward the restaurant entrance. *He's mine now, Audrie. You can bet your ass on that.*

*A*udrie pissed me off, and it took all I had in me not to tell her where she could go. The scene came close to becoming extremely ugly. I was just glad I got out of that restaurant without totally losing my cool. Audrie didn't even bother to come after me. In my opinion, she had confirmed her guilt by staying there with Rodney. Embarrassed or not, if she didn't have anything to hide, she should've been on my heels, begging me to listen.

She tried calling me a few times that Saturday night, but by then, I really didn't want to hear anything she had to say. I figured she'd try to pop over since I wasn't answering her calls, but she didn't. The next day was rough for me. I couldn't get seeing her in that restaurant with her ex off my mind. I felt deceived. I'd been putting my all into our relationship. There shouldn't have been any reason she needed to see Rodney.

Monday morning, Audrie tried to barge into my office. Still pissed, I wasn't ready to hear anything she wanted to say. I cut her off every time she tried to speak, asking her to leave my office. After pleading for a minute or two, she finally turned and walked out. She didn't bother coming back. I gave her the cold-shoulder treatment the rest of the day.

Karma had been very attentive and comforting after seeing Audrie at Ruth's Chris. I totally expected her to want to be there for me, considering her obvious crush. Since she'd been containing herself and seemingly had begun to accept my relationship with Audrie, I was confident she could continue to work for me with no issues. She wanted to wait on me hand and foot for five days straight while I sulked over Audrie. At times, I wanted Karma around, but there were also times when I wished she would go to her own place for a bit. I remained nice because as much as I hated to admit it, having her around helped keep my mind off Audrie.

Karma knew how to be a useful distraction. We played cards, watched movies with the kids, and she even had me helping with dinner a couple of times as the week progressed.

By the close of the day on Thursday, I couldn't wait to get home. I had just spoken to Karma, and she informed me that the kids would have a pleasant surprise waiting for me. I began to count down the clock and was feeling good—that is, until my attorney called me.

"How are things going for you these days?" Lewis Fisher, my good friend and attorney, asked.

"It is what it is, Lewis. I guess I can't complain. What's up with you?"

"I'm afraid I'm calling you with a bit of bad news, my friend."

I stood then went to look out my office window. "I don't know if I'm ready to hear any bad news, Lewis, but if you must, then hit me with it."

"I'm pretty sure the district attorney's office is getting ready to make a move on you."

"What?" I yelled. "Where'd you get that from?"

"An inside scoop came by and told me confidentially, so I'm just giving you heads-up."

"How can that be? You mean at this point, all they could conclude is that I must've had something to do with the shooting? They can't possibly have evidence on me. I didn't sit on the driver's side and shoot out the passenger side window. My kids were in the car. C'mon, man, that's ludicrous."

"I know. Cole, all I can tell you is to hold on. If you have to do jail time—"

"Jail time?" I screamed.

"Hold on, Cole. Let me finish. If there's any jail time required during or before the trial, I'll make sure it's minimal."

I hit the wall with my fist. "Lewis, I have children. I can't afford to do jail time."

"I know, Cole. You haven't been indicted yet, so right now just let me find out what they have or think they have, and then I'll do what I can to fix things from there. I'm hoping things will be squashed before we spend time and money on a trial." I was quiet. I just didn't know what to say. "Cole?" Lewis called. I couldn't speak. "Cole?" he called again.

"I'm here," I uttered.

"Keep your head up, man. Everything's gonna be alright. You hear me?"

"Yeah. I hear ya." I sighed. "Well, let me go, man. I've got to get home to my babies and kiss them."

"A'ight, man. Peace," Lewis said then hung up.

I paced in my office for nearly twenty minutes. I looked at the clock then realized it was only 3:00 P.M. I couldn't focus, so I called my supervisor's office to let him know I was taking an early out. I grabbed my jacket and briefcase then locked my office behind me. When I turned around, Audrie was behind me, staring as if she wanted to say something but couldn't.

"Excuse me," I said, making my way around her. I left the office without saying another word or looking back.

Perhaps if my mind hadn't been so filled with what Lewis told me then I might've given Audrie a little time. I had to get out of there. I wasn't in the mood for conversation or anything else. All I wanted to do was see my children.

Karma and I pulled into the driveway almost simultaneously. I greeted the children as soon as they stepped out of her car.

"Daaaddyyy," they both sang as they ran to me.

I hugged and kissed them both. Karma seemed shocked to see me. "You're home early," she said. "You've sort of spoiled your surprise."

"Yeah? Well, I'm sorry. I just felt like being home with my folks," I said, pulling the kids to my side then reaching out to hug Karma.

I could tell by how quickly she pulled away then looked at me that I'd confused her. I put on a brief smile then asked them all into the house.

"Cole, is everything alright with you?" Karma asked.

I shook my head. "No. I'm just praying everything will be alright though."

Karma looked at the kids. "Children, why don't you two go get out of your school clothes while I talk to Daddy? I'll bring your afternoon snacks up to you in a bit."

They did as told then Karma escorted me to the living room to have a seat. She sat next to me, rubbing my back and staring as I sat with my elbows on my knees and my hands under my chin in deep thought. When I felt I was ready to talk, I looked at her. She was beautiful. Her long eyelashes batted on top of a striking set of almond-shaped eyes. Concern shielded the boldness I once knew in them. I couldn't speak right away because I couldn't help admiring her glow. She wore a cranberry-colored lip gloss that begged for me to kiss her. I cleared my throat then looked into her ebony eyes once more.

"Your hair looks nice. Did you go to the beauty salon today?"

"No," she said, patting her hair.

"No?"

"No. You know ever since school started back I haven't been able to spend much money. I had to get books and supplies for this semester. I did my hair myself."

"Well, it looks great. And as far as the beauty salon is concerned, all you have to do is come to me. You take great care of me and the kids. I wouldn't mind scrapping up the extra change so you can pamper yourself. Okay?"

She did a double take then got up. "Hold on. I'm calling the police because I don't know who you are or what you've done with Colby Patterson, but you're obviously an imposter."

I laughed then went over to her as she stood near the cordless phone. She picked it up then started laughing, too. I grabbed her hands and begged her to put the phone down. She finally put it back on the charger after a few tugs back and forth.

"You make it seem as though I'm mean as hell," I said.

"No. Not mean, but the Colby Patterson I know wouldn't have hugged me on the way into the house, complimented my appearance, or offered to take care of my pampering fees."

I chuckled a bit, realizing she was right. Something about hearing there was a possibility I could go to jail made me understand I needed to savor every opportunity of freedom, including letting Karma know how much I appreciated her.

I took her hands again. "I don't know how to tell you this."

Her eyes widened. "What's wrong?"

"My attorney called me this afternoon saying I might be charged with my wife's murder. I may be going to jail for a little while."

"Cole, no," Karma screamed. She squeezed my hands. "That can't happen. What are . . . what . . . I mean why—"

"I don't know anything else right now. Lewis is not just my attorney. He's a very close friend. I know he'll think of something to get me out of this mess."

Karma dropped her head. "Cole, you can't go to jail," she said, speaking toward the floor.

"Hey, you think I want to."

108

Karma broke from me then ran upstairs. I paced the living room for a few minutes then started behind her. Just as I reached the top of the stairs, she was coming out of the bathroom. The beautiful eyes I admired were tinted with a shade of red. It was too obvious she'd been crying. I didn't know what to say, so I dropped my head as I started into my bedroom. She stopped me as I was about to close the door. "Cole, we need to talk. Do you mind?" she asked.

I hesitated because I wasn't sure that inviting her into my bedroom would be smart. "Um . . . no. I don't mind," I answered, beckoning her in.

She went over to sit on the bed. I left the door wide open in case the kids started down the hall to my room. Karma could barely hold her head up as she spoke.

"So, when will you know if they're going to arrest you?"

"That's the killing part. I don't know. I guess I'm supposed to just wait it out."

She sighed as she picked at her pants leg, a sign of nervous energy. "I'm crushed at the idea that you may be taken away from your kids."

"Yeah, well, that makes two of us." I began to pace, expressing my own nervous energy.

"I know you didn't have anything to do with Glenda's murder. Why can't the police understand that?"

"I don't know. This whole thing has been like a bad dream. I still can't believe Glenda is gone."

"Cole, I was thinking, perhaps you need to take off work to spend time with the kids. You know . . . like an extended vacation or something. I can go, too . . . to help out with the kids."

The idea was tempting, but I didn't see how I could make it happen. "I can't pull those children out of school. Their grades would be affected."

"No. That's why I said I can go, too. I could ask their schools for an approved family leave and upcoming assignments so they won't fall behind. I'm sure I could make the same happen for me."

The thought of having a real vacation with my children seemed wonderful. "You know, Karma, that's why I like having you around. You know how to help me figure out things. I'm going to call my boss to see if I can get time off. Once that's done, I'll get on the Internet to search a few options. Let's not tell the kids until we can see if we can make this happen."

Karma's face lit up. "Okay. I'm going to get them, so we can put the finishing touches on dinner. They're helping me today. We're cooking up and garnishing the rice pilaf with love— literally. We have enough raisins to spell love with. That was your big surprise."

I smiled. "I can't wait," I said, dialing my company's number.

Karma headed out of my room, switching that apple bottom of hers. *Good thing the kids will be going on this vacation or else I might get carried away,* I thought.

Cole made me cry. It never crossed my mind that one day he could possibly be implicated as the one responsible for his wife's murder. He didn't do it. I knew he didn't. He was a good man. I didn't want to see him go to jail. His kids needed him. *I* needed him. His news couldn't have come at a more opportune time though. I had been thinking of how I could get him to agree to do a vacation with me and the kids, and after going upstairs to let off some steam, it came to me. It was time to address taking a retreat.

On Friday morning, Cole had gotten his days approved then went to finish last-minute business for our trip. He told me he'd give me the details once he returned. I went to the children's schools to get their leave of absence situated then to my apartment to pack. I was certain we were going somewhere warm, so I grabbed plenty of shorts and halter tops, some swimwear, and a couple of evening items in case he had a notion to go to a formal spot.

I finished packing just in time to pick the children up from school. On the ride home, I decided to share the good news.

"Shawna and Gavin, listen up. Your father has decided this family needs a break, so we're all going on an extended vacation."

They cheered and clapped. "No school?" Shawna asked.

"Well, there will be some studying for you guys, but for the most part we're going to have fun."

"Where're we going?" she asked.

I forgot I hadn't gotten that information from Cole yet, so her question threw me. "Um . . . well . . . um . . . it's a surprise. Daddy will tell us when we get home, okay?"

They cheered some more and bounced in their seats. I drifted into a daze, wondering if Cole had arranged something in Bermuda or maybe even Hawaii. I had never been outside of the forty-eight states before so both places seemed enticing.

When we pulled into the driveway, Cole wasn't home. I sent the kids upstairs to pull out their summer gear so I could help them pack. I started toward the kitchen, but the house phone rang, stopping me in my tracks. I went over to answer it.

"Patterson's residence," I answered.

"Karma, it's Cole."

I panicked because I didn't recognize the number he had called from. "Cole? Are you okay? Where're you calling me from?"

"Calm down, Karma. I'm fine. I just got in a bit of a hurry and left my cell at home somewhere." I let out a sigh of relief. He laughed. "Relax. No one has picked me up and thrown me in the slammer."

"Well, that's a relief," I said, sitting down to calm my nerves.

"I'm at the travel agent's office trying to get things squared away. We're just about set to leave tonight for a ten-day luxury vacation. We've got a short layover, but at least we'll be to our destination by morning."

My heart fluttered, and I wanted to jump up and click my heels. I tried to sound relaxed though. "Good. Glad to hear it. By the way, where are we going?"

He chuckled. "Gosh, you mean you can't wait to discuss it when I get home?"

"No, I can't wait. You knew this morning where we were going, but you didn't tell me. I've been in suspense long enough."

"Okay . . . okay. I've found a spot where I can enjoy one of my favorite pastimes."

"Really?"

"Do you play golf?"

Suddenly I felt let down. "Golf?"

"Yeah. Golf. If you don't, I can teach you."

I didn't want to sound ungrateful, so I masked some excitement in my voice. "Sure," I answered, elevating my tone. "Sounds great."

"Karma, you don't sound too pleased."

"Oh, I'm cool. I just kinda thought we were heading out of the country. I mean, that's what I already told the kids."

"Hmm. Last time I checked, Costa Rica wasn't anywhere inside the United States."

A huge smile quickly spread across my face. I fell back on the couch, giggling into the phone and kicking my feet rapidly into the air. He called my name a few times before I could gather my composure. "Um . . . yes. Costa Rica will be fine," I said, trying to sound calm and proper.

Cole laughed at me. "You're a trip, you know that?"

"Well, a good trip I hope."

"Yeah . . . yeah . . . yeah. Anyway, I hope you've got your passport ready."

"Yes, it's ready. It's never been used before. I got one just before moving to Memphis. I had wanted to take a trip to Cancun, but decided against it."

"Get ready to break it in with Costa Rica. I'll see you when I get in, okay? Do me a favor and charge up my cell phone."

"Okay. See you soon."

I hung up the phone then waltzed around the living room with my arm stretched as if I had a partner. I was so excited I couldn't focus. I didn't know what my next move was—fix dinner or help the children pack. *Oh, find Cole's cell then plug it up,* I finally remembered.

As I looked around the living room, the house phone rang again. I thought it would be Cole, but the caller ID revealed it was Audrie. I decided to let the phone ring. Cole wasn't there to talk to her anyway.

I wrapped my mind around the fact I'd be in Costa Rica soon, and what a pleasant thought it was. I heard a ring tone coming from the laundry room. I went in and noticed Cole had left his cell sitting on top of the shelf with the dry-clean only clothes. I glanced at the caller ID and noticed Audrie was again trying to reach him. Something came over me, and I decided to answer it.

"Hello?" I said sweetly.

"Hello?"

"Yes? I said hello."

"I'm looking for Colby Patterson. Did I call the right number?" Audrie asked.

I huffed into the phone. "Yes, Audrie. You called the right number."

"Well, may I speak to him?" She sounded agitated.

"Sorry, Audrie. Cole is away right now getting his golf clubs cleaned, and even if he was around, I wouldn't let you speak to him."

"Excuse me?"

"You heard me. I didn't stutter. We're in Costa Rica on our family vacation for ten days, and I promised Cole I wouldn't let anything or anyone stress him out while we're away. I'm afraid that hearing from *you,* my dear, might be undue pressure."

"Look, little girl, let me speak to Cole. I don't have time for this. Why do you insist on playing childish games?"

"Childish? Games? I don't have to play games with you, Audrie. What part do you not understand—the part about me being on vacation in Costa Rica with my family or about not letting you speak to *my* man?"

"Bitch, put Cole on the phone," Audrie screamed. "I don't feel like entertaining you."

"Then don't. Just understand, Audrie, that you had your chance. The best woman won, and so that's me. If you don't believe me then call our house." She was quiet. "Judging by your silence, I'm assuming you have already. We're not there, are we?" I enjoyed taunting her. "Now, as I stated before: Cole is away getting his golf clubs cleaned. Costa Rica is our home for a while. I suggest you do whatever it is buzzards do to have a vacation of a lifetime. As for me, a swan—well, I'm having mine. Gotta go. Ta-ta now." I hung up before she could say anything else.

Although I had been mean to Audrie, I felt pretty good about setting her straight. She didn't deserve Cole. I did, and at least for ten glorious days in Costa Rica, he'd belong to me.

I invested a little time erasing all the missed and incoming calls Audrie had placed on Cole's cell and home phones before going upstairs to help the children pack. Dinner would have to wait. Besides, I also knew Cole wouldn't mind if I went to get takeout for once.

Cole came home in good spirits. He called the children downstairs to reconfirm our vacation. We were all ecstatic.

"Is Princess going?" Gavin asked.

Cole picked up Gavin. "She sure is, buddy. I have a new kennel for her and everything. What do you think of that?"

"Cool," Gavin yelled. "I love Princess." Gavin asked to get down from his father's arms then called to Princess. "C'mon, girl. We've got to pack your favorite dish."

Cole stood, smiling as he watched Princess and the kids run off. He turned to me then raised his hand for me to give him a high-five. I had to pat myself on the back for bringing the vacation idea to Cole's attention.

I had time to make a few sandwiches before we were to catch our nine-forty flight. I heard Cole calling my name, interrupting me. I went upstairs to see what he needed.

"Cole, did you call me?" I asked, peeping into his bedroom. He stopped packing then turned to me. "Yes. I just need to address a couple of things with you."

"Okay. Shoot."

"First, I just want to let you know that I only reserved a two-bedroom suite, so you'll have to sleep in the room with Shawna. There will be two beds in the second room. Will that be okay?"

I nodded. "That's perfectly fine."

"Good. The next thing I need to know is what your professors said about you having to be out of school for so long."

I took a deep breath then released slowly, killing time as I thought of a response. "Well, they all pretty much understood. I have the assignments and materials I need to complete them, so I should be good."

"So they were all understanding?"

"I had one teacher try to give me some grief, but after explaining about my sick uncle in Costa Rica, she gave in."

Cole frowned then laughed. "Young lady, you could go to hell for that lie." He shook his head.

"Well, it was either that or tell them all your business, and my professors don't need to know your history."

"Okay. I just wanted to be certain that turning in your papers late or doing makeup work wouldn't be a problem. Education comes first, you know?"

"I know. I'm going to help the kids study while we're away, too, so don't worry."

The doorbell rang. My heart fell. I had a gut feeling that Audrie had made her way over to wreck my happiness.

"I wonder who that could be," Cole said.

"I don't know, but you wait right here," I said, turning to leave the room. "I'll get rid of them."

"I'll go with you," Cole said, attempting to follow me.

I held my hand to his chest. "No. It could be the detectives. You don't need to talk to them right before your vacation. Let them see you when you get back. Stay up here and be quiet."

Cole looked a little apprehensive, but he went ahead and nodded then backed away. I peeped into the children's rooms and told them to stay upstairs and be quiet. I headed downstairs then pulled the curtain back to see who was standing outside the door. To my surprise it wasn't Audrie or police detectives. I went to the door then opened it.

"Yes," I said to the older gentleman and woman staring at me. "May I help you?"

They looked at each other before the woman decided to answer. "Yes. We're the Carters, parents of the late Mrs. Glenda Patterson, and grandparents to her children, Shawna and Gavin."

It was pretty cold outside, but despite the draft that smacked me in the face, I couldn't seem to get myself together. "Um . . . um . . . okay. Well, um . . . come in," I said, motioning.

"Thank you," they said simultaneously.

Before I could close the door all the way, Mrs. Carter was in my face. "Where is Colby and my grandchildren?" she asked.

"He's um . . . well . . . they're um—"

"Right here," Cole yelled from the top step. He came down to greet them. "I'm right here, and the children are in their rooms. How may I help you?"

"Cole, you no-good bastard," Mrs. Carter yelled. "You know we love those children, and you're intentionally keeping them away from us." She turned her attention to me, looked me up and down then asked, "And who is this? The woman you cheated on Glenda with?"

Cole grunted then answered, "I don't have to take this. Not in my own house. I've stayed away from you all because I don't have to put up with your foolishness. You don't have to believe I'm innocent, but God knows. He's the only one I have to answer to."

"And answer to Him you will," Mrs. Carter spat back.

"Good day, people. I was a little busy, so I'm going to have to cut this reunion short."

Mr. Carter spoke up. "Wait, Cole. We just want to see our grandkids. They're all we have left of Glenda."

"Yeah? Well, they're all I have left of Glenda, too. Despite what you believe, I loved that woman. I loved her more than I loved myself," Cole said via a cracked voice. "My children are doing fine, and I'm not about to let the two of you poison their minds against me."

"Now wait just a minute—" Mrs. Carter started.

"Honey, hold on," Mr. Carter said, cutting her off. "Cole, we realize their minds are young, and we wouldn't do anything to turn them away from you. Please . . . just let them spend this weekend with us."

Cole sighed. "I can't. We're about to go out of the country for a while."

"You're kidnapping my grandkids and taking them to a foreign country? How dare you—"

"Thelma, please," Mr. Carter yelled. He turned to Cole. "What's going on? Don't they have school? Why are you going away?"

Cole shook his head. "You know . . . I really shouldn't have to stand here and explain this to you, but I'm taking a stress leave. I need a break. I miss my wife, and instead of the district attorneys trying to find out who killed her, they're doing everything they can to implicate me as the culprit. I just need some time alone with my kids, that's all." Cole paused then looked at me. "And by the way, this is Karma Jolley, my nanny and personal assistant. We're not sleeping together or whatever you think— strictly business."

Mrs. Carter stood with her arms folded and mouth twisted as if to say, "Whatever."

"So where are you going?" Mr. Carter asked.

"Costa Rica, but I'll be back. I promise."

"Promise Thelma and me you'll let the children spend time with us once you get back."

118

Cole looked up at the ceiling as he huffed and puffed before answering. "I can't promise. All I can do is tell you I'll think about it."

"May we see them for a minute?" Mr. Carter asked.

Cole looked at me then nodded, gesturing for me to get the children. Once they were halfway down the steps, they saw their grandparents then nearly lost their minds.

"Grandpa . . . Grandma," they chimed.

Cole didn't budge. He wasn't going to let the children out of his sight no matter who it hurt. I stood watching the entire scene then realized I had to utilize the Carters to my advantage. *So you'd like to spend time with your grandkids, huh? I'll make sure you get all the time you want.*

We landed and arrived at the beautiful Villas of Hotel Cala
Luna bright and early Saturday morning. We had a two-bedroom
suite fully equipped with a bathroom in each room, satellite TV, a
private pool, and an espresso machine and microwave in the
kitchen. Karma and the kids were running around like they
owned the place. I set my bags in the middle of the living room
floor then went and stood on the patio to take in the fresh air.

I noticed on the ride to the villa that the land was surrounded
by beautiful tropical rainforests and marine parks. I knew the
children were going to have the time of their lives. The golf
course wasn't too far away, so basically, I planned for most of my
mornings to be in heaven as I combed the grounds.

On our first night there, we went to a restaurant that placed
families at tables with other families so we could have an opportunity to know who we were sharing the land with. For the most
part, all the people we met were cool.

I should've known it would happen, but it didn't take Karma
long to begin her little seducing game. She must've packed the
skimpiest bikinis she could find. If the kids hadn't been with us, I

believe she would've opted for a g-string. I tried to keep her out of my way as much as possible. I sent her on activities with the kids while I played golf and enjoyed alone time in saunas and bath houses. I almost felt guilty, but I decided I'd just have to make things up to her by giving her one whole day to herself before we left.

I woke up early Sunday morning, preparing for a day of golf. I offered Karma money to take the children shopping, but she declined, adding that she'd like to get in some studying with her and the kids before we became too preoccupied later in the week. I was proud she wanted to be so responsible. The children didn't hear my offer, so it didn't hurt them not to go shopping that day anyway.

Just before stepping out of the suite, my cell rang. I looked at the ID and noticed it was Lewis. I took a deep breath before answering.

"G'on hit me with it, man," I said just after pressing the talk button.

"Hit you with what?" Lewis responded.

"You're calling to tell me when I can expect to be put in handcuffs, right?"

He laughed. "Relax, Cole. I was only calling to ask how things are going for you."

"I'm okay . . . I guess. You've got a brotha's heart rate elevated right now though. I was afraid you were calling to tell me more bad news."

"No. The only news I know can be considered good news actually."

"Oh, yeah? What's that?"

"The only information the detectives got on you is circumstantial. Basically, they have nothing, and they won't be arresting you on insignificant details."

"Umph. I don't know whether to laugh or cry. I guess I should be asking what minor details they're holding on to.

Obviously at one time the DA thought it was enough to push forth with a trial."

Lewis sighed. "All they had was Glenda's cell phone records."

"Okay . . . and?"

"It seems Glenda reported harassing calls to her cell phone carrier. The calls they traced were all made from a payphone."

"I don't know if I want to hear any more, Lewis. I have to tell you I'm relieved the DA is off my back for now."

"Yeah. Enjoy your vacation, man. We'll talk more when you get back."

"Will do," I said just before hanging up.

On my third day there, I had the pleasure—or should I say non-pleasurable opportunity—of speaking to Audrie. She called as I headed to the golf course.

"Where are you?" she snapped shortly after I answered the phone.

"Why does it matter?"

"Cole, you're being very immature about everything. Why can't we be adults about this?"

"I'm being immature, huh? Then why did you even bother to call me? Didn't you know I'd only continue being a big kid?"

Audrie huffed into the phone. "Fine, Cole. Be a big kid, but we need to talk."

"Please explain to me why you figure we need to talk? Your actions said everything there needed to be said. What on earth do we have to talk about?"

"Cole, things weren't the way they seemed."

I got fed up with Audrie's conversation quickly. "Audrie, I think you've already said that, sweetie, so unless you have something new to add, I'm going to have to let you go."

"Well, let's talk face-to-face. By the way, why haven't you been to work?"

"I'm on vacation."

ALISHA YVONNE

Audrie's tone went from frustrated to hurt. "Cole, please don't tell me you're in Costa Rica."

"How did you know?"

"That . . . that . . . nanny of yours. I called you the other day and she told me, but I didn't want to believe her. Cole, I don't believe you."

I didn't care how Audrie felt at the time. She couldn't have possibly felt the aggravation I did when I saw her with her ex on my birthday. I just held the phone.

"So you don't have anything to say?" Audrie fussed.

"What do you want me to say?"

"Well, you can start by explaining why you took that skeezer to Costa Rica with you."

"Did you forget she renders services for me?"

"Yeah, I bet she does." I sat quietly, holding the phone, awaiting Audrie's next low blow. "Go ahead," she said. "Keep talking."

I sighed. "Look, Audrie, I don't know what you want me to say. It's over between us anyway. Why do I need to say anything? Huh? What do you want me to say, Audrie? Tell me quick because my cab is pulling up to the golf course."

"Nothing. Don't say anything, Cole. Fine. Have things your way. I hope you have a grand time in Costa Rica with your little girlfriend."

Audrie hung up on me. In a lot of ways I missed her. Before my birthday, things were good between us. She was my friend, and considering she knew all I'd been through, she was the last person I expected to cross me. I still loved her, but I began to push my feelings for her to the back of my mind.

I left my issues and all other bullshit back at home in the States. If Audrie calls back, I'm going to have to ignore her, too. This is going to be a stress-free vacation, I vowed.

123

Karma 16

Costa Rica was everything I expected. I never knew I'd get to see such a marvelous place, and I loved Cole so much for choosing the villas to share with me. The kids were a handful, but I wouldn't have traded the experience for the world. As far as I was concerned, I was right where I needed to be—in a tropical spot with my man and my family.

On the fifth night there, we sat at a table with a couple who seemed to be around Cole's age, but their two children were a couple of years older than Gavin and Shawna.

"So where are you from?" Cole asked the gentleman.

"Humboldt, Tennessee," the dark-skinned man with broad features answered. He could've fooled me. Before he spoke, I thought he was from Africa.

"Humboldt? I'm from Tennessee myself, but I live in Southaven, Mississippi—just outside of Memphis," Cole replied.

"Oh, I know where Southaven is. I've been to Memphis and Southaven plenty of times."

"Hmm . . . I don't think I've ever heard of Humboldt," Cole said, setting his glass of water on the table. "It must be a small town."

The man nodded. "Yes, it is. It's known as Gibson County with a population just under ten thousand."

Cole gasped. "You've got to be kiddin' me."

"Nope," the man said, shaking his head. "And you best believe everybody knows everybody." A woman came over, kissed him on the forehead then sat down next to him. "Hey, baby," he said to her then quickly turned his attention back to us. "So, you're living in Southaven, Mississippi, but where did you say you folks are originally from?"

Cole had just stuck a roll into his mouth, so I answered for him. "Memphis, Tennessee," I said. "Shelby County."

"Oh, how nice," the lady said. "And who are you? His daughter?"

I had a notion to kick her ass under the table and pretend it was a mistake, but I refrained. Cole spoke before I had a chance to reply. "No. This is Karma Jolley, our nanny and a good friend of the family."

The woman raised her eyebrows then nodded. "Oh . . . I see. You must really do a good job, Karma, if you get to tag along on extravagant vacations." She turned to Cole. "So, will your wife be joining us for dinner?"

Cole cleared his throat. "Ahem. Um . . . no. She won't be joining us," is all he said.

Poor Cole probably didn't feel like going through the motions of explaining Glenda's death. He picked up his fork, which indicated he'd much rather eat than talk. I picked up my glass of tea then took a sip. I knew I'd need something stronger if I was going to have to spend another moment at the table with that hag. Just after setting my glass down, I attempted to be cordial.

"Your husband introduced himself and the children before you came to the table, but I didn't catch your name. You are?"

She looked at her husband. "You didn't tell them about me before I got here, dear?"

I wanted to tell her she was probably just as unimportant to him as she was to me at the moment. He quickly chewed the bite of salad he'd placed in his mouth before responding.

"I assumed you'd show some manners by introducing yourself once you took a seat, dear," he said.

I wanted to say, "That's telling her skank ass." I kept quiet though, trying my best to keep from having to look in her face. She had beautiful toffee-colored skin, but her little beady eyes told off on her. I knew she was going to be a nuisance for the remainder of our trip, so I had to keep my guard up. I glanced up when I saw her hand stretch toward me.

"I'm Patsy," she said, shaking my hand, and this is my family—Jerry, Jerry Jr., and this here is Felicia." She placed her hand on the girl's shoulder.

"Um, baby, they already know that," Jerry told her. "We all made our introductions before you came to the table."

"Well, Jerry, I didn't get to meet anybody."

"It's not my fault you decided to stay in the mirror fifteen minutes longer this evening."

"I know, but I would like to know who I'm sharing the dinner table with tonight, if that's alright with you," she said.

Jerry looked at us. "Sorry to have to put you good folks through this again, but do you mind introducing yourselves to my wife?"

Cole wiped his mouth, set his napkin on the table then stretched out his hand. "No, not at all," he said, shaking her hand. "I'm Colby Patterson . . ."

I rolled my eyes then asked to be excused shortly after all the re-introductions. I gave Cole my request for dinner then headed to the bar. I had the bartender give me a shot of Courvoisier straight up then I asked for a Long Island Tea. I took my glass then headed out to the patio. I just didn't feel like going back to the table with that talking-ass woman from Humbug or whatever the hell the name of her little town was.

I leaned across the railing and sipped my drink as the wind stroked my face. It felt good to look out across the water as the waves rippled toward the shore. I became excited as I imagined playing in the sand with Cole and the kids the next day. My peace was short-lived when Patsy decided to join me on the patio.

"Whatchu drankin'?" she asked.

I contemplated answering her for a few seconds. "Long Island Tea. Why?"

"How old are you? Aren't you too young to be drankin'?"

I looked back out at the ocean then took another sip before answering her. "The legal drinking age in the States is twenty-one last I heard. I don't know what it is over here in Costa Rica." I took another sip.

I could feel her eyes piercing the side of my head. I turned to look at her. She stood with a pruned face and her arms folded across her chest. *This can't be good,* I thought.

"Something wrong?" I asked.

"Really . . . who are you?"

"Excuse me?"

"Don't pretend you didn't hear me. Why on earth is a little girl like you here with a grown man and his children? Are you his mistress, and where is his wife?"

I got off the rail then stepped closer to Patsy. "First off, I'm nobody's mistress and never will be. Second, let me say that what goes on between Cole and me is none of your damn business. As for where is his wife, dead and in her grave—where you're gonna be if you don't stay in your place."

"Say what?"

"Oh now you want to pretend you didn't hear me, huh?"

I was just about to cuss her out, but then Jerry came out onto the patio. "Dinner is at the table, ladies," he said then went back inside.

I walked over and leaned in to Patsy's ear. "Stay out of my way, beyotch." I smashed her toe as I walked off. She screamed in pain. "Oh, I'm sorry. Did I do that?" She started limping. "Here," I said, reaching for her arm. "Let me help you."

"Don't touch me," Patsy screamed. "Don't you touch me. I'll be fine." Her face was stern and had pruned even more than it was before she came outside to chat with me.

After dinner, Cole and Jerry suggested we all go out on the beach for a late-night stroll. Patsy excused herself to the bathroom while we all left the restaurant to head toward the beach. The children had all rolled up their pants legs to feel the cool water and wet sand between their toes.

Patsy was out on the beach with us about ten minutes later. Jerry had been talking with Cole about corporate America and didn't seem to notice the length of time Patsy had been gone. In fact, if I read his face correctly, he looked as if he didn't miss her until she came strolling up.

"Ah . . . there you are?" Jerry said to her just after she walked up. "Glad you joined us. You left poor Karma here to suffer listening through all of the boring talk between Cole and me."

Patsy put on a fake smile. "Sorry," she said, merely glancing at me.

Since I had made it clear I didn't want to have anything to do with Patsy, she bid us all good night minutes after being on the beach with us.

"Jerry, baby, I'm going back to our suite," she said.

Jerry looked concerned. "Something wrong, baby?"

Patsy looked at me. "Yeah," she answered. "Something's very wrong, but I'll talk to you about it later."

"Are you feeling okay, Patsy?" Cole asked.

I intervened. "Must be one of those days, huh, Patsy? You know . . . a feminine thing." I smiled. "If you need some medicine, I have some in our suite. As a matter of fact, why don't you come with me to get it then I'll make sure you get to your suite safely to lie down?" I reached behind her back to escort her, but she jerked from me.

"No," she yelled then tried to compose herself. "No . . . no," she said much calmer. "I'm fine. I don't need any medicine, but I do want to lie down." She turned to Jerry. "Don't have the kids out too late, dear. I'll see you all in the room shortly." She turned to walk away.

"Bye, Patsy," I said. "We're all meeting up here tomorrow afternoon. I'll see you then."

Patsy turned around to look at Jerry. He confirmed my revelation. "Oh yeah. Patsy, I told Cole that I'd meet him in the morning for a couple of rounds of golf while you and the kids do your thing, and then we can all meet up here in the afternoon. What do you think?"

Patsy seemed at a loss for words. "Um . . . okay. Sounds good."

"Great," Cole replied. "Good night, Patsy."

She walked off without another word. I rolled my pants legs up and joined the children in the water. I couldn't thank Cole enough for taking us to Costa Rica, away from the freezing cold temperatures back home.

Forty-five minutes later, it was dark and getting chilly. The kids and I left Cole and Jerry on the beach to talk while I took them in for a little studying and then play time with Princess before going to bed.

By the time Cole came in, it was nine o'clock and the children had been asleep for thirty minutes. I had showered and was in my robe, watching TV.

"The kids in bed?" he asked as he entered the suite.

"Yes, they've had their baths, and we even studied a bit before nodding off. Oh, and so you know, Gavin had a fit to sleep in the room with Shawna tonight."

"Wow. I guess he didn't want to be in the room without me. Was I gone that long?" He looked at his watch.

"Yes, you sure were. I was wondering if I needed to go check on you. Jerry seems nice and all, but we don't know those people."

Cole laughed as he pulled his shirt over his head, exposing his bare chest. "Now what did you think a man like Jerry was gonna do with me?"

I could hardly keep my eyes off Cole's chest and rock-hard abs. Before I knew it, I was thinking out loud. "A man like Jerry can't do *shit* with you."

Cole's eyebrows grew together, making him look as if he didn't know if he'd heard me correctly. "Huh?"

"Well, um . . . I mean, you're in shape, Cole. Jerry doesn't look like he could tussle with you long."

Cole smiled briefly then headed into his room and closed the door. I took a deep breath, trying to calm my nerves. We had been in Costa Rica for five days, and Cole hadn't made a move on me despite my two-piece swimsuits and sexy lounging attire. I had to have him. I was going to have him whether he wanted me or not.

I sat patiently watching TV until Cole reappeared from his bedroom. In five days, I had his routine all figured out. I knew he had gone to take a shower then at some point before laying his head down, he would be face-to-face with me again, even if only to say good night. So I waited.

I sensed this was the night we'd have our uninterrupted moment. And just like I thought, he opened his bedroom door then stood staring at me for a minute before he said anything. I wanted to look toward his midsection, but I knew I had to do it subtly. I didn't want to do anything that would shoo him.

He was shirtless, wearing only his navy silk pajama bottoms. I loved the way his PJs hung loosely off his waist, exposing muscle after muscle rippling down to a fine hairline. He looked delicious. I'd be in heaven if I could only take one lick. Before I looked away, I caught a glimpse of his bulging muscle. An uncontrollable flow of moisture began to coat between my legs. I pretended to be looking at TV, hoping he'd just come sit next to me.

"Don't forget to turn the television off before you go to bed. You left it on last night," he said.

I turned to look at him. "I won't," I replied.

We stared into each other's eyes for a few more seconds then that was it. He closed the door. I threw myself back on the couch, damn near ready to cry. I tried to ease the yearning by fingering myself, but that wasn't enough. I needed to be close to Cole, have him rub me between my thighs, put his shaft in me as far as it would go, and then feel him throbbing as he released in me.

Princess came over and began licking my feet. "Move," I said, quickly pulling my foot up on the couch. "Why aren't you asleep?"

I got up then headed toward the bedroom I shared with the kids. I opened the door then beckoned for Princess to go inside. Once she did, I closed the door behind her. I started back over to the couch, but then it hit me. Cole wanted me to go crazy over seeing him half-naked. *He wants me to make the first move again,* I thought. *That's it. He's ready for me.*

I made my way over to Cole's bedroom, and just as I had expected, the door was unlocked. I entered the room slowly. It was dark, but I could see Cole lying on his back with his hands behind his head. He confirmed he wasn't asleep when he turned his head in my direction. I closed the door behind me then started toward him. I moved at a snail's pace, thinking he'd stop me in my tracks, telling me to leave, but by the time I made it over to the bed, he stared silently, apparently awaiting my next move.

I dropped my robe beside his bed, revealing my short, black, see-through chemise then climbed on top of him. I only wore a black thong under the chemise, and I could tell by the glare in Cole's eyes that he was pleased. I sat up straight, grinding and massaging my breasts. He seemed awestruck, finally removing his hands from behind his head to slide them up my waist. I decided to help him by pulling the chemise over my head. I could tell Cole wanted to touch my breasts, so I grabbed his hands to show him it was okay to caress me.

I leaned over to kiss him, but he turned his head. I was very disappointed. We'd come so far. I didn't think we'd have any trouble going to the next level.

"What's wrong, Cole?" I began kissing his neck.

He didn't answer. He moaned instead. I knew I had his spot, so I wasn't backing down. I kept kissing and nibbling on his neck and ears. His moans became louder, and he became more aggressive with fondling my breasts. I slid down to face the tool I desired. I needed to taste him, and so I did. I took him into my mouth like a hungry dog. His wetness on my tongue drove me crazy. I would have completely devoured him if I could've. Before long, his dampness turned into a gushing river. The first mission was complete, and so I headed for another level of ecstasy.

I inched back up to his neck then nibbled some more. I made another attempt to kiss him in the mouth, but that was the move that deadened everything. Cole just wasn't going for it.

"Get up," he said.

"No, Cole. You want this," I whispered, still kissing his neck.

"No, Karma. I mean it. Get up," he said, raising his voice.

I sat up straight to look at his expression. He looked serious, so I got off him. He got out of bed then turned on the light switch, practically blinding me.

I stood one thong away from being totally nude. "Cole, why are you stopping us again? Don't worry . . . I'll help you get it back up."

Cole seemed suddenly disgusted by me. "Put your robe back on," he said, turning his head.

"Why? It's too late. You've already seen me and felt me up, too."

Cole looked at me like he hated me. "I shouldn't have ever brought you here with us. First thing when we get back to the States, I'm letting you go."

Stunned, I asked, "Excuse me? And after sucking your dick. . . you wanna let me go? Why didn't you stop me while my head was bobbing down there?" I quickly grabbed my robe and chemise then threw them back on. "There. Is that better? I'm covered up now."

Cole walked around me then went over to the door and opened it. "I need you out of my room, Karma."

Before I knew it, I had slammed the door shut then put my finger in his face. "This is some bullshit, you know? You coat my tongue with your semen, and then punk out of having sex with me?"

He bit his bottom lip then said, "Are you crazy?"

"Yeah. Something like that, and tonight I might as well be after the way you're treating me."

"You're going to wake up my kids, Karma."

Tears fell from my eyes. "So what? All the fun is over anyway. Besides, I think they need to know their father is firing me." Cole just stared at me. More tears fell. "I do a lot of shit for you, Cole, and I don't even bother to ask for what it's worth. You know why? Because I love you. Audrie may care for you, but she clearly doesn't love you like I do. Yet, you'd rather be with her lying, cheating, whoring ass than to be with me—a woman who is willing to give you her all." He remained silent. "It's jacked up that you'd let our age difference get in the way of what's real."

"What's real is that you're young, and you're not ready for the world."

"I'm not trying to be ready for the world, Cole. Just for you," I said, stabbing him in the chest with my finger.

"Karma, you can't even stick to a vow to respect my wishes."

133

"Don't you stand here and act innocent. You knew what the hell you were doing when you stood in this doorway half naked. You wanted me to come bother you. Now say you didn't."

I stood crying, waiting on Cole's reply. He didn't seem to know what to say. When he finally said something, it wasn't what I wanted to hear.

"You're right, Karma. Part of me wanted you tonight, but it wasn't for the right reasons. I'm sorry, but when we get back to the States, I'm going to have to terminate your services. We can no longer work together under the circumstances."

"What circum—" I cut myself off. "Never mind. I understand." I walked out of his room, letting him have the last say.

Terminate my services? We'll see about that!

*K*arma had to go. *What in the hell was I thinking by taking her out of the country with me and the kids?* I asked myself on the shuttle ride to the golf course with Jerry. He was rambling on and on about nothing, but he soon got the hint that I wasn't interested in his conversation so early in the morning.

"You seem to have something on your mind, my new friend. What's eatin' at you?" Jerry said, snapping me out of my trance.

"Oh . . . um. Well, I was just thinking about some things I need to tend to when I get home, that's all."

"Home? Aren't you here because you were running away from stress back home? I mean, you're here because you wanted to get away from the ole ox for a while, right?"

I was perplexed, and I huffed to let Jerry know it. "Ole ox? What are you talking about?" I said, elevating my voice just a notch below shouting.

"Your wife. Isn't she the reason you're here with your nanny and kids—to get some peace? I mean if I could've left my baggage at home, I would've." He winked. "But she wasn't having it."

Suddenly, I realized Jerry was not as smart as I thought he was. He sounded rather stupid, and it took all I had in me to refrain myself. I wanted to choke the living daylights out of him. "Jerry, my wife is dead." His dark complexion went white within a matter of seconds. "She was killed—not by me, but by some creeps who felt like acting a fool that night by taking an innocent life—on our anniversary."

Jerry seemed apologetic as he stammered to speak. "I'm . . . um . . . I . . . I'm sorry. I didn't know or else I—"

"Don't worry about it," I responded, cutting him off. "You couldn't have known unless I told you. And for the record, I'm not sleeping with my nanny. She is who we say she is—the nanny."

Jerry shrugged. "A'ight. I'll say no more about the subject then."

We were both silent for the remainder of the trip to the course. Once the shuttle stopped, Jerry motioned to let me off first. I threw the club carrying case over my back then headed off. I turned to Jerry just after stepping off the last stair. "I hope you don't take this ass whippin' personal, Jerry. I came here to play golf, and that's what I intend on doing."

He cracked a smile then burst into a loud country laugh. "I like that. A man with a sense of humor," he said, chuckling. "Let me see. How about a little friendly wager?"

"No problem. What do you have in mind?"

"If I win, you owe my family and me a movie rental package and room service for the evening. If you win, I'll do the same for you and your folks."

"Bet," I said, sticking my hand out to shake his.

Just then my cell rang. *Oh no . . . not another call from Audrie,* I silently hoped. I looked at the ID, but I didn't recognize the number. I decided to answer anyway.

"Hello?" I said after hitting the talk button.

"Colby Patterson?" a male voice said.

"Yes. This is he. How may I help you?"

"Mr. Patterson, this is the hotel manager at the villas where you are staying. Sir, I'm sorry to report there has been a serious accident in your suite."

My heart fell, and I stopped in my tracks. "Accident? What type accident?" Jerry stared at me, obviously perplexed.

"Sir, it seems your son is having trouble breathing and . . ."

The shuttle had just begun to pull off, but I dropped my clubs and ran behind it so fast my feet didn't know they had ever touched the ground. I banged on the back of it.

"Waaaaiiit," I screamed then banged some more. "Waaaaiiit." The shuttle came to a halt.

Jerry was fast behind me. "Cole," he called, "what's going on?"

We both jumped back on the bus. "Take me back to the villas," I yelled to the driver.

After Jerry and I took a seat, I remembered the hotel manager was still on my cell. I put it back to my ear and told him I was on my way. I closed the flip then Jerry kept asking what was going on, but I found it difficult to talk. I felt like I couldn't breathe, and I could hardly keep still, repeatedly standing then sitting as we rode. The driver didn't seem in a hurry despite my frantic behavior. I lost it.

"Man, drive this damn shuttle, would you?"

He looked at me in the rearview mirror. "Sir, I'm gonna have to ask you to keep your seat, or else I'll be forced to pull over. It's against company policy that I drive while you're standing."

"A'ight . . . a'ight! Just get me back to the villas as quick as you can," I replied.

Once we were back to my suite, I noticed medical emergency workers everywhere. The entrance to the suite was blocked by many of them. I began to pry my way in, pulling the men out of the way, one by one.

Karma was sitting on the floor with Gavin's head in her lap. Tears streamed down her face. Shawna was on the floor, too, with her head propped on Karma's shoulder and her arms wrapped around Karma's waist. The minute they both looked up and saw me, they seemed relieved. Shawna was the first to jump up.

"Daddy," she screamed, grabbing at my leg.

I bent down to hug her, glancing over at Gavin who was lying still with an oxygen mask on his face. His eyes met mine, then he attempted a weak smile. I squatted then reached over to rub his leg.

"What happened, buddy?" I asked.

"You forgot to tell me about his allergies, that's what happened," Karma snapped. Another stream of tears fell from both eyes. "I cooked crab cakes for breakfast . . . in peanut oil."

I gasped. "He can't have shellfish, tree nuts, or anything cooked or made with those foods!"

"Well, why didn't you warn me?" She cried some more.

I had to check myself. Karma was right. I had failed both her and Gavin. I released a loud sigh, more out of frustration at myself than anything. "I'm sorry, Karma," I said in a much calmer tone then turned to my son. "I'm sorry, Gavin."

Karma wept uncontrollably. I slid closer to her then put my arm around her as she continued to hold Gavin. She looked up then put her head on my shoulder.

"I was so scared, Cole. I didn't know what to do," she said.

A medical worker kneeled to remove the oxygen mask from Gavin's face. "Oh, but ma'am, you have to give yourself a little more credit. At least you remembered to bring his Epipen on vacation with you."

EpiPen, I thought. *How did she know that?* Karma seemed at a lost for words. "Oh . . . yeah . . . right," she said.

I slid back and looked at her. "How did you know about the EpiPen if you didn't know he had allergies?"

Her mouth opened and closed a few times before she ever said a word. "Well, I uh . . . I just uh . . . thought I'd better search the medicine cabinet for a few items that may be needed for a first aid kit. I also grabbed cough medicine, eye drops, and a few other things. The EpiPen was among the things I raked into a large Ziploc bag. I had forgotten all about it until Gavin had that reaction. I meant to ask you what it was for."

Gavin began to sit up, so I directed my attention to him. "Are you alright now, Gavin?" He nodded. I reached for him. "That's what I'm talking about. C'mere, son." I held him close.

Karma jumped up then stomped into her room, slamming the door behind her. I wanted to call out to her but the medical techs interrupted before I could say anything.

"Sir, we gave your son a shot of epinephrine and then a little oxygen," the man said. "He'll be just fine, but you might want to make sure you ask what's in your meals throughout the remainder of your stay here."

I looked at Gavin then kissed his forehead. "I will," I said. "I'm not going to let anything happen to my little man." I kissed his forehead again.

Glenda wouldn't've forgotten to tell the nanny about Gavin's allergies. What kind of father am I? The EMT snapped me out of my trance.

"We've been around for quite some time, so I doubt if he'll have another episode. You might want to take him over to the local clinic to get a prescription . . . just in case."

"Sure, I'll do that."

My suite was clear about fifteen minutes later. I told Jerry to give me some time and perhaps I'd be back with him in a few hours. When I went to tell Karma I was taking Gavin to the clinic, I noticed the door was locked. I knocked, but I didn't get an answer.

"I tell you what: we'll talk when I get back," I yelled through the closed door. I never got a response.

Shawna went with me to take Gavin to the clinic. She was being a little woman, concerned for her brother. She even asked if she could hold him while we waited on the doctor to see him, but Gavin was far too heavy for her.

139

The doctor had agreed with the EMT that Gavin shouldn't have another allergic reaction or trouble breathing, but he gave me a few more EpiPen refills just in case. After more than two years of taking shots of epinephrine into his thigh, Gavin had become use to the treatment. I felt better after seeing the doctor and having the prescription.

The kids and I headed back to the suite. Once there, the place was silent. I didn't know if Karma was lying down or what. I opened the patio door then asked the kids to sit outside until I came to get them. I wanted to speak to Karma in private. Considering how angry she was at me from the night before as well as after the episode with Gavin, I knew she might have a mouthful to say to me.

I headed to knock on her bedroom door, but as I tapped on it, it pushed opened. Karma's suitcase was on top of her bed nearly full. From the looks of things, she had almost finished packing. I stood, blinking in disbelief as she exited the bathroom then headed over to the bed to pile more stuff into her luggage. She glanced at me, but she didn't say a word.

"Are you going somewhere?" I asked.

"I'm going home," she replied then headed back into the bathroom.

I wondered if I was hearing and seeing things. *How is she going back to the States without me and the kids?* I questioned her on her way back out of the bathroom.

"Karma," I called. She ignored me, walking about the room, picking up this and that, stuffing her suitcase. I called her again. "Karma." Still no reply, not even a glance at me. I walked over and grabbed her hand, forcing her to stop what she was doing. "Karma, I'm trying to talk to you."

"Why? What do you want?"

I couldn't speak for a moment, but I knew I needed to say something. "I wanna know why you're packing. Our vacation isn't over."

"Your vacation isn't over," she snapped, jerking her arm from me. "I've had it with you. Not only did you treat me like something dirty last night, but today you made me feel like I wasn't worthy to be around your kids." She paused and looked away then turned back to me and began to yell. "I didn't mean to cause Gavin harm, Cole. It's not my fault you didn't tell me what his allergies were."

Karma was crying again. I looked into her eyes, which always made me weak, then mustered up the words I didn't know if I should say. "I don't want you to go, Karma."

She looked confused. "What? Aren't I this huge distraction for you? Don't I always seem to find a way to corrupt your mind, have you thinking and doing things with me that you really don't want to do? You panted . . . your actions practically begging me to stuff your dick in my mouth last night, and then you had the audacity to hint I shouldn't be here." She turned to zip her luggage.

I put my hand on hers. "You were right in what you said last night. I'm also at fault for you ending up in my bed. I'm sorry for that. Karma, I don't want you." Her neck snapped around. I had to clear my throat. "Ahem. I mean, at least not in the same manner you want me, and it's not fair that I lead you on. The only way we can continue working together is if we both work at being more careful."

Karma finished zipping her bag. "I've arranged the change on my flight so I can leave today. I've paid the extra fees and everything."

"So . . . call 'em back and change it again. I'll reimburse you and pay the additional fees." Karma shook her head. I grabbed both of her hands then pulled her to me. "Please, Karma . . . stay. The kids and I need you," I said, squeezing her hands.

She dropped her head then squeezed my hands back before looking in my eyes to answer. "Okay," she whispered. I sighed out of relief. I released her hands, but not a moment too soon. Karma put her pointer finger to my forehead then began poking me. "The next time . . . you insinuate . . . I tried to hurt . . . one of the kids . . . I'm walking out . . . and I'm never coming back. You hear me?"

Five was the number of pokes that gave me a complete headache. I cupped my forehead with my palm. "Gotcha," I responded. She brushed past me, heading out of the room. I called to her. "Karma." She stopped and turned to me. "Thank you— for everything—being here for my children, and for being here for me, too."

She put on a slight smile then answered, "You're welcomed," then walked out of the room.

I looked at her suitcase on top of her bed. *Cole, you know you should've just let her leave, right? Now let's see you make the best out of the remainder of this vacation without screwing her.*

Karma 18

Someone once told me a sucker is born every day. After putting on the Oscar-winning performance with Cole, which led him to begging me to stay, I came to know he was more of a sucker than I had imagined. That damn EMT almost blew me up. I thought an intelligent man like Cole would at least put two and two together, but he didn't. *Oh, well…game isn't over yet.*

I knew my plan would work. I knew that in order for me to have Cole eating out of the palm of my hands for the remainder of the vacation, I'd have to show him that he needed me around after all. Gavin couldn't have been a more perfect tool. I knew the little brat wasn't going to die, but if he had, oh well—shit happens. My mission was to get Cole back on my side, and it worked.

A few hours after the incident with Gavin, he was up and ready to roll. Cole had second thoughts about going out to the beach with Gavin, but I convinced him everything would be fine. He called up Jerry and Patsy to let them know we would still be meeting them.

I decided to take it easy on Cole by wearing a one-piece halter swimsuit with an ankle-length wrap. I could've messed up his mind with one of my skimpy bikinis, bringing thoughts to surface of the skillful blow job I'd given him, but that would only make him mad at me again. I placed a bottle of suntan lotion in my tote before heading out the door. Once we made it to the beach, Jerry and Patsy were stretched out on beach chairs. We got cozy right next to them, unpacking our towels and beach toys. After pumping air into some floats, Cole took all of the kids out into the water. Jerry followed him, to help with his children, I assumed.

Patsy placed a large hat over her face pretending to be asleep. I began to ramble about nothing, just to aggravate her and to make certain she didn't get any sleep. Only five minutes had passed before she rose and looked at me, frowning.

"Is something wrong, Patsy? You don't look well," I said as bubbly as I could.

She sucked her teeth. "I'm trying to sleep here, if you don't mind."

"Really? I didn't know you were trying to sleep. I thought you were only trying to keep the sun out of your face. I'm sorry," I lied.

Patsy rolled her eyes then relaxed back on the chair. She placed the hat over her face again, which pissed me off. She clearly wanted nothing to do with me, but since rejection is not my thing, I went on with rambling again.

"You know, Patsy, I think you and I can be friends. You're a good ol' country girl, and so am I at heart. Plus, Richmond, Virginia, where I'm from, has its rural parts, too. What about you? Don't you think we could be friends?" She didn't answer, so I kept going. "I mean, I can see me bringing the kids up to Tennessee to visit you and your kids, and we could all go to—"

Patsy sat up straight. "Did I just hear you say something about being from Richmond, Virginia?"

I'm sure she could tell my face went blank. "I live in Memphis, Tennessee."

"Yeah, but you said you were from Richmond."

"And? What if I did?"

Patsy stood then set her hat on the chair. "Karma Jolley . . . I knew you looked familiar."

"What's that supposed to mean?"

"Melvin and Della Jolley were your parents, right?" I just stared at her. I couldn't say a word. "I know who you are. I have a sister who lives in Richmond. I was visiting her the weekend of the fire. Your parents' death was all over the news, or should I say their murder?"

For the first time in a long time, I was speechless. Patsy had gotten the last word and was on her way out into the water. I had to make certain she wasn't heading to tell Cole about her revelation. I jumped up and started behind her.

"Hey, where are you going?" I asked.

She turned and noticed me following her. She didn't respond. Instead, she turned back around and called to Jerry as she entered the water. Jerry started her way, and so did Cole and the kids. We were waist deep in the water by the time they all reached us. Jerry began talking nonstop.

"Baby, doesn't this water feel good?" he said. "The kids are having the time of their lives out here. How about you and Karma take the floats and go on out some more. The waves are mild. I think you'd like the sun. Here, get on this one and lie flat on your stomach," he said, assisting her onto the float.

Cole assisted me on the one he had. "Here, Karma. You can use this one," he said. "Jerry and I will take the kids onto the sand for a game of volleyball. Relax and enjoy yourselves."

The men gave us both a push farther into the water. Patsy tried to object, but the waves had already started to carry her. I wanted to be close to her, but for some reason, the push Cole gave me sent me floating in a different direction. I remained calm, especially since Patsy was nowhere near the men. I knew she planned to let her little discovery about my parents out of the bag, and I couldn't let that happen. She didn't know my parents. They deserved what they got.

Melvin Jolley wasn't my biological father, but he was the only dad I knew. He spoiled me rotten when Momma wasn't around, but when she was, he'd act tough and strict on me. I could hardly tell he actually loved me at times. I lived for the times when Momma was out of the house, and he and I would be alone. I still remember the first touch, the first kiss and how soft his lips felt on my thirteen-year-old virgin lips. His tongue tasted like candy as he wiggled it into my mouth. I didn't know what to do, but Melvin soon taught me, and soon I couldn't get enough of French kissing him.

I was the sharpest dressed teen in Richmond. Melvin would buy me nothing but the best in the latest fashions. My Sweet Sixteen party was held at his sports bar. The two hundred Dooney & Burke card holders with a credit-card-sized invitation in them cost a little more than ten thousand dollars by themselves. Momma fussed about him spending twenty-five thousand dollars on my party, but I think she was jealous because he never made a fuss over her like he did with me. Plus, he stopped sleeping with her just before my birthday because I gave him everything he needed—at least that's what he was telling me.

Melvin was in love with me, and I loved him. He'd continue to prove his love every time he'd lay me down—that is, until after I got pregnant at seventeen. We had been using the withdrawal method for years, so I don't understand why it didn't work that last time. Melvin was pissed at me because I wanted to keep the baby. He said that if I loved him, I'd get an abortion, so I did, but even after the abortion, Melvin stopped coming into my room. Despite my crying and pleading, he just kept saying he just needed some time.

I had had it when I got up to use the bathroom in the middle of the night and heard Momma's moans. I confronted Melvin the next day. His only response was that it was time for him and me to stop having sexual relations, and that I should start seeing other boys. Not only did the sex stop, but so did the fancy clothes and money.

Melvin was forty-one when he began to reject me. He should've been glad a young, beautiful woman like myself wanted him. I looked better than Momma, a woman well into her forties, but he started giving her all of his attention. Melvin was my man, and I'd had enough of sharing him. If he couldn't be mine, he wouldn't be with anyone. I didn't know any other way of knocking him off except to set the fire. I knew Momma would be killed, too, but they wanted to be together anyway.

A big wave came by, lifting me and dropping me like a roller coaster. I shook off my trance immediately then looked around for Patsy. She continued to float farther away from me, lying on her stomach with her head facing the opposite direction. I utilized the opportunity to paddle toward her.

As I eased toward her, she didn't notice. I decided to whisper her name to see if she was asleep. I saw her flinch, but she remained silent, seemingly ignoring me. I looked around to see if anyone was paying attention to me. Cole and Jerry were too into the kids and their game of volleyball to notice Patsy and me.

I reached over and pushed Patsy with all my might. She fell off the float and into the water. My push had caused me to fall into the water also, but that was right on time. When Patsy floated up for air, she immediately began to scream for help.

I grabbed her. "I've got you," I said just before dunking her again.

I tried to hold her down with my hand covering her mouth and nose for as long as I could. Once I had to come up for air, Patsy was back to screaming. I looked up and noticed Cole, Jerry, and a few other people swimming our way. I pressed my luck and dunk Patsy one more time. I heard Patsy swallow a lot of water as we went down. I held a firm grip on her. By the time I got ready to come up for air, she was dead weight. I let her go then floated to the surface.

147

Jerry called for Patsy. She was nowhere to be found. Cole grabbed me and helped me on the float while several men began to dive, looking for Patsy. I began to act innocent.

"Cole," I panted. "Patsy . . . she . . . she . . . where is she?"

"I don't know, Karma. They're looking for her. Let's get you back to shore."

Once on the shore, I turned, hoping to see everyone still in havoc, looking for Patsy, but to my dismay, I saw them lifting her into a boat. She seemed to be lifeless. I could tell the lifeguards were working on her as the boat made it back to safety. A huge crowd had formed. Cole held on to me and his children as he bowed his head to pray for Patsy. I continued pretending to be shaken as Cole began questioning me.

"Karma, what happened out there? The waves were low," he said.

"They were low, Cole, but they must've picked up. I woke up and collected myself after a big one hit, but Patsy must've forgotten where she was. Before I knew it, she rolled over into the water. I jumped in to help her. She seemed to be panicking because she kept saying she wasn't a very good swimmer and pulling me down with her." I placed my head on his shoulder. "Cole, I thought I was gon' die. I couldn't get her to turn me loose."

I heard Patsy cough a few times then the crowd began to cheer. *Well, I'll be damned. I guess God does listen to some people's prayers.* The ambulance came then Patsy was placed on a stretcher and put into the back of the ambulance with her crying family behind her.

Cole escorted me and the kids back to our suite. "It's been such a long day already," he said just after opening the door to the suite.

"You can say that again," I responded, stepping inside.

Princess immediately ran to the kids and Cole to greet them, but she acted like she didn't even know me. My feelings were a little hurt, but I had other things on my mind to be too bothered. I wondered what if anything Patsy was telling people at the moment.

We had been settled for about fifteen minutes when the phone rang. Cole and I looked at each other before he walked over to answer it. "Hello. This is Colby Patterson," he said just before pausing. "I'll be right there." Cole hung up the phone then started out the door.

"Wait," I called. "Where are you going?"

"To the manager's office. Apparently the police want to speak with me."

"Why? I was the one nearly drowning with her."

Cole shrugged. "I don't know, but I'll tell you when I get back."

Cole still had on his swim trunks and a pair of flip-flops. He and all his sexiness went out the door as I headed to give Gavin a bath. The children had sand all over them. Once Gavin was out of the tub, I placed his clothes on the end of the bed then helped Shawna with her bath water. Shawna could bathe herself, so all I had to do was help Gavin get dressed then turn on the TV in the bedroom for him. He went into a world of his own while watching cartoons. He didn't respond to anything I said to him once the TV came on.

I headed into the kitchen and was hit by a foul odor. I looked down and noticed Princess had pooped on the floor. I could've killed that dog. I didn't go into the kitchen to clean up dog mess. Princess came trotting around the corner. As soon as she got within close reach, I grabbed her by the throat then shook her violently just before throwing her into the wall. When she began to limp, I almost felt sorry for her, but then getting a whiff of the mess she'd left for me to clean up quickly changed my mind.

I was done cleaning when Cole walked in with his eyebrows dipped toward his nose. I wanted to pretend I didn't notice, but he began barking at me soon after slamming the door.

"I wanna know what happened out there on that water, Karma, and this time try telling me the truth," he yelled. The children came out of their room. He turned his attention to them. "Go back into the room and watch TV while I have a grown-up conversation with Karma, kids." They turned and did as they were told. "Karma, I wanna see you in my room, please," he said without looking at me.

"You sure about that? Last night you made it clear I wasn't welcomed in there, remember?"

His face clearly expressed he wasn't in the mood for sarcasm. "Fine," he responded, planting his feet. "Have it your way, but you're going to tell me what happened at the beach."

"I've already told you what happened."

"Yeah, but is there more?"

"More? What do you mean? You were there, too. There's nothing else to tell."

He rubbed his forehead. "Karma, for some reason, people keep accusing you of doing mean things to them."

"Who are these 'people,' Cole? Audrie? Patsy?" He didn't say anything so I continued. "I think we both have learned what kind of woman Audrie is, and as for Patsy—" I sighed—"who believes a woman from a place called Humboldt, Tennessee?"

"Where she's from has nothing to do with it, Karma."

"It does to me. Her country ass is just probably delusional from the trauma she suffered. I can't image why she would say I'd do something bad to her when all I was trying to do was help her. Hell, I almost lost my life trying to save hers. Some thanks I get, huh?" I rolled my eyes and folded my arms.

"Karma, I want to believe you. The police say once Patsy was able to talk she just kept screaming that you tried to drown her. I really want to believe you, Karma. Please tell me I can trust you're telling me the truth."

"I'm telling the truth, Cole," I said as convincing as I could.

ALISHA YVONNE

Just then, Princess came limping up to Cole, whining. He picked her up. "What's d'matter, girl? Was she limping just now?" he asked.

"Um, I think so. I saw her run into the coffee table earlier, so she might be a little sore."

"How'd she do that?"

"I don't know. I wasn't paying attention. Anyway, can we get on with our day?"

He paused then took a deep breath. "Go pack everything."

"For what?"

"We've got to get out of here before things continue to heat up. I don't know whom the police believe, but I didn't come way over here to have you go to jail. There's been nothing but drama ever since we got here. Let's just catch a flight back to the States tomorrow."

"Cole, the kids are gonna be crushed. We only have a few more days left, maybe four, right? Let's just stay."

"Karma, I'm so ready to go right now, you just don't even know. I'll find something for us to do when we get back."

"Do you promise?"

"I do," he said.

I do? Hmm . . . just the words I wanna hear.

*I*t was a long ride back from Costa Rica. It was Friday—three days shy of our original return date. Karma hardly said two words to me. I knew she wasn't ready to leave, but I just couldn't stay after all that had happened with Gavin nearly suffocating from a closed throat after an allergic reaction and Patsy accusing Karma of trying to drown her, all in the same day. In fact, I had completely scratched Costa Rica from my list of perfect spots for vacation. I didn't think I could bear to go back there considering all the drama that had surfaced.

Jerry and I traded business cards before I left. I told him to keep me posted on how Patsy was doing. As soon as my plane landed in Memphis, I checked my voice mail and discovered I had one new message, which was from Jerry. He said Patsy was going to be fine, and they, too, were headed back to the States. I felt awful. Not only had my family vacation been short-lived, but I felt at fault for Jerry's vacation being cut short as well.

I needed a break from Karma, so after dropping her and the children off at home, I went for a drive. After circling for a while, I ended up at Platinum Rose, a strip club on Third Street, which wasn't too far from my home and even closer to where Audrie lived. I'd been in there once before with Lewis and Nick, so I knew exactly what to expect. I went in and sat at the bar then ordered some Crown Royal and Coke. Before I knew it, I was broke and had a hard-on that was out of this world. The African-American beauties in Platinum Rose performed their asses off. Good thing I only had a few hundred dollars on me because had I had more, they surely could've gotten it all.

I jumped into my car then had a notion to drive by Audrie's house. I was horny and didn't have anywhere else to turn. Something kept telling me to go home, but I couldn't until I had at least driven down her street. Once I got there, I noticed a car parked in her visitor's spot. I became ill and cursed myself for having even gone by there. I became as angry as the day I saw her with her ex, Rodney. I had a notion to get out and cause a scene, but that concept helped me to realize I wasn't as sober as I had thought when I left the club.

I contemplated parking my car then calling a cab, but then I decided I could make it home safely. *Shame on you, Cole,* I said to myself as I headed home. *You promised to never be like other people who drink then drive.* Suddenly, I didn't feel so good about having gotten behind the wheel. I turned off my radio then said a prayer, asking to make it home safely.

I looked at the time on the dashboard and noticed it was only eight o'clock. I felt pretty good about going home because I knew the kids were probably still up. As I pulled into the driveway, I noticed a car parked on the curb in front of my house. The lights were on in the living room, which suggested there was really company at my house. I reached into the glove compartment for a mint then got out of the car. I looked back just after stepping onto my porch and noticed my nosy neighbor, Ms. Willis, peeping out her window. I imagined she knew who was at my house before I did. I waved at her then went inside.

Karma met me at the door with a worried expression. My heart dropped because I'd been hit with a notion some detectives were there to arrest me. Karma backed away to let me in. As soon as I closed the door, I stepped farther into the living room and noticed Mr. and Mrs. Carter sitting on the sofa. I was very disappointed to see them, especially so soon after getting home. Mr. Carter got up to greet me.

"Colby, how was your trip?" he asked.

I couldn't have made a smile if I had wanted to. "Fine," I answered abruptly.

"Glad to hear it," he said, reaching to shake my hand.

I gave him a firm shake. "What can I do for you, Mr. Carter?"

"Well, I'd love for you to allow the kids to spend the weekend with Thelma and me. We miss them terribly, Colby."

I sighed. "Mr. Carter, we just got back. Anyway, how did you know we were here?"

Mr. and Mrs. Carter looked at each other then Mr. Carter turned back to me. "We just took our chance. C'mon, Colby. We'll have them back home by Sunday evening," he said.

I looked at Karma. "Have the kids already been down to see them?" I asked her. She shook her head.

"No, Cole," she answered. "The Carters just got here. I asked them to have a seat until you came home."

I felt stuck. I didn't want to deny the Carters visitation with the children, but I just wasn't ready to let the kids out of my sight. Plus, while they seemed calm and kind, I knew deep down they hated me, and I feared they'd fill my children's heads with a bunch of crap about me and what happened to their mother. I huffed, sighed, and even paced a bit before finally giving in.

"Sunday evening, Mr. Carter," I told him.

"You got it, Colby." He shook my hand fast and hard, nearly giving me whiplash. "We promise to have them back on time. No problem."

I sent Karma upstairs to pack for the children and get them ready. When they came downstairs and saw their grandparents, they were excited. A part of me was jealous, but I knew I had to get over it. I watched my children pull away in the car with the Carters then went back into the house wishing I could cry. I felt somehow that would make me feel better.

I closed the door then turned around to find Karma close up on me. She stood silent with the tip of her fingernail in her mouth. Then it dawned on me.

"You called them, didn't you?"

She shook her head vigorously. "No . . . no, I didn't. Cole, why would you say that?"

"I don't know. I guess I just find it too much of a coincidence they'd show up the day we got back from our vacation, not to mention we're early."

"Cole, you're paranoid, and you're being ridiculous. I don't have the Carters' phone number, and if I did, what good would it do me to call them and risk pissing you off? I do enough of that unintentionally. No need in creating deliberate mistakes."

Karma seemed angry as she stormed off. She headed up the stairs. "Where're you going?" I yelled to her.

"To pack and get the hell out of here," she answered, pouting.

I went upstairs behind her. She was in her room stuffing a bag. "You don't have to pack everything. It's not like I'm firing you or anything," I told her.

"Whatever," she answered shortly. "At least not this time you aren't."

I really didn't have a response for that. "Will you be able to pick up the kids after your classes on Monday?"

"Sure."

I leaned against the dresser and watched as she moved quickly, sorta like she couldn't wait to get away from me. I noticed she had on a pair of shorts and a fitted T-shirt, both items being a perfect blend of blush red. "Are you going out with that on? It's pretty cold outside. We're not in Costa Rica anymore, you know?"

She shrugged. "Don't remind me."

155

I decided to give her some space. I went downstairs to fix myself another drink. I opened the cabinet to find a bottle of Absolut Ruby Red. I poured a splash of cranberry juice in a glass then filled the rest with the vodka. I retreated to the den. My glass was just about empty when Karma came down to let me know she was on her way out.

"Leave the credit card on the kitchen counter Monday if you want me to get some groceries for dinner," she said.

I couldn't respond. She still had on those tight red shorts and that fitted top with a pair of black, thigh-high boots. I was mesmerized. She went to the closet and took out her full-length leather coat then put it on. Just before turning around, she picked up Princess then turned and walked over to where I sat on the sofa. She set Princess on the floor near me.

"Is it okay if she stays here with you for the weekend? I didn't unpack her food and bowls, and I don't have money to buy more right now."

Flashes of the sexy women at Platinum Rose came to mind. I couldn't ignore my arousal as I glanced toward Karma's warm spot. I stood then went over to her. She looked confused as I stepped into her face.

"Sure. Princess is welcomed to stay." I then took a sip of my drink. Karma nodded. "You don't have to leave either," I said smoothly.

She smirked then turned to walk away. I was horny as hell, and I knew if Karma left, I was going to be sorry. I grabbed the back of her coat, forcing her to stop. As I tugged on the coat some more, it slid off her shoulders. Karma turned around slowly then looked at me.

"What're you doing?" she asked.

I set my glass on the coffee table then tossed her coat on the couch. I motioned with my finger for her to come to me. At first she hesitated, and she then slowly but surely started my way. I began to tongue her with slow, sensual strokes. Her moans let me

156

know how much she enjoyed it. She seemed stunned once our lips unlocked.

"Cole, why are you teasing me?" she asked. "You know I want nothing more than to make love to you, but you always get me riled up only to let me down."

I stopped. She was right. I wondered who I thought I was fooling. Karma and I both knew I would probably only allow just enough to happen to where I wouldn't feel guilty. Then I wondered why I even felt at fault about anything. Audrie and I were over. She was at her home doing her thing. It was time to do mine. Still, I hesitated.

Karma reached up to stroke my face with the back of her hand. "Baby, take me," she said, placing my hand on her ass. "I want you to take me, Cole. Please, Cole. You can't imagine the heat I'm feeling right now. Just take me," she pleaded.

I didn't move. As sexy as she was, I still couldn't bring myself to advance. Karma decided to take matters into her own hands. She unbuckled my belt then unfastened my jeans, sliding them to my ankles along with my underwear. I thought about stopping her, but my body wouldn't let me. She'd pleased me like I'd never been pleased before in Costa Rica, and I wanted more. I needed more.

Karma pulled her shirt over her head, exposing her perky, round breasts then squatted and took me into her mouth. There was no turning back now. She began to massage me as she swallowed me inch by inch. I bit my bottom lip as a tingling sensation ran through my body. The warmth of her tongue was just what I needed. I looked down at Karma as she did her thing. Her eyes were closed, and she seemed to enjoy giving me the sexual favor as much as I enjoyed receiving it.

After noticing her hardened nipples, I could feel myself oozing, but she didn't stop until I begged her.

She stood smiling and fondling her breasts. "Take this off," I said, tugging on her shorts. "Slowly," I commanded. She lifted her leg to take off her boot, but I stopped her. "No, please. I want you with the boots on." She nodded then slid her shorts down, revealing a red satin thong.

Karma looked just as good as the women I'd seen earlier at the club. She helped me take off my shoes and socks then pulled my jeans and underwear from around my ankles. We left them in the middle of the floor as we retreated upstairs. I motioned for her to go first so I could watch her strut naked from the back.

When we got to her room, I asked Karma to get on the bed and fondle herself while I took off my sweater. Her sexiness made me want to taste her, but my first mind told me not to go there. This was only supposed to be a fuck. Oral sex was something I only wanted to do with the woman of my dreams. I ignored my urge to go down on her, but she couldn't seem to get enough of me.

"C'mere, baby," she called seductively. "I need to taste some more of you."

Before I went to her, she removed her fingers from herself then placed them into her mouth. I gladly went over to the bed to grant her wish. She pulled my face to hers then kissed me, flavoring my tongue with her moisture. I was so turned on, and I knew it was time to break my rule. I pushed her back on the bed then got into the sixty-nine. I slid her thong to the side and began to do an oral slow dance with my tongue between her thighs. She squirmed so much she could hardly tend to me as I began to do a leisurely grind.

When I felt myself going there again, I made Karma stop. I wanted us to take our time, but she began trembling before I had a chance to really get into what I was doing. I wasn't ready to stop, so I held her down and kept going until she had reached a second climax.

I could tell Karma was spent, so I went into my room to retrieve the condoms I'd purchased for use with Audrie. When I rejoined Karma, I found her spread eagle in the middle of the bed. I put the condom on then sat on my knees between her legs. She opened her eyes then looked at me.

ALISHA YVONNE

"Are you too tired?" I asked.

"No," she responded sweetly.

"Then c'mere," I said, pulling her toward me. I placed her petite frame down on me as I sat on my knees, gripping her ass as I rocked her back and forth. I questioned whether she could handle all of me because she screamed really loud upon my entrance, but then she started grinding as I rocked her.

"Oh, this is so good, baby," she said, moaning. "I can't believe this is happening." She wrapped her arms around my neck then kissed me. "I've been wanting this for so long, baby. Yeeeesss. Give me more." She grinded harder.

Why did she have to demand more? I placed her flat on her back then put her legs on my shoulders. It was on. Once I got my next release, I went down on her some more to make it up to her. She seemed to love my face between her legs, so I gave her as much as she wanted. By the time we both were done, we were tired and thirsty. I got up to get us something to drink.

"You want water, soda or juice?" I asked.

"Orange juice if we have any," she said in a low whisper. The poor girl was worn out.

"Okay. Be right back."

I headed downstairs and realized we'd left several lights on. I went to the kitchen to fix our beverages then circled through the living room turning off lights. The last one was on the phone stand near the stairs. As I set one of the glasses down to turn the lamp off, I noticed my phone book opened to the page with names beginning with C's. I skimmed over the content, coming to a halt on the inscription reading the carters.

I swear that Karma is a sneaky little lying-ass ... ooooo, just wait, I thought as I headed upstairs.

"Karma," I called out to her as I entered the room.

She sat up in bed. "Yes, baby?"

"I'm not your baby, Karma." She frowned. I set our glasses on the nightstand. "You mind telling me what my phone book

159

was doing open on the page with the Carters' phone number on it?" She opened her mouth to speak, but I cut her off. "And don't bullshit me. You knew I wasn't ready to release my kids in anyone's care. Those are my babies, Karma. What in the hell were you thinking?" I yelled.

She scratched her head and batted her eyes a few times as if she was looking for the right response. "Are you gonna let me talk now?"

"Yeah . . . go ahead. This ought to be good, especially since you just got through giving me a spiel about how you wouldn't intentionally piss me off."

Karma threw her hands in the air and raised her voice. "I thought you were gonna let me talk," she said. I remained silent. "Sheesh. I don't know why I'm wasting my breath because you're probably not going to believe me anyway, but Gavin accidentally bumped into the table on his way upstairs, knocking over the phone book. I picked it up and set it back on the table. I didn't pay attention to how I placed it. I didn't think it would matter whether the book was opened or closed. I'll be more careful next time since it makes a difference to you."

I sat on the bed. "I didn't say it made a difference, Karma. The only thing that matters to me is if you called the Carters over."

"No, Cole," she yelled. "How many times am I gonna have to say that? I told you earlier I didn't."

Her response seemed genuine, but a little inkling told me not to be so sure. I picked up her juice then tried to hand it to her, but she refused it.

"So now you're not thirsty?" I asked.

"Not for orange juice. I'd rather take another drink of you," she said, sliding closer.

She put my third leg into her mouth, causing an immediate erection. *Aw, what the hell . . . I can let bygones be bygones.*

On Saturday morning, I woke up to an empty bed. I wondered if the night before had been a dream. I looked down at myself and noticed I was nude then smiled. *Oh, it was real,* I told myself. *Real good in fact.* I rolled over and looked at the clock. It was only eight-thirty, so I wondered why Cole was up, considering the late night we'd had.

I jumped out of bed and grabbed my robe to go look for Cole. The first stop was his room. He wasn't there. I went downstairs, calling his name, hoping he'd answer. He never did. I took a peep out into the driveway and realized his car was gone. He didn't leave a note or anything letting me know where he was or when he'd be back. I wanted to call him, but I felt I should wait a while to see if he'd return.

In two hours I had taken a shower, washed and curled my hair then dressed in jeans and a fitted pull-over sweater. I still hadn't heard from Cole, and I had begun to feel my waiting hadn't paid off. I went to use the phone downstairs near the steps, but just as I began to dial his cell, I heard his keys rattling in the door. I put the phone back on the receiver then anxiously awaited his appearance. I feared he wouldn't be in a pleasant mood after realizing what occurred between us the previous night.

"Morning," he said, closing the door behind him. He had several bags in his hand. He gave me one.

"Morning, Cole. Are you okay? I've been worried about you."

"Why would you worry about me? If the Feds had shown up to take me to jail, believe me, I would've woken you." He laughed—a good sign he was in a good mood.

"Stop talking about jail," I said, clinging to his arm. "You're not going to jail, and if you do, I'll be right down there with explosives to get you out." We both laughed. I looked down at the bag he handed me. "What's this?"

"Breakfast from IHOP. I thought you might be hungry."

"Oh, yes—extremely. It's almost lunchtime now."

"It's not even eleven yet."

"Some people eat lunch around this time, you know?"

"Well, I would've been back sooner, but you looked like you needed to sleep in."

"You could've gotten me up," I said, heading toward the kitchen. Cole followed me. "I would've loved to have tagged along with you—wherever you went."

"Believe me. You didn't wanna sit and go through what I have this morning." Cole shook his head.

"Well, what do you mean?"

"Lewis, my attorney, had me hemmed up for a while, going over the old police reports and the day of Glenda's murder."

"Cole, don't tell me you're still listed as the key suspect."

"I'm afraid so, but they don't have enough to go on. That's why I haven't been arrested yet. Lewis just told me."

I pulled down some plates and set them on the table. "Well, that's good news, and considering I know you had nothing to do with Glenda's murder, I'm not worried about them arresting you."

Cole sat down and pulled his plate closer to him. "Well, I know I had nothing to do with it, but what makes you so sure of my innocence?"

I paused then put my hand on my hip. "Cole," I said.

"I'm listening," he answered, sticking a fork into a couple of pancakes then releasing them on his plate.

I walked over and stood beside him, pulling his head to my side. I kissed his forehead a couple of times then said, "Because I know you wouldn't harm a fly." I kissed him again and rubbed his head. "I just know it."

He turned his head then began to pull away from me with sly moves. Despite his effort to not seem evasive as he began to eat his food, I could tell he didn't want me close to him.

"Aw, shit. Here we go," I said, stepping away from him.

"What?" He shrugged.

I shook my head. "Sometimes he feels like being down with Karma, then at other times, he doesn't wanna *fuck* with her." I sat down to eat my food.

"What are you talking about? Who the *fuck* is 'he?'" Cole frowned.

I snapped. "You, and who are you cussing at?"

"You, because you started it. You cussed at me first, little lady."

We stared each other down for about fifteen seconds then burst into laughter. I had to shake my head some more.

"And I'm not a little lady," I told him. "I think I proved that to you last night."

"Well, excuse the hell out of me." He stuck a forkful of pancakes in his mouth.

"Did you say your grace?"

"Of course not," he mumbled with his mouth full. "I was too busy arguing with you. Did you say yours?"

"I haven't started eating yet. Now be quiet."

"You be quiet," he mimicked.

"No, you be quiet."

163

"No, you—"

"Coooooole. Please," I yelled. We both laughed again.

"A'ight . . . a'ight. Eat your food. You might need some energy for something else."

"Sounds promising. Let me hurry up."

I hung out with Cole all day. We made love off and on through the afternoon. I finally felt like I had conquered him. He was mine. He was really mine. He wasn't as well off as my stepfather, Melvin, had been, but Cole looked just as good and had the same mannerisms. Cole was the man of the house, and there was no doubt about that. He could be the boss of me anytime.

Cole drove me to my home later that evening to pick up some more clothes and "school supplies." I couldn't believe how he still hadn't caught on to the fact that I wasn't enrolled in school. I hurriedly packed some things while he browsed around. Once I was ready, I found him in my bedroom staring at the only black dress in my closet.

"Where'd this come from?"

I didn't quite know what he was getting at, so I'm sure my face displayed my confusion. "Excuse me? What do you mean?"

"Seems like I've seen this dress before."

"Oh, I'm sure there're other women out there with the same dress."

"Mm-hmm. I was trying to remember if Glenda ever had one of these. I know I've seen this dress on somebody before."

He was getting too comfortable, and I was ready to go, so I hurried him. "Um . . . don't you have better things to do than size up hanging clothes?"

He knew I was being smart. "Yeah. I've got plenty of things to do. One of them is to put something in your mouth so you can't be such a smart aleck," he answered, unzipping his pants.

"Well, c'mon then. I thought you were about to issue a real threat. I've had that before," I said, pointing at his midsection. "I'm not scared of that."

He zipped his pants and laughed. "C'mon. Let's go."

Gladly, I thought. I was relieved to get him out of my place before he found something else to question. The newspaper articles I had preserved were well hidden, but I still wanted to be careful.

When we got back to Cole's place, his mood had taken a turn. He became quiet and not so playful anymore. Every time I'd question him, he'd say it was nothing. I offered to put in a movie and cook some popcorn. I didn't realize it at the time, but he had reluctantly agreed.

Cole lay across the couch in the den with me. We watched two DVDs before he finally told me he wasn't in the mood to see movies.

"Would you please tell me what I've done to alter your mood? You were doing fine until the ride home. What's wrong?" I demanded to know.

"I've already told you nothing."

"Don't lie to me, Cole. Just get it out in the open."

He sat up then stared at the floor. When he decided to speak, it came out as mumbling. "I need some space," he said.

"What? Did you say you need some space?"

He looked up at me and nodded. "You're crowding me, Karma."

I put my hands on my hips. "You asked me to stay last night, Cole. I didn't force anything on you."

"You knew what you were doing . . . wearing those tight-ass shorts."

I couldn't believe my ears. He suddenly had regrets about what we'd shared, and he wanted to blame it all on me. I didn't set out to entice him, but I wasn't going to let him win the argument.

"So, it's all my fault, huh?" Cole kept silent. "You don't re-member forcing your tongue down my throat first, right?" He still didn't say anything. "You know, Cole, I'm starting to think you like picking arguments with me. We were having a good day, and now for some reason, you've flipped on me. So, you and I screwed . . . a few times or more. Now you're sorry it happened. It's not the end of the world. Get over it. Is there something else going on with you I should know about?"

He looked me square in the eyes then said it. "I still love Audrie."

I don't know what he expected me to say or do, but I gave him no reaction at all. I sat still just looking at him. He stared back until he couldn't take the silence any more. He stretched out on the couch then stared at the ceiling. I got up then went to the kitchen to refill my glass with soda. I thought about what he said while pouring the orange Fanta into my glass. I didn't know how to feel. I knew he wasn't completely over Audrie, so his words didn't come as a total surprise.

When I came back into the living room, he looked at me. "Don't you have anything to say?"

I shook my head. "Un-un."

"Why not?"

"What's there to say?"

"I don't know, but I thought you'd have some type of re-sponse. Are you hurt, angry, what?"

"None of the above. I can't tell you how to feel about some-one else. All I want to do is work on us."

"That's what I'm telling you, Karma. There isn't an us." He paused before continuing. "Audrie is more like my speed, and she was the first woman to make me feel it was okay to love again."

Suddenly, I knew what I felt—disgust. I gave him much atti-tude. "Do you really want to be with a woman who can't be faithful to you?"

"No. I don't. I'm not saying I'm going to take Audrie back. I'm just saying the same thing I've said for months now. You and I have fun together, but that's all. It was a mistake to be intimate with you last night and earlier today. I realize I need someone more my age to—"

"Save it," I said, giving him the talk-to-the-hand sign. "I've heard enough. Do you want to watch another movie or not?"

"Not," he said, getting up. "I'm going upstairs for a bit. Knock yourself out."

I heard him close his bedroom door once he was up there. My feelings weren't hurt that he didn't want to continue a vibe with me through the night. I blocked out all the things he had just said then turned on the stereo just before heading into the kitchen to cook dinner. It was when dinner was done that my feelings got hurt. I went upstairs to let him know he could eat.

"I'm not hungry," he said through the locked door.

I knocked on it again. "C'mon, Cole. I cooked everything especially for you."

"Karma, I said I'm not hungry."

"You mean to tell me you let me cook all of this food for nothing?" I said into the door.

"Why don't you eat it then? Leave me alone, Karma. I don't want to be bothered."

"So, you gon' let love bite you in the ass, take your appetite, and treat me like shit?" He didn't answer me. "That's alright, Cole. I'm gon' remember this," I said just before hitting the door then walking away.

Be depressed all you want, but when it's all said and done, you're mine, Colby Patterson. Ain't no mistake about that.

*S*ince I had decided to lift my leave of absence and return to work on Monday, I was in bed at the same time as the children Sunday night. Karma left and headed to her place, arguing that I was just going through another phase where I didn't want her around, but that was only partially true. I enjoyed her company over the weekend, but to be completely honest with myself, she could only be a time filler compared to Audrie.

Karma was like an exciting and fun youngster, who by the way knew how to lay it on a man in bed, while Audrie was more tamed and possessed all the womanly qualities I loved and longed to be around. Audrie could hold an intelligent conversation about news, politics, football, the industry in which we worked, and more. Karma basically wanted to talk about Princess and what new dog food we should let her try. She even turned her nose up at me when I changed the TV channel to the news station. I learned there were some things about me Karma probably would never understand.

I woke up on Monday feeling pretty good. I got the kids dressed then off to school. I made it inside my office about forty minutes later. Everyone seemed surprised to see me, but I expected it since I had returned to work earlier than I intended. I pretty much stayed in my office the whole day. I dreaded having to look at Audrie.

Monday went by with a breeze, and so did Tuesday and Wednesday. I had even convinced Karma she should leave at night rather than sleeping over at my house. Karma not being there in the morning made for a good start to my day. I could wake up with a clean conscience, knowing I hadn't used her the night before, although I'm sure she wouldn't have minded. Karma took my rejection like a champ. Audrie, on the other hand, kept leaving me voice messages every day of the week after she discovered I'd returned on Monday.

When I stepped into work on Thursday morning, Audrie was waiting near my office, pretending to be having conversation with a coworker. I made a mistake by glancing at her, and she took that minuscule eye contact as a sign that I wanted to talk. I left her standing outside my office door as I shut it in her face.

I was a little late for work on Friday. The place seemed pretty quiet, and I wondered where everyone was. As I unlocked my office door, Nick stepped outside the conference room and greeted me.

"Colby Patterson? What's up, man?" he said, heading toward me.

We did the soul man handshake then slapped each other on the back once. "You got it, man. I think I can help you with that project today, so hit me up before you get started.

"Word? Yo, that's what's up. Thanks."

"Anytime, man. So, where is everybody?"

"Oh, we're just beginning a meeting. You need to join us. I was just stepping out for a second to get some coffee. I think it's gonna be a long one in there."

"Aw, hell. Well let me join you in the break room before I go in."

I opened my door, set my things down then grabbed a notepad and pen. Nick and I fixed ourselves some coffee then joined everyone else in the conference room.

Audrie tried several times to get me to make eye contact with her. She made sure to be the first one to ask questions and give her two cents on everything. Despite everything she did, I kept my eyes focused on the slides from the projector.

Before the close of the day, Audrie had had enough of the cold-shoulder treatment. She barged into my office like she owned it. Nick was standing next to me, looking at a chart on my computer. We looked up as soon as the door opened.

Audrie tucked her purse under her arm then pointed at me. "You're going to listen, whether you like it or not."

"Audrie, I'm busy. Nick and I—"

"Well, he needs to leave because I'm not going anywhere," she snapped.

Nick looked at me with raised eyebrows, patted me on my back then gathered his file. "We can pick this up tomorrow, man," he said.

I nodded then sat back in my chair. When Nick closed the door behind him, I motioned for Audrie to have a seat.

"I'll stand," she said. "I don't feel welcomed anyway."

I leaned forward. "Why should I welcome you?" Audrie didn't respond. "Don't you have a man somewhere waiting for you?"

"No," she yelled. "The only man I want seems to be diggin' another woman."

"What are you talking about?" I frowned.

"Costa Rica, Cole? You took her to Costa Rica?"

"I needed to get away from stress for a while. It was a family outing."

Audrie's eyes bucked. "So, she's family now? Exactly what does that mean?"

"C'mon . . . you know most households with hired help like nannies and maids and people like that are considered family.

170

And, why am I sitting here explaining anything to you? You were the one caught enjoying yourself with a so-called ex. Do you know how much you hurt me?"

Audrie's face softened. "No, but I can imagine. I'm here to explain, Cole. Even if you feel my excuse has no validity, you should at least want to hear me out. You deserve to know why I was at dinner with Rodney."

"You're right. I do deserve an explanation of why my woman was having dinner with her ex and receiving roses from him on my birthday. Please let me hear this."

She sighed. "Rodney didn't buy them."

"Really?" Skepticism bellowed in my tone. I couldn't believe she hadn't come up with a better response. "And I suppose that wasn't his car I saw out in front of your place last Friday either, huh?"

"Last Friday?" She frowned. "Last Friday . . . Cole, last Friday I didn't have comp—" She stopped. "Oooohh, that was my sister's car. Was it a white Ford Taurus?"

"I don't know. Maybe."

"My sister from Jacksonville, Florida was visiting."

"Okay, Audrie. Fine . . . if you say so."

"Why won't you believe me?"

"The same reason I don't believe Rodney didn't take you out on my birthday and buy you roses. I guess you want me to believe the flowers were compliments of the restaurant or something. If that were the case, I wonder why they didn't bother to send me some. It seemed like I was the only one there celebrating a birthday," I said sarcastically.

"No. Seriously, Cole. There's something strange going on here. All this time I had been thinking Rodney sent flowers to my home and office, but he says he never did. Even though the cards were saying they were from him, they weren't. I don't know what's going on, but I believe him."

"So how did you end up at dinner with him?"

"That's the strangest thing to explain. I received an urgent letter in the mail saying I needed to meet him at Ruth's Chris Steak House." She removed her purse from under her arm then pulled out a piece of paper. "You'll see it seemingly is from his attorney stating some type of estate is involved and that I should share this information with no one. It turned out to be a fraud. Rodney had the same false letter."

I took the paper, read it then slammed it on my desk. "And you didn't feel you could even talk to me about this?"

"I didn't know how to explain it. You had already been thinking there was something going on between Rodney and me because of the flowers."

"Well, what about his attorney? Did you even bother to call him?"

"What're you thinking—I'm stupid? Of course I tried to contact his attorney. He was out of the country until yesterday. Rodney and I both just found out that someone has been playing games with us."

A thought came to mind, and I began to feel sick. "Whoa," I said, holding my head. I leaned back in my chair.

"What?" Audrie came around the desk then sat on my lap. "Are you okay, Cole?"

I nodded. "Yeah. I just had a thought that was really crazy."

She looked at me suspiciously. "You're not thinking that Karma—" she stopped herself then gasped. "Cole, I betchu that's what's been going on. Your little admirer has been trying to break us up. She even tried to make me believe the two of you were an item now."

My silence almost told off on me. Audrie turned my head toward hers and made me look her in the eyes. "What?" I asked.

"I am still yours, aren't I?"

I paused and stared into her eyes. She was even more beautiful than I last remembered. "Yes," I said softly. She gave me a peck on the lips.

"That Karma bitch is crazy, Cole. I'm telling you . . . she's behind all of the foolishness that's been going on. How was your trip? Did she do anything strange or out of the ordinary while you were there?"

"Well, yes and no. I mean, a couple of things happened, but I don't want to go into all of that. She just has a tough time making friends, I guess. I know a lot of things point in her direction, but I don't know that she's behind all the accusations, Audrie. A moment ago was the first time she crossed my mind as being guilty of sabotaging my birthday night, but we have no proof."

"I'm telling you, baby. I bet she—"

I shut Audrie up with a long, passionate, I-miss-you-like-crazy kiss. When we let up for air, her eyes were still closed as she said, "I miss you, too." She rested her forehead on mine.

I began to feel an enormous sense of regret for having slept with Karma. I knew at that moment I wanted to be with Audrie, but how could I tell her I'd crossed the line with Karma? I looked into Audrie's eyes again.

"What?" she asked, rubbing my head.

"You really miss me?"

She sighed. "So much."

"How much?"

"I can show you better than I can tell you."

I gave her a peck on the lips. "When?"

"Come home with me. I swear you won't regret it."

"Give me five minutes to wrap up then I'm heading to your place."

Audrie kissed me. "See you soon."

She got up then left my office.

♦

"Aaahhh, yeeeesss," Audrie moaned as I tasted her honey. Less than five minutes after I was in her house, we were at each other like dogs in heat. I missed her terribly, and I'm sure it showed through my rough lovemaking. I climbed on top of her after she'd reached two orgasms then vigorously tapped her insides. She continued to moan and dug her nails into my back, turning me on even more. It was my turn to moan.

"Ooohhh, yeeesss, baaaby," I cooed. I pounded her some more. "Shiiit, yes. Let's break up then make up again. This feels soooooo goooood." I was almost there. "Get one with me, Audrie. Can you get one with me, baby? Pleeease."

My pleading worked. "Here it comes, Cole. Yes, oh yes," she said, gasping. "Yeeeeeesss, baby. Here it cooooomes."

Her walls were wet and warm as they tightened around me. I lost it. I screamed like a bitch as she gripped me and bulked her hips into me. I had no problems filling the condom. *Damn, she was good. Where the hell did she learn to do that shit?*

We lay cuddled, our bodies sticking together on top of Audrie's wet sheets, evidence of our extreme workout. She missed me. I knew because of the many sweet kisses she began to plant on my lips and face, seemingly every time she had to blink. I lay still, hoping for a break because I felt like I had given all I had during round one.

I felt a faint wind on my cheek then my neck. *Hell, she may as well go to sleep because I'm spent,* I thought. "Must you do that?" I said out loud before I knew it.

I opened my eyes. Audrie seemed shocked. "Do what?"

"Was that your breath I felt?"

"Um, duh . . . I have to breathe, Cole."

"You were blowing on my neck, trying to get me aroused again."

"Was not. I was about to go to sleep. I didn't know you could feel my breath."

"Liar," I said teasingly.

"Am not. And what if I was trying to get some more? What would be wrong with that?"

ALISHA YVONNE

"Get some more? Audrie baby, I'm afraid I ain't got none left." She laughed at me.
"Oh, yeah? Wanna bet?"
"Really, I don't." We both laughed.
"You *will* give me some more, even if I have to take it."
"Is that right?"
I turned over and closed my eyes. Wrong move. Audrie was in a playful mood. She straddled me as I lay on my side then began grinding on my hip. I wanted to laugh. I opened my eyes then looked up at her.
"Is that that new sex I've been hearing about?" I asked. She said nothing. She just kept grinding. "I hear a man's hip can give a woman one hell of an orgasm, so just go right ahead. Knock yourself out."
I dropped my head back on the pillow, closed my eyes then pretended to be snoring. Wrong move. Audrie inched her way up to my face then continued her slow grind. I tried to be strong and act like she wasn't there. Ignoring her soon became difficult for two reasons: the stubble between her legs began to aggravate me and despite how tired I was, her stuff being that close to my face was a huge turn on. Playtime was over.
When I turned to face her, she almost smothered me with that thang. "Okay . . . okay," I exclaimed although my tone was somewhat muffled.
"Okay what?"
"Okay, I'll give you some more, but for future reference, you might want to shave that thang before you sit on my face. You almost cut my lip," I teased.
"Shut up and just eat me," she said, grabbing the back of my head, pushing it into her.
She took charge, and I loved it. I let her have her way with me all night. We stopped to eat dinner then we were back at it again. Before I realized it, time had flown. It was midnight, and I hadn't called Karma or checked on the kids. As Audrie lay

175

asleep with her arm across my chest, I eased it off me then got out of bed to retrieve my cell. Audrie must've been sleeping lightly.

"Where're you going, baby? I thought you were going to spend the night."

"I am—I mean I was. Well, I forgot to call Karma, and I'm sure the kids are probably mad that I didn't wish them good night, too. I should leave." I grabbed my underwear then put them on.

"I'm sorry. It crossed my mind to wake you so you could call home, but I slept longer than I had intended."

"Well, better late than never, I guess. I'll just call now and let Karma know I'm on my way."

I picked up my phone and noticed ten missed calls from my home number. I knew Karma was probably pissed, so I pondered whether calling so late was a good idea. I figured she'd be mad if I waited till morning to call, so since I was damned whether I did or didn't, I decided to climb back into bed with Audrie.

"On second thought, I'll just wait until morning."

"Why? What's wrong? You don't feel like hearing your other girlfriend's mouth?"

I smirked. "There's no other girlfriend, but if you're referring to Karma, I do feel her attitude can wait till daylight."

I pulled the cover over my head, but Audrie snatched it back down then straddled me. We went for another round of hot, sweaty sex. *I must've been a fool to think about leaving this tonight,* was all I could think.

The kids were in the den, watching Saturday morning cartoons when Cole came into the house. I heard them clapping and singing "Daaaddyyy" soon after the door closed. I heard him ask where I was, and the kids told him I was in the kitchen. I was just about finished with washing the breakfast dishes when he walked in. I kept on with my chore without acknowledging him. Princess was no longer limping and had followed him into the kitchen. She came over and stood on her hind legs, scratching at my shin.

"Princess, quit it," I snapped.

Cole didn't like my tone. "I know you're mad at me for not coming home or calling last night, but don't take it out on Princess."

I looked at him then rolled my eyes. "Her claws hurt. Why don't you try pulling *your* pants legs up so she can scratch you," I said then returned my attention to my chore.

He pulled out a chair then sat down at the table. "Princess, c'mere, girl." Princess did as told then Cole picked her up.

"Your momma's not happy right now, but she doesn't mean to take it out on you," he told her, rubbing her coat.

I knew Cole had spent the night with Audrie. Truth is, there wasn't anywhere else he'd be. The fact that he didn't answer my calls or bother to call me further confirmed my suspicion of his whereabouts. I didn't like the fact that he was with Audrie the night before, but what could I really do about it?

Without looking at him, I said, "Did you even bother to check the messages I left on your voice mail last night?"

I turned to look at him. He seemed at a loss for words, but he managed to answer. "You left me messages?"

"Well, never mind. I guess you didn't listen to them."

"Anything you'd like to tell me now?"

"Not really. I guess I should at least let you know about the important phone call from your attorney's office."

"Really? Was the call from Lewis?"

"I don't remember his name, but I wrote it down."

"I wonder what he wants now. What did he say?"

"He didn't say anything. He just asked if you were here and said it was important that you get back to him as soon as possible."

"Hmph. This sounds important. I hope he's not calling to say new evidence against me has somehow surfaced. I'm really getting sick of being questioned over and over."

"The caller didn't say, but his name and number is on the piece of paper attached by the magnet on the refrigerator."

Cole put Princess down then got up to retrieve the number. Just like that, he forgot about me. No "I'm sorry for leaving you with the kids last night", no "can I make it up to you", no nothing. Cole grabbed the phone to call the attorney then headed out of the kitchen.

I finished the dishes then headed upstairs. Once I got to the top of the stairs, I could hear Cole's voice as he talked on the phone in his bedroom. Judging by the sound of his tone, I immediately sensed he wasn't talking to the attorney. He was talking to Audrie.

"Yeah, it just seems as if Lewis wants to update me three times a week now, but he's saying the same thing: there aren't any new leads," I heard Cole say. "I'm getting tired of hearing that. Who knows? This case could never be solved. There are a lot of cases that go unsolved, you know?" He paused then continued. "I was in a pretty good mood until I returned that call . . . sure I'd like to spend more time with you. Bowling? Sure. I think I might be able to whip your butt. Let's do it. How about that Winchester Bowling Center closer to the Hickory Hill area?" Cole paused. "No. The kids can come with us at a later time. Let's just make this our day. I'll ask Karma if she's got anything planned. If she doesn't, I'll pick you up in a couple of hours."

I eased back downstairs to the den. I whispered to the children. "Hey, kids." They looked at me. "How would the two of you like to go to the arcade to play games and have some fun today?"

"Yeah," they both screamed. I shushed them.

"When Daddy comes downstairs, ask him if he'll take you guys, but listen to me carefully. Don't tell Daddy I told you to ask him, okay?"

"Okay," they said in unison.

When I heard Cole's footsteps coming down the stairs, I headed toward the kitchen. He called out to me, "Karma, can I talk to you for a minute?"

I stopped just short of the kitchen entrance then turned to him. "Yes, Cole?"

"I've got something to do today, and I was wondering if I could pay you double time to sit with the kids."

Before I could answer, Shawna walked up and interrupted her father. "Daddy, will you take us to the arcade today?"

"Yeah, Daddy, pleeeease," Gavin sang.

Cole seemed speechless. When he finally spoke, he began to stutter. "Um . . . well, um . . . not today, kids. I um . . . I've got some running around to do."

"Aw, you gotta work today, too?" Shawna whined.

"Well, yeah . . . I . . . I'll take you guys to the arcade tomorrow. How about that?"

Gavin and Shawna remained silent with their mouths poked out. Cole looked at me for some help. I shrugged then patted him on the back.

"They'll be okay. I'll make sure we have fun while you take care of business."

"Thanks, Karma."

Cole turned then went up the stairs. I looked at the pouting children. "Hey, you guys. We'll still have some fun today," I said. "Just give me a little while then I'll tell you when we can begin." They nodded then started back into the den.

I waited until Cole had been gone about half an hour before getting the kids dressed to go out. Boy, was he in for a surprise. What Cole didn't know I knew was that the Winchester Bowling Center not only had bowling, but it was equipped with an arcade as well.

An hour and a half after Cole had gone, the kids and I were pulling up into the parking lot of the center. I circled to see if I noticed Cole's car, and I did. I made certain to park on the opposite side so I could declare I had no idea he was there.

The children practically skipped all the way inside. I knew Cole said he would be bowling, so I led the children to the bowling lanes first. To my dismay, there was no sign of Cole or Audrie. Shawna questioned my intentions.

"I thought we were going to play games?" she asked.

"We are. Just hold on a sec." I gave the place a once-over again then grabbed the children's hands. "C'mon."

As we walked toward the arcade, the children began to skip again. After a few minutes of walking around, I spotted Cole and Audrie playing a pinball machine. Cole stood behind her, apparently attempting to assist her with the game. They were giggling like they were in love. I made certain to bring them to the children's attention.

"Hey, kids. Look over there," I said, pointing. "Isn't that your father?"

"Yes," Shawna answered.

"What's he doing here?" I asked. "He told you guys he had to work, didn't he?" Shawna's face turned sour and so did Gavin's. "Let's go over and talk to him."

Of course I didn't just walk up to Cole. I pretended to stumble up on him. "Cole?" I asked, adding a surprised tone to my voice. He did a double take. "What're you doing here? I thought you had to work."

Cole looked down at his angry children who didn't bother to speak to him, then looked back up at me. "I've got a better question," he said, frowning. "What are you doing here with my children, Karma?"

"I told you I'd make sure they'd have fun while you were away taking care of business."

He pointed his finger as he spoke. "Why didn't you call and let me know you were leaving the house? You had no right bringing them out of the house without my permission. Who the hell do you think you are?"

I was ready to answer that, but then Shawna broke out in tears. Cole kneeled to console her, but she jerked from him. "You said you had to work. You just didn't want to spend time with us today," she cried.

"Shawna, sweetie," Cole started then stopped. He looked at Gavin then pulled him near. "C'mere, kids. Let me talk to you outside for a minute." He took the children by the hand then led them to the door.

Audrie stood in front of the pinball machine looking stupid. "Bitch, what are you doing here with my man?" I asked her.

"Your man?" she asked with raised eyebrows.

"Yes, my man. Is there too much noise in this place or something, or are you just plain deaf?"

She stepped closer to me, shaking her finger. "Let me tell you something, you delusional little—"

I slapped her finger down, startling her. "Oh, I think you better step off. You don't want none of this. I'll have your tall lanky ass hemmed up between one of these pinball machines. Black-ass bitch." I rolled my eyes then started off to look for Cole.

"Black is beautiful, sweetie," Audrie yelled.

I turned to face her. "You wish."

"It's a fact. You haven't figured it out by now? Why else do you think Cole loves me so? You ain't dark enough. Chocolate is his flavor, sweetie. Grow up then go get you a tan or something. Maybe then you'll be able to give me a run for my money."

I stepped back over to her. She took a step backward. "We'll see about that. If I were you, I'd stay the fuck out of my way." I walked off again.

"You don't scare me, Karma," she yelled again. "Find you some kids your own age to play with and leave me and Cole alone."

I ignored her last comment because I really wanted to see where Cole and the kids had gone. I found them just outside the door, standing against the wall.

"Don't you guys want to come in? It's too cold out here," I said, rubbing the sleeves of my jacket.

The children's eyes were fixed on the pavement. Cole looked at me like he could kill me. "You are so through," he said through clenched teeth.

"What did I do?"

Audrie stepped outside. "Is everything okay, Cole?"

Cole passed her Shawna and Gavin's hands. "Take them inside for me. I'll be in shortly," he said. Audrie nodded then headed off with the children.

I repeated my question. "What did I do now, Cole?"

"Where the hell do you get off taking my kids out of the house without my permission?" he scolded.

"Oh, c'mon, Cole. This isn't about me leaving the house with the kids. This is about me having exposed you as a liar to your children. I didn't know you were coming here to be with Audrie. I heard the same lie those kids heard—your ass was going to work. Don't blame this on me."

"Come get your shit out of my house tomorrow. I want you gone," he snapped then tried to walk past me.

I pulled his arm. "Um, so when were you gonna tell me you got back with Audrie?"

"I don't owe you a damn thing. You and I laid a few times and that was it. I made no commitment to you, and you know that."

I shook my head. "Wrong. You didn't have to say it with your mouth. You committed to me the first time you stuck your dick in me. You're mine, Cole."

He looked dumbfounded. "You're crazy, you know that?"

"Yes, and so I've been told many times before." He jerked his arm from me. "Don't do that," I said. "Listen. I'm willing to overlook this little weekend fling you got going with Audrie, but I expect you to bring your ass home by tomorrow."

Cole didn't seem to know what to say. I began to walk back inside. "Where're you going?" he asked.

I looked over my shoulder as I kept walking. "To get my children."

He grabbed my arm and pulled me back. "No, you're not. Stay the fuck away from my children, Karma. I mean it. Your ass is out. Don't come around us."

It was my turn to jerk from him. "Those are my babies, too, Cole. They love me. You can't do this to us."

He began to breathe hard. "Give me my keys, Karma."

"No," I stated simply.

He looked at my purse then lunged for it. I held on for dear life. Before I knew it, he had my purse high in the air with me dangling from it. Audrie and the children ran over about the same time security did. When the guards pried us apart, I had my purse so I went about my way.

I jumped in my car then headed to Cole's house. I grabbed any and everything he still had that reminded him of Glenda then destroyed it, including the one picture in Shawna's room. I even crashed the anniversary clock Glenda had inscribed before she died.

I grabbed up as much of my belongings as I could because I knew I'd probably go to jail for vandalism if I tried to come back. I picked up Princess then took one last look at the mess I'd made before heading out. *Who's got the last laugh now, Cole?*

I took Audrie and my children to her home before heading to my house. I didn't know if Karma would be there, so I figured things would pan out better if I didn't have them all with me. Audrie was very understanding, but very concerned at the same time. She and I had come to the same conclusion: Karma wasn't operating with good sense.

I had told Audrie about Karma claiming me as her man, and all she could say was that she had told me so. I could kick myself for being so trusting and allowing such a madwoman around my children, but Karma had me fooled. She knew how to turn on the charm when she wanted to. She cooked, cleaned, and was very good at being my nanny and assistant. I figured out how I went wrong though. I shouldn't have ever let her begin working for me without reviewing her references. I guess I was just vulnerable without Glenda and needed immediate help with the kids.

When I pulled into the driveway, Karma's car wasn't there. I felt a sense of relief because I really didn't want to go toe-to-toe with her again. I began dialing Audrie's number as I got out of the car.

"Audrie, it's me," I said just after she answered.

"Are you home already?"

"Yes, but Karma's car isn't here. I'm going inside right now. Why don't you and the kids come on over?"

"Okay. We were about to pop in a movie, but we can head out now."

I opened the door then stepped inside to an utter mess. Karma had completely trashed my place. "What the—"

"What? Is everything okay, Cole?"

"No," I yelled. "That crazy heifer trashed my place, and oh hell naw."

"What? What is it?" Audrie asked in a panicked tone.

"My clock! She broke the anniversary clock Glenda had inscribed for us before she died. It was the last thing my wife ever gave me."

"You've got to be kiddin' me? Cole, what did you do to make her so mad?"

I couldn't tell Audrie every reason Karma was mad, so I sugarcoated the truth. "Well, for one thing, she's mad that I told her she's too young, and I want to be with you."

"When did you tell her that?"

"It hasn't been too long ago. Anyway, listen. I'll call you when I get things cleaned up here. I don't want the children coming home to this mess. Plus, I need to get my head straight. I'm pretty torn about the clock. I also need to get my locks changed."

"Sure. We'll hold tight. Call me as soon as you get done."

"Thanks, Audrie."

We hung up then I took another look around. Flashes of the broken pieces of Glenda's pictures came to mind. I looked down at the shattered clock next to my foot. I became enraged. I headed toward the door, but then stopped after realizing I didn't need to be over to Karma's place making trouble. If I ended up in jail, the Carters would probably get custody of my children, and

ALISHA YVONNE

I'd catch hell getting them back. I dialed Karma's number instead.

"Hellooo," she sang with a soft, innocent tone. I could sense a sinister smile on her face.

"I had no idea you were so crazy," I told her. "I shouldn't have ever let you in my home without checking the proper references, if you ever had any."

Karma laughed. "C'mon, Cole. What did you expect me to do—walk away quietly?" She paused. "I'm a mad black woman. When we find out there's another woman keeping our man from being dedicated to us, for the most part, we tend to cut up in some fashion."

"Think practically. Audrie has always been there," I screamed. "What are you talking about?"

"Un-un. You and Audrie had a break up. Remember the whole roses-from-the-ex-at-the-restaurant scene? How could you forget it? You were crushed."

"I guess you haven't figured out that by now I know you were behind the making of that scene, huh?"

"Now what are you talking about?"

"I know everything," I yelled. "For some off-the-wall reason, you've set out to ruin my life ever since you got here, Karma. You knew my wife's pictures and belongings were all precious memories for me, but you've destroyed them. And to blame things on an innocent child . . . you went too far. I can't believe I went for that crap about Gavin smashing those pictures. Everything was destroyed by your psychotic ass."

"Hmph. Name calling isn't nice, Cole," she answered calmly.

I huffed. "Karma, I hope you've gotten what you need from here because I'm having my locks changed in a minute. I don't want you back here. I might do something bad to you."

She laughed, sending a wicked sensation through my body. I felt sick to my stomach thinking how I ever laid with her. She laughed some more before she finally spoke.

187

"You act like you don't hear very well. You're mine, Cole. I can't stay away from something—or in this case—someone who's truly mine. I'll give you some space to cool down, but we'll meet up again. Okay, baby?"

I hung up in her face. I paced the floor, trying to decide if I should report her to the authorities. I really didn't have much on her except the vandalism, and since that could easily be resolved with me cleaning up and having my locks changed, I decided against calling the police.

I called a locksmith then began straightening up the place. It took me an hour to clean and salvage what little things I could. My clock was beyond repair, and that depressed me immensely. I fixed myself a drink then sat on the couch to wait for the locksmith. I only had a little bit of Absolut Ruby Red left, but it was the remedy that calmed my nerves.

Once the locksmith had changed all the locks and gone, I called Audrie and the kids over. Audrie had only been inside my place one other occasion. For the most part, we had been spending our time at her place. She walked around the den, glancing and touching things before she finally sat down.

"The place looks different since I was last here," she said, getting comfortable on the couch.

"Well, the time you came here a few months ago, you were in and then right back out," I lowered my tone before finishing my statement, "and let's not forget a certain person helped rearrange things also." I looked over at the kids to see if they were paying attention. They were arguing over the remote. "Shawna and Gavin, do me a favor. How about going upstairs to study a bit?"

"Aw, Daddy," Shawna said. "It's almost bedtime, and we haven't watched TV yet. Ms. Audrie said we had to go home, so she turned off the TV."

"I know. I'll double your television time tomorrow. Right now I need to speak with Ms. Audrie in private, okay?"

Gavin got up then started up the stairs with no problem. Shawna followed, pouting.

"Night, children," Audrie said to them, but she failed to get a response. "They're not happy with you, Cole." She turned to me. "It's not the first time, and I can promise you it won't be the last."

"I've always wanted children, but the Lord knew best. Rodney and I would still have to deal with each other—tied." Audrie shook her head. "Sometimes I think about the what-if, but then I start shouting and giving out praises. Children with Rodney would've been an eighteen-year sentence."

I sat next to her. "I know Rodney wasn't that bad. You told me he had his issues you couldn't deal with, but what would make you think having his children would've been hell?"

"I know Rodney . . . those kids would've probably turned out like Karma—troublesome and alone with no friends. That girl is coo-coo. You know that, right?"

I released a long, deep sigh as I sat back on the couch. "Yeah, I know."

Audrie slid closer, placing her head on my shoulder. "I know the clock is upsetting you, but just think about it like this: It could've been worse. It took some time to figure Karma out, but at least now that you have, you're rid of her, and your family is safe." She lifted her head then planted a kiss on me.

Safe, huh? Something tells me Karma meant what she said about not letting go. I better brace myself for this ride.

*C*ole needed a cooling-down period, so I gave him a couple of weeks to collect himself. Nearly fourteen days without hearing or seeing me gave him a sense of security, I'm sure, but I was restless without him. Two weeks was far too long to be Cole-less. I missed everything about him—the way he complimented my cooking, his smile when he greeted me, and oh, the way he touched me and kissed me sent chills up my spine.

I needed to be close to him again, so I did the next unthink-able thing—applied for a position at his company, Essential Software Development. The interview was a breeze. Luther Bonner, the interviewing manager, was turned on by my charm. He knew this would be my first position in such a company, but just as I had convinced Cole, I had managed to spark something in Luther.

I researched as much as I could about software development and referred to the textbooks I'd bought off a few college students so I could be prepared for the interview. I was more than ready when Luther told me I had the office assistant position.

ALISHA YVONNE

I made sure to be there bright and early that clear, sunny morning in March—my first day as office assistant. I didn't have my own office like some of the team, so I went straight into Luther's office to go over some things before Cole came in. Once everyone had made it to work, Luther called a meeting.

"Um, Luther, do you mind if I step into the ladies' room," I said just after grabbing his arm to stop him. "You can go ahead and get started. I promise I'll only be a minute."

"Okay," he answered. "I won't get too detailed about anything until you return. Plus, I need to introduce you to everyone, so try not to be very long."

"I won't."

I went inside the restroom then began grooming my hair. *Karma, girl, you are too much,* I thought as I looked in the mirror. *You are going to totally rock some people's world once you step into that conference room.* I laughed out loud at the thought of the look I'd see on Cole's face. I refreshed my lip gloss then headed to join the meeting.

I purposely opened the door slowly. Luther was standing within view. He beckoned me in. "Ah, here she is now. Our new office assistant," he said with his hand stretched in my direction. I went ahead and stepped inside. "Everyone, this is Karma Jolley."

I looked around in time to catch Cole's head coming up from his writing pad. He made no attempt to hide the fact of being disturbed; neither did Audrie. I smiled and waved at everyone.

"Hello," I said, cupping my hands in front of me, pretending to be shy.

Cole's friend Nick threw his head back then burst out laughing. Luther looked as if he didn't have a clue as to what was going on. "What's so funny, Nick?"

Nick shook his head as he continued to laugh. "Nothing. Don't worry about it. It's nothing."

Cole intervened, "It is something. Luther, may I have a word with you in private?"

"Sure," he responded. Cole slid his chair back. "After my meeting, of course." Luther was stern. "Have a seat over here, Karma," he said, gesturing toward a vacant chair.

"Thanks, Luther."

"How about telling everyone a little about yourself before I begin the meeting," he added.

"Sure." I smiled then went on a short spiel of introduction.

No one seemed excited about my presence, so I assumed they all remembered me from the skating rink, when I tripped up their beloved Audrie. I just kept smiling and pretending to be elated about being there. Well, I was sort of excited. I had just come face to face with Cole. He looked like a chocolate hunk—so worth the wait.

Audrie kept eyeing me as Luther spoke. I eyed her right back. She should've known she couldn't scare me. If I had nerve to seek a job at Cole's place of employment, then that should've been a sign to her that I was playing for keeps and I meant business.

After the meeting, Cole went straight into Luther's office. They were in there for quite a while, but I couldn't be too sure how everything would turn out, so I was nervous. I went around to various desks, chatting with the employees, trying not to think about whether Luther was going to fire me. When his office door flew open and Cole came storming out, I could only hope for the best. Luther soon appeared in the doorway then beckoned me.

"Yes, sir. Is there a problem?" I asked just after closing the door behind me.

"Who are you?" he asked, sitting behind his desk.

I played dumb. "Excuse me? I'm Karma Joll—"

"No. I hear everyone except me has met you. I was out on vacation during the company outing in December. Who are you to Colby?"

"Apparently I'm nothing to Colby. I use to work for him, but he fired me over a minor misunderstanding."

"So why are you here, Karma?"

"To work."

"Is that all?"

"Yes, sir."

"Have a seat, Karma." I did as he said. "Are you sure that's all? Are you planning to start some kind of trouble in my establishment?"

"Not at all," I stated innocently. "I came here because I want to work. As I stated in my interview, I need a job, and this time I prefer it be something that will develop me toward my field of study. I want to grow and learn, Luther. If it'll help, I won't even go near Colby."

Luther nodded. "I think that will be best. He's very upset about you being here, and although I'm quite sure he hasn't shared the full story, I know him well. I feel like his anger might be somewhat justified. I'm sure you know the man recently lost his wife. He's a single father, and stress is the last thing he needs."

I nodded. "Enough said. I'll stay out of his way."

"I appreciate that, Karma. That'll be all."

"What about my assignments for today?"

"I'll partner you up with Nick Murphy for a while. Let me get him on the line."

Nick, eeewww. I smiled as if there was no problem. Within a matter of seconds, Nick was at Luther's door. Luther called for him to come in. Nick dragged his boney ass in the office, grinning as he reached for my hand.

"I'll be happy to show you the ropes, Karma," Nick said.

"Thanks, Nick." I turned to Luther. "Thank you, too, Luther," I said just before exiting the office.

Nick escorted me into his office. We were there most of the morning going over charts and graphs. Nick explained various ways I could assist him and the other associates.

"I've wanted an assistant for a while," he said.

I nodded, letting his words pass through one ear and out the other. As long as I pretended to be interested in what he had to say, he kept talking. I repeatedly nodded as if I understood him, but all the while I wondered what Cole was doing, and if he was thinking of me.

Before I knew it, it was lunchtime. Nick invited me to join him, but I made up a lie about having to run some errands. I sat in my car, slumped down, listening to the radio as I waited for Cole to come out to his car. I finally heard his voice. He was speaking to someone on his cell. I turned my radio down, but as soon as I rose to get out of the car, Audrie trotted up behind Cole, visibly shaking him up.

"Boo," she screamed.

"Girl, you almost got it from me," I heard him say.

Audrie laughed. "You thought I was your deranged admirer, didn't you?" She laughed some more.

"Yeah, and that's not funny. I have a huge headache behind her drama. The nerve of her—applying to work for this company."

"You know what that's about, baby. She doesn't give a damn about working here. She just wants to be near you."

Audrie put her arms around Cole's waist as they stood next to his car. He hugged her back then kissed her forehead.

"Everything's going to be okay," she said, barely audible.

He kissed her nose then her lips. Then I saw my man's tongue enter her mouth. *Aw, hell naw.* I reached for the latch on the car door, but stopped when I heard Nick's loud mouth.

"Get a room, you two," he yelled. "Please . . . before you get fired. You know how the company is about public affection. It's camera's and shit out here in this parking lot."

Cole and Audrie broke their kiss, but held on to their embrace. They all laughed as they got into Cole's car. I hit my dashboard as they pulled off. I was livid. I wanted to speak to Cole, but Audrie and Nick had deprived me of my opportunity. I went back inside to wait for Nick.

I fiddled around on Nick's computer, killing time as I awaited his return. I played Solitaire and surfed the Internet for Cole's new home number. I came up empty, but I planned to continue my search once I got home.

Nick came into the office an hour later, smiling and touching me. His breath reeked of alcohol. "Have you been drinking?" I asked.

"Shhh." He cupped his hands then blew into them and sniffed. "You can tell?"

"Can't you?" I frowned.

He opened his desk drawer, pulled out a huge bottle of Scope, threw a large gulp into his mouth then began swishing it. He mumbled something that sounded like, "I'll be back" as he held up his finger and stepped outside the office. Once he returned, he blew a strong gust of air into my face.

"Is that better?" he asked.

I jumped back. "If you ever do that again, I'll knock all of your teeth to the back of your throat."

"Oohh, feisty, eh?"

I rolled my eyes. "I don't care if your breath smells like heaven. It's not cool to blow it into people's faces."

He sucked his teeth. "What would you know about heaven?" He sat at his desk. "There's nothing angelic about you anyway."

I sat in the seat next to him. "Whatever, Nick. You should never believe everything you hear. I'm sure Cole only told you half of the story."

"Well, why don't you try telling me the rest?"

"Why don't you show me what I'm supposed to be learning?" I said, tapping on the computer monitor. "How about that?"

Nick shook his head then continued with my lesson. We only left the office once to get printing paper then we were hemmed up once again. I excused myself to the restroom while Nick printed out our documents. After passing Luther's office, I noticed he seemed to be gone for the day. It was three o'clock in the afternoon, but his office lights were off and his door was shut.

On my way out of the restroom, I made a convenient stop at Cole's office. His door was unlocked, but he was on the phone.

If looks could kill, I would be dead. I stood patiently waiting for him to get off the phone. I could tell by the conversation that he was stretching the call, so I began to do things to aggravate him, like sitting on his desk, fondling with things.

"Let me call you back later," he finally told the caller as he snatched his paperweight from me.

"How have you been, Cole?" I asked just after he hung up.

"I was fine until you pulled this stunt. How dare you come into my workplace?" he said through tight lips.

"I needed work. I got fired, remember?"

"Karma, I don't know why you're here, but I swear—"

"Aw, c'mon, Cole. I don't wanna cause you harm. I love you. I thought you knew that." I reached to stroke his face, but he slapped my hand away.

"Get your ass off my desk. You're not even supposed to be in here. Luther said you promised to stay away. What do you think you're doing?"

"I just wanted a little time to talk to you alone. What we talk about is our business . . . and just so you know, I'm still willing to let you play around with Audrie for a minute, but pretty soon, she's got to go."

"Karma, get your ass out of here," he said, standing and pointing toward the door. "You're a psycho. You need help. Get out of my office—now!"

I kept smiling as I headed toward the door. "You know," I said, pausing to scratch my head, "I'm feeling really unappreciated lately, but nevertheless, I love you, Cole. I can't wait until we're happy together again."

"Out, Karma."

"Kiss my babies tonight and tell them I love them, too." I blew a kiss to Cole then left his office.

As soon as I closed the door behind me, Nick started out of his office. "Karma, I was just about to come looking for you," he called over to me.

"Coming," I sang.

I quickly walked toward Nick then a loud bang sounded as if Cole had thrown something against the inside of his door. Nick looked at me with raised eyebrows. "What was that about?"

I shrugged. "I don't know." I eased toward Nick's office as he stood staring over at Cole's door.

"I'll be back," he said over his shoulder.

I knew he was going to check on Cole. It took him about ten minutes to get back. I sat at the computer, clicking on buttons.

"Karma, you're playing with fire, girl," he said as he sat down.

"No, I'm not. I did everything you showed me this afternoon. See," I said, scrolling on the computer.

"You know what I'm talking about."

I sighed. "All I did was stop in to say hello."

"That's not all you did, and you know it."

I placed my hand on my chest as if I was offended. "I don't believe you said that. Are you accusing me—"

"Listen. Just stay out of Cole's office. You say you want to keep your job here, so I suggest you don't bring attention to yourself. I like you, and I'd love to see you hang around."

A wide smile crept on my face. *He likes me. Hmmm, I wonder if I can make Cole jealous by starting a relationship with Nick.*

*T*hree weeks later it was early April, and Karma was still secure in her position on my job. I avoided her as much as possible—or should I say for as much as she would allow me to. She had won everyone over with her charming ways, including Nick. He seemed to think having Karma around was the best thing since the invention of external computer drives, claiming she'd been able to help him better multitask. Some of the other associates said the same thing, but I didn't care what she was good at. I didn't want any part of her.

I got up one Monday morning, struggling with getting the kids ready. They fussed and cried about missing Princess.

"Where's Karma and Princess?" Gavin cried.

"They're still on vacation, son. I don't know if they'll be back," I lied. "But hey, we're getting along without them, right?"

Shawna began to whine, too. "Daddy, I miss Princess. She was my best-est friend."

I sighed as I handed Shawna the tie to her uniform shirt. "She was your best friend, Shawna, not best-est."

"Well, can't we see Princess just one time?"

I was frustrated. "I don't know where they are, Shawna," I yelled. She poked her mouth out. "I'll buy you a new dog. How about that?"

"We don't want a new dog," Gavin said. "We want Princess."

There was a knock at the door. I shook my head then walked over to answer it. I looked through the peephole then unlocked the latches. I opened the door then stepped back to allow Audrie inside. "Shawna, have a seat. Audrie is here to comb your hair." After letting Karma go, I took Shawna to the beauty shop for braids as we'd done in the past. Audrie offered to step in so the beauty shop visits wouldn't get too costly. This was very gracious of her, and I thanked her every time I thought about it.

Shawna sat with her arms folded, looking mean as Audrie approached. "What's wrong, Shawna?" Audrie asked. "I'll only put two pigtails in your hair today, okay?"

Shawna didn't answer. "We've all had sort of a disagreement this morning. They both miss Karma and Princess."

Audrie gasped. "Oh no," she said.

I nodded. "Exactly. That's what I'm saying."

"Well, why don't we just get them a new dog? I'll help pick one."

"It's not that simple," I replied. I stepped over and rubbed Gavin's head. "My son here has made it very clear he only wants Princess."

Audrie picked up the comb then sat next to Shawna. "Hmph," she said. She seemed to be at a loss for words.

After finishing Shawna's hair, we packed up to leave. The children got into the car with me, and we headed to their schools. Audrie went on to work ahead of me.

Once I got to work, Nick met me at my office. "Yo, Colby, let me holler at you for a minute," he said as I unlocked the door.

"A'ight. Give me a minute to set my things down."

I entered the office, set my bags down then opened the blinds. Nick had taken a seat in the chair in front of my desk. I turned on my computer then logged onto my system. Once I'd had a chance to catch my breath, I turned to Nick.

"What's on your mind, bro?" I asked.

He turned to look behind him then got up and closed the door. "Well, it's about Karma," he said, heading back to the chair.

I shrugged. "Okay, and?"

"I just wanted to ask what do you think about her joining us for lunch today? I really think she's much different now."

I must've looked like the Rock with one eyebrow raised. "Karma? Are you serious? Please. Different how?"

"Just trust me."

I shook my head and began crossing my hands in front of me like a baseball referee motioning a player safe on base. "I don't know what y'all selling, but I don't want none. Forget about whatever it is."

"Colby . . . man, you're not being fair. Can people not change?"

I began rambling through my desk drawers, trying to signify he needed to leave without me saying it. "Where did I put that thing?" I said with my head buried in my drawer.

"People can change, Colby, and what would it hurt to invite her to lunch with us? Audrie's going to be on your arm anyway, right?"

I sighed as I slammed the drawer shut. "You're not going to let this go, are you?"

"She's changed, I'm telling you. Just trust me on this one. She's got other things taking her attention off you now."

I raised another eyebrow. "Interesting."

"What?"

"Well, you are a pretty good judge of character, and I'd love to know what finally made her have some sense."

"So, it's okay for her to join us for lunch?"

I felt sick to my stomach thinking about sitting across the table from Karma, but something told me to go along with Nick. "A'ight, but if she—"

"I know what you're going to say. She won't cut up. I promise."

"I wanted to believe Nick, but deep down I couldn't. He left my office then I called Audrie to break the news to her. She, too, was very skeptical and questioned Nick's motive.

"I don't think Nick would have a motive, baby," I responded. "Why on earth would he want you and Karma to be cordial? Didn't you explain to him all she's put you through?"

"I did, but I have to admit, he's got me curious as hell about why I need to sit across the table from Karma. I'll do it this time, but I swear if she acts up, I'm done with Nick and her."

"I don't know why we need to trust them. Nevertheless, I'll be at lunch, sitting right next to you, babe."

We hung up then continued with our work day. I didn't see Nick or Karma come out of his office for the first part of the day. When it was time for lunch, I called Nick to let him know he'd have to transport Karma to the restaurant. He cheerfully agreed then hung up with me.

We met at an Applebee's not far from the office. Audrie and I were seated in a booth near the window when we saw Nick's car pull up. My stomach turned when I saw Karma stepping out of the car, grinning like the Cheshire Cat. At one time, I had thought she was a gorgeous young lady, but there I sat wondering how I could've ever been attracted to her. She was still pretty, but her ways had thrown me.

Nick held Karma's hand as they walked up then slid into the booth. "What's up, you guys?" Nick asked.

"Hello, Audrie and Colby," Karma spoke.

Colby? When did she start calling me that? "Good afternoon," I responded. Audrie didn't bother speaking.

As the double lunch date progressed, Karma was very cordial and extra friendly toward Nick. Audrie had been pretty quiet, then out of nowhere she decided to talk to Karma.

"So, Karma, how's Princess?" Audrie asked.

"Princess is doing well. Thanks for asking," Karma responded.

"Shawna and Gavin miss her, you know?" Audrie added.

"I can imagine. The children had grown very close to her. I can bring her by to see them if you'd like," Karma said excitedly. I shook my head. "No, but thanks for offering."

Audrie continued. "How much time do you have for her? Would you ever consider selling Princess?" I squeezed Audrie's knee under the table, hoping she'd get the hint to stop, but she pushed my hand away and continued. "I mean, we were thinking of getting the kids another dog, but think of how happy they'd be if Cole and I brought Princess home to them."

Karma looked as if she would give the idea some serious thought. "Hmm," she responded, smiling. "I hadn't thought about selling her, but if I did, there wouldn't be more deserving kids than Shawna and Gavin. Give me some time to think about it. I just might let them have her." Up went that strange grin again.

I changed the subject. We were into a conversation about our projects when I heard something that led me to believe Karma and Nick must've been fooling around.

"Naw, baby," Nick said. "I meant our other client . . . you know . . . the one we just landed."

Baby? I thought.

"Oh, that's right, boo," Karma answered then leaned on him. "I don't know how I got the two mixed up." Their lips met for a few instant pecks.

Audrie and I looked at each other. "So, Nick," Audrie said, "I take it you two are dating now."

He put on a huge smile. "Karma's my baby." He looked into her eyes. "This girl's all that and a bag of chips, I tell ya."

Karma laughed. "Thank you, boo. You're all that to me, too."

They leaned in and locked lips for several seconds. While their eyes were closed, Audrie made a gagging gesture with her finger toward her opened mouth. She tried to hold back her laughter, so she turned and looked over her shoulder. I couldn't believe what I was seeing. I put my fry down then interrupted their kiss.

"Yo, Nick man, let me talk with you outside for a minute," I said. Audrie shot me a confused look. "I'll be back, sweetie." I gave her a soft peck on the lips, but I could tell it didn't help clear her confusion.

Once Nick and I were outside, I questioned him. "Man, you have got to be kiddin' me. I've told you that girl is off her rocker. What on earth would possess you to fool with her? This has got to be a joke."

"Why it's gotta be a joke?" he asked with his arms stretched wide. "Just because you can't see yourself with her?"

"No . . . just because of all the crazy shit I've told you she's been up to lately . . . and trashing my place. Hell, no . . . I can't see myself with her, and neither should you."

"Man, I told you a long time ago if you didn't want her, pass her to me—or was that Audrie?" He laughed but soon stopped after he noticed I didn't see anything funny. "What's up with you? You been screwing Karma or something?"

I began to stutter, having a difficult time telling a straight lie. "Huh? Na . . . naw. Un-un," I said, shaking my head. "I ain't . . . I ain't slept with her. Are you crazy?"

"Well, why aren't you happy for me?"

"Man, that girl is young, and let's not forget a bit unbalanced, too."

Nick shook his head then laughed. "Colby, Karma talked to me about the quarrel between you two. It was just a misunderstanding, that's all." Nick sounded so naïve, it was sickening.

"She's really laid it on you, huh? You use to warn me to be careful with her, remember? Now you're the one who can't see through her."

He shook his head. "I can't explain it, man, but Karma's changed. She's a good girl, Colby."

I could see there was no getting through to Nick, so my instinct told me to just leave him alone. As long as Karma had found someone else to direct her attention to, I had no real reason to worry.

"A'ight, man. I can see this is why you wanted us all to have lunch, huh?"

"Yep. She finally realized you're happy with Audrie and decided she wanted to be happy with me. The best part about that news is she won't be bothering you, right?"

"Right. I'll let it go. You're a grown man, and I can imagine you know how to handle yourself."

He slapped me on the back. "Man, do I? You should see the tricks this girl got. I'm telling you, deep throating is a trade—"

"Um . . . that's a little too much information for me," I said, cutting him off.

I don't know what came over me, but once we got back to the table, I noticed Nick and Karma with what seem like sincere happiness on their faces, causing me to reek with jealousy. I tried to finish my meal, but I couldn't. Audrie noticed.

"What's wrong, Cole? Aren't you gonna finish eating?"

I shook my head. "I can't," I said, wiping my mouth with the napkin. "Let me take care of our tab then we can get out of here."

"Heading back to the office so soon?" Karma questioned.

"Um, no," I said, beckoning the waitress. "Can I get the check for me and my lady here?" I told the waitress as I put my arm around Audrie.

"Yes, sir. I'll be right back," the tanned blonde responded.

When I looked across the table, Nick and Karma were seemingly awaiting me to finish my statement. "Oh, well, I just kinda want to spend some time with Audrie before we head back to the office. We'll probably go by the bookstore for a bit."

Karma nodded while Nick responded. "Sounds cool. We'll catch the two of you later then."

Audrie and I had barely pulled off the parking lot when she began attacking me. "What's wrong with you?"

I glanced over at her then kept driving. "Nothing."

"Colby Patterson, don't you tell that lie."

"Lie? What makes me out to be a liar? And please call me Cole. Glenda use to call my whole name when she was mad, too."

"Sorry, Cole, but it's your face. It has liar written all over it. Ever since Karma and Nick sat down at the table you've been acting funny."

"Did you really expect that to be comfortable for me? I could tell you weren't at ease either. You hardly said anything until the Princess conversation."

"But why so much awkwardness, Cole? You even had to get up to have a private conversation with Nick after finding out he and Karma are a couple."

I sucked my teeth. "Nick's my boy. I had to make sure he had his head on straight. That girl is dangerous, but for some reason he can't seem to see that."

Audrie began to sulk, reminding me very much of Glenda. I shook my head then turned up the radio, hoping to be distracted from the aura she gave. I knew Audrie could see through my jealousy, but despite what she said, I had no plans of confessing the truth. Once I got close to the bookstore, I turned the radio down a bit to speak to her.

"Are you gonna go in the store with me?" I asked.

"For what?" Her head snapped around so fast, she scared me.

"Well, never mind. I'll just head back to work."

I drove past the bookstore then started toward the office. Audrie turned the radio all the way down and angled her body toward me. I glanced over at her then quickly put my eyes back on the road. She wasn't going to let me ignore her.

"I've been sitting here thinking." She paused.

"Mm-hmm. I'm listening."

"Something happened between you and Karma during our brief separation, didn't it?"

Aw, shit. Get your lie together, Colby. "Huh? That's what you've been sitting here thinking about?"

"Admit it. You slept with her while you were in Costa Rica, didn't you?"

Audrie began to sound more and more like my beloved Glenda on the day she died. I couldn't answer right away because I was torn, and I was shaken. I pulled into the company parking lot, tuning out a ranting and raving Audrie. I parked then got out of the car.

"Why don't you just answer me, damnit!" Audrie got out of the car then darted in my face.

I had to get myself together, but I didn't know how. I stood staring at her. Just before she got ready to walk off, I grabbed her arm. "Please," I managed to say.

"Please what?" she snapped.

"Please don't walk away, Audrie."

"Give me one reason to stay."

"I love you. Is that not enough?"

Audrie stepped in my face close enough for me to smell a hint of strawberry in her lip gloss. "Answer my first question, Cole."

I dropped my head and squeezed her hands. "Audrie, I didn't sleep with Karma in Costa Rica."

She jerked from me. "You're a liar," she yelled. "If you love me, you'll tell me the truth." She began to walk away.

"You wanted me to answer your question, and I did. It's the truth, Audrie."

She started back toward me. "Look me in the eye and tell me you didn't sleep with Karma."

I dropped my head. "I didn't sleep—"

"Un-un . . . look me in the eyes, Cole," she said, lifting my chin.

I began to yell out of frustration. "I'm trying to tell you I didn't sleep with Karma in Costa Rica." Tears welled in Audrie's eyes. I could see she'd gotten my hint, so I continued. "It happened the weekend we came back from Costa Rica."

Audrie's knees seemed to buckle. I reached to catch her. "Why? Why, Cole?" Her tears began to fall.

"I . . . I . . . Audrie, I was still pissed at you over what I thought you had done to me . . . and . . . and . . . well, Karma, she was convenient . . . there for me at the time. I'm sorry, babe."

I found it very difficult to look into Audrie's eyes. I pulled her into my chest and caressed her back while she wept. I didn't know what to say to her. I imagined her pain to be ten times worst than what I felt when I saw her at the table with Rodney. Several minutes went by before Audrie pried herself from me.

"Do you love her?" she asked.

I huffed. "C'mon now—"

Audrie stomped her foot and yelled at the same time. "It's a simple yes-or-no question, Cole."

"No! Hell no," I screamed. We both stood quietly for a few seconds. "There . . . happy now? I don't love the girl. I never did."

"You have no idea how much pain I'm in right now—"

"Why did you insist on me answering a question you didn't want the answer to?" My arms began flying loosely with my frustration. "I didn't want you to know, Audrie. She got me in bed with her because she's conniving. No . . . I don't love her." I pulled Audrie to me and squeezed her hands. "I love you, and I want you to forgive me." Audrie stood crying. "Please, baby. I can't lose you, too. Just when I didn't think I could love another woman as hard as I loved my wife, you came along and proved me wrong. I can't lose you. I can't lo—"

She buried her head into my chest and cried some more. "A'ight," she mumbled. "Okay. I'm not going anywhere."

I held her tight, hoping she understood my love would be forever. I looked up into the sky then sighed. *If that Karma ever comes close to me again, I'll spit in her face. I can't lose my woman.*

*M*y plan worked. I knew Cole wanted me. Jealousy was written all over his face when he found out about me and Nick, or whatever perception I had created about us. Only six days after that lunch outing, I had Cole right where I wanted him—with his face between my legs.

"Oh, daddy, I love it when you do it like that," I said, grinding into Cole's face as he sopped my juices.

"Do you? You like that?" he said, licking and teasing me.

I spread my legs even wider. "C'mon, now. Don't stop. I'm almost there."

"Get it, baby," Cole said just before diving nose first back between my legs.

Then it came—the orgasm of the year—and I held Cole's face right there. "Yeeeeessss . . . oh yeeeessss," I screamed as I trembled and climbed to the head of the bed.

"Where're you going? Huh? You wanted this. Where're you going?"

"Cole, stop. I can't take—"

"What did you say?"

Oops. "Huh?" I said, panting.

"What did you just say?" Nick asked.

"I said stop."

"No, what did you just call me?"

"I didn't call you anything. I just said stop."

"I could've sworn you just called me—"

"Turn over," I interrupted. "It's my turn."

Nick still looked a little perplexed, but I made him forget all about what I had possibly said when I took all of him into my mouth. He moaned, hissed, panted, and even inched about the bed before leaking like a running faucet onto my sheets. *This nigga pisses me off when he does that.*

I got up to change the sheets. Nick questioned me because he was spent. "What're you doing? It's Saturday. We don't have to go to work."

"I know. Now get up."

"Why are you making me get up?"

"Because I've got things to do. Now move so I can change the sheets." Nick sluggishly got up then headed for the shower. "And don't be in there too long, wasting up all the hot water. I've got to shower, too."

I huffed and shook my head. *I'm never nice to him. Why does he believe I even like him? I'll give any sugar daddy some ass. He's just plain dumb.* I continued to make up the bed then pulled out an outfit for the day. I was on a mission, and Nick couldn't be with me to see what I was up to.

As soon as he finished in the bathroom, I headed to the shower. "You know how to let yourself out, right?"

"You don't want me to wait for you?" he asked, buttoning his shirt.

Hell naw, you six-foot-four Slim Jim. "No, I'm good. I'll catch up with you later," I said, smiling.

I rounded the corner into the bathroom. After starting the water, I jumped in and began masturbating, thinking of Cole again. I missed him so much. Me getting kicked out of his life just seemed to have happened so fast. I hated fooling around with Nick just to try to get Cole's attention. I thought it would make Cole run back to me. It worked with my stepfather, Melvin, when I began dating a boy at school—well, at least it worked temporarily.

Cole meant everything to me. Until I could get him back, I had to make do with Nick. At least I could fantasize and pretend he was Cole. Plus, Nick would tell me everything I wanted to know about Cole and what he was up to each day. Poor thing never caught on that my line of questioning was because I loved Cole and wanted to be with him.

After reaching another climax, I washed off and jumped out of the shower. When I stepped into the bedroom, Nick nearly scared the living daylights out of me. I screamed.

"Sorry . . . didn't mean to startle you," he said, holding one of my newspaper keepsakes in his hands.

"I thought you were leaving," I fussed.

"I was, but then I realized you'd probably rather I'd wait so we could leave at the same time." *Yeah, what the fuck ever,* I thought as I opened my panty drawer. "Baby, did you know Colby's wife, Glenda?" Nick asked, looking at the newspaper.

I couldn't move. I stood hovering over my drawer unable to say anything. When he looked up at me, I just shook my head. He buried his head back into the article. I closed the drawer then snatched the newspaper from him.

"Why are you snooping in my things?" I fussed.

"I wasn't snooping. I was looking for something to occupy my time until you got out of the shower, and that's when I noticed a stack of old newspapers in your closet."

I had glanced at the newspapers the day before. I could've kicked myself at that moment for having forgotten to place them back into their original hiding space in the closet. I huffed and stomped my foot before responding to Nick.

"You said the key word—closet. You don't have any belongings in my closet, so you shouldn't have been in there."

"The door was open. Sorry. I didn't know it would be a problem."

I had to hurry and get dressed so he could get his ass out of my place. Judging by how calm and collected he was, he didn't see that most of the papers on the floor all had some type of article dealing with Glenda's death. They were all part of my keepsake articles just as the ones I'd kept on my parents' death. I dressed in such a hurry, I didn't bother to put on eyeliner and lip gloss. I still looked cute though. Nick walked me to my car, begging to hang out with me during my chores. As bad as I didn't want to, I kissed him and convinced him to just come back over later in the evening. He was cool with that idea.

I hopped in my car then circled the block a few times to be sure Nick wasn't following me. Once I was certain he was gone, I headed toward the Dixie Homes housing projects for some assistance. When I got there, Hercules and Boo-bay were standing against the same building I'd met them at just before Glenda's murder. They looked at each other when they saw my car then smiled. I beckoned them over.

"What's up?" Hercules asked me as he approached my car. His pants hung so low, I kept thinking they'd fall to his knees before he could reach me.

I leaned out the window. "I see y'all ain't got shit better to do than to stand around holding up the brick wall, huh?"

"Naw. Not unless you got somebody else you want us to knock off," Boo-bay said.

"No. I think I can handle the next one myself," I replied.

"Why?" Hercules questioned. "We did exactly what you said. We left the kids and the man without a scratch on 'em."

Boo-bay added, "Yeah. You can thank me for that. They don't call me sharp-shooter for nothing," he said, brushing off his shoulder.

"Well, I gave y'all the last of everything I had, so the favor I'm asking today is a small one."

"You did hook us up," Boo-bay said. "You stepped into a nigga's life right on time last year, just when I was strapped for cash. Tell me what you need. I gotchu."

"I'm looking for a pregnant woman," I said.

"You looking for one in particular," Hercules asked.

"No. I'm just looking for a pregnant woman who would be willing to give me some of her urine."

"Oh . . . I get it. You tryna fool ol' dude into thinking you pregnant, right?" Hercules asked, showing both top and bottom rows of grills. I nodded. "Yo, that's some fucked-up shit you women be pulling on us, but whatever. It ain't me, so how pregnant you want this lady to be?"

"It doesn't matter as long as her urine can produce what I need."

Boo-bay turned to Hercules. "Ey, man. What about your sister Tameka? Tameka is about five months, right?" Hercules nodded. "I know her piss oughta be good and hot by now." They both laughed.

"A'ight. Pull over there and follow me," Hercules said, pointing toward a Dumpster.

I parked my car then got out to follow the men. They were pretty rough around the edges so I had my hand on my Mace, which was attached to my key chain, just in case. We walked about half a block then went inside an apartment. Surprisingly, the place was neat and well furnished. It was only ten-thirty in the morning, but the stereo was blaring as if it was well into the afternoon.

Hercules asked me to wait in the living room while he went to get his sister. He began yelling her name. "Ey, yo, Tameka . . . Tameka. C'mere a minute," he called, heading toward the back of the apartment.

I figured Boo-bay either lived there or was treated like family because he walked straight to the kitchen and helped himself to what he wanted in the refrigerator. He stepped back into the living room, smacking on crackers and holding a half-empty jug of milk. He swallowed the contents in his mouth then turned the jug up, gulping nonstop.

"Hey, muthafucker, that's my milk you're drinking," a petite, dark-skinned woman yelled. Her belly sat high and round. She hit Boo-bay on the back of the head, causing him to spit on the floor.

"Look what you made me do, black-ass girl," Boo-bay said.

"So! That's my gotdamn milk I went and stood in the WIC line for. You ain't bought shit up in here," she said.

"Eeeyyy," Hercules yelled, shushing them. "Where's y'all muthafuckin' manners? We got company?" He turned his attention to me. "Sorry about that, um . . . um," he said, snapping his fingers. "Damn, I done forgot cho name."

"Kelly," I lied.

"Yeah. Kelly. Give Kelly some respect." Hercules looked at Tameka. "Kelly got a proposition for you."

Tameka gave me a long, hard look then turned up her lip, awaiting my response. I broke it down to her that I wanted to pay her for some of her urine. By the time I left there, I was minus fifty dollars, but two medicine bottles of pregnant piss richer. It was time to attempt turning my fifty-dollar investment into a lifetime of happiness.

I stopped by Walgreens and purchased a home pregnancy test. I was so excited, I cracked open the box once I got back into the car. After opening one of the medicine bottles, I held the test out the window then poured the contents on stick. The instructions said the test would take about three minutes to turn colors, but by the time I pulled it into the car, it had already changed. *Well, that ain't no whole cantaloupe Tameka swallowed. That there is a baby,* I thought then laughed out loud. *Time to go find my man.*

I drove around the back of the pharmacy, threw out the empty medicine container then headed to Cole's house. Just as I was pulling down his street, I saw his car leaving the driveway, heading in the opposite direction. I slowed a bit then cautiously followed him. I could see Audrie sitting on the passenger side of the car.

We only drove about five minutes before pulling into the lot of a different Walgreens than the one I'd been in earlier. I started to stay in the car and wait for them to come out, but something told me to go inside. Once they were in the store, I got out and walked in. It didn't take me long to find them on the hair product aisle.

"Baby, you only have one little gray hair on your right side. I say cut it out rather than color your whole head," Audrie said, not noticing me approaching.

"Are you sure?" Cole asked.

"Gray hair is sexy on a man," I intervened. They both turned around, surprised by my presence. Since neither of them could seem to talk, I spoke again. "Where're my babies, Cole?"

He frowned then took a deep breath. "Look, don't refer to my children as your babies . . . and thanks to you, I have to share them on the weekends with the Carters."

"Well, it's the right thing to do, don't you think?"

"What do you want, Karma? I'm sure you followed us here for a reason," Cole said.

"Followed you?" I let out a tsk. "Puhleeze. I just left Olive Garden down the street. I was having a bite to eat with some friends when I became nauseated. I figured I better ask the pharmacist a few questions before taking any medication, considering the fact I'm pregnant." It rolled off my tongue cool, calm, and collected.

They both were quiet. Audrie looked as if she was going to faint. Her face went white. She set the box of hair dye back on the shelf then started to walk away. Cole pulled her back.

"Hold on, baby," he said, pulling her into his arms. "Can't you see this is another one of her many ploys to break us up?"

I didn't respond to his comment because I had the proof that was going to not only break them up, but it would also break their faces. Audrie seemed speechless. She just laid her head on Cole's shoulder and blew out deep breaths.

"Even if you are, how would I know it's mine?" Cole asked. "We practiced safe sex. I would've known if any one of those condoms had broken."

"You would know it's yours because I'm about seven weeks pregnant. I didn't start sleeping with Nick until a week ago. Besides, condoms are only about fifty percent effective, Cole," I said, placing my hand on my hip. "Lord knows we screwed enough times for you to rough ride a hole into one of them."

Audrie took a step back from Cole. "You slept with her more than once?"

"Off and on for an entire weekend, honey," I answered for him. "Didn't he tell you? Shoot, the man can put it down, girl. Oh, but I'm sure I don't have to tell you that, right?"

Audrie seemed to be having trouble breathing. Cole tried to pet her up. "Baby . . . baby . . . don't let her get to you, baby." He redirected his attention to me. "I want some proof, Karma."

"Hmph. I thought you'd never ask," I said, reaching into my purse. I handed him the positive test.

"This doesn't prove shit. For all I know you got this off another pregnant woman," Cole replied.

I became very dramatic, flailing my arms about. "Well, what do you know . . . we're right inside a pharmacy . . . hmm . . . think maybe perhaps if he buys his own test he'll believe me," I said, speaking wildly into the air. I rested both hands on my hips then stared Cole down.

He frowned even more. "Damn good idea," he said, walking away, holding Audrie's hand. I followed them. We ended up on the aisle with all the pregnancy tests. "Which one, Audrie?" Cole asked.

I stood laughing while Audrie scanned over a few boxes then picked out one. "This one, Cole," she said. "It's more accurate, and early morning pee isn't necessary for it to work. It can be used any time of the day."

Without a word, Cole led us to the cash register where he paid for the product. The cashier started to bag the item, but Cole stopped her.

"That's okay, ma'am. We won't need a bag," he said. She nodded. "Do you have a restroom she can use?" Cole asked, pointing at me.

The cashier told us where to find the restroom. Audrie took the test from Cole then opened the package in front of me. She handed it to me before I entered the restroom. She and Cole stood outside the door. Thank goodness I thought to pay Tameka for two samples of urine.

This time I only poured half the contents onto the stick. I didn't know if I'd need more urine or not, but I figured I'd rather play it safe than to be sorry. When I exited the restroom with the stick, having fully changed into the positive shade of pink, Audrie broke down and cried. Cole slapped the stick out of my hand then pulled Audrie to him and hugged her.

I was pissed. "Muthafucka, you're the one who wanted me to take another test. Don't be slapping it out of my hand now."

"Get out of my face, Karma," Cole yelled.

A small crowd began to stir. I turned around and noticed the cashier who had directed us to the restroom staring at us. From behind her came the manager and a so-called security guard.

"Is there a problem, folks?" the manager asked.

I looked at Cole as he consoled Audrie. "No, sir. No problem here," I said, walking away. I headed out the door.

If this nigga chooses Audrie over me like Melvin did my mom, I swear he's gonna pay.

I dreaded going in to work on Monday morning. I knew I'd have to face Karma at some point during the day, and that was a task I just wasn't looking forward to. I kept waking up in the middle of the night from dreams of Karma chasing me. For most of the dream, she was herself, but during parts of it, her body was shaped like a serpent. The more I ran, the closer to me she got. Each time I'd awaken then go back to sleep, the dream would pick up where it left off. My nerves were on edge by morning. I couldn't get Audrie's tears out of my head.

I had spent about ten minutes in that store after Karma left, trying to calm Audrie down and convince her the weekend I'd slept with Karma meant nothing. She said she believed me, but her tears kept flowing. Hearing Karma could possibly be pregnant with my kid was a bitter pill for me to swallow. I could only imagine how Audrie must've felt.

I managed to drag myself in to work despite my throbbing head. Once I got comfortable in my office, I began calling around to other desks, looking for some type of pain killers. I knew I wouldn't be able to last the rest of the day without some headache medicine. After having no luck, I called Audrie's desk again.

"Hey, baby," she answered. "Did you find some medicine?"

"No . . . no. I feel like I'm about to pass out," I responded.

"Well, have you eaten anything?"

"A little. I ate a bagel and some juice this morning, but I know this isn't a hunger headache. I'm stressed out."

"I can imagine, baby. Look, I told you we're going to be fine. Shit happens. The bitch had you, but she won't be getting you again. We're on to her, so she can go piss on somebody else's lawn. Our grass is green, and it's going to stay that way."

"Glad to hear you say that, sweetie. Listen, I need a favor."

"Anything for you, baby."

"Will you drive over to the Exxon across the street for some Aleve?" I asked.

"Say no more. I'm on my way out, and I'll be back shortly."

"Thank you, sweetie."

After hanging up with Audrie, I began to massage my temples, but it wasn't helping. A knock at the door startled me just as I was about to rest my head on the desk. I sighed then answered, "Come in."

My worst nightmare walked in. "I hear you're looking for some aspirin," Karma said, holding out an opened palm with two pills on it.

"No thank you," I answered dryly.

She put her hand on her hip. "You'd rather suffer than take help from me?"

I dropped my head back on my desk. "Karma, please leave my office."

I heard her footsteps coming closer, and then I could feel her presence next to me. "I just want to give my love to you, Cole, and have you love me back. What's wrong with that?"

"Please leave, Karma."

I heard her blow out a long sigh. "Not until we discuss what we're going to do about our baby. I think we should be a family.

Shawna and Gavin are already use to me, and I'm sure they'll welcome our new addition to the family. You wanna touch my stomach?"

"No. I want you to leave," I said, slowly lifting my head. Karma's gaze was creepy. She looked as if she was trying to stab me with her eyes. It was hard to keep looking at her. "So what am I supposed to do? I'm carrying your child."

"Abort it," I said calmly then placed my head back on my desk. There was a long, eerie silence in the room before Karma finally said something. "A'ight. I need fifteen hundred dollars—five hundred for the abortion and another thousand for my pain and suffering."

I didn't hesitate going into my briefcase for my checkbook. "Who do you want this made out to?" I asked, filling out the check.

She waited a few seconds then snapped at me. "To Karma Jolley, you sorry muthafucka."

I didn't look up until I had completed the check. She snatched it from me then stared me down before stomping toward the door. She met Audrie on her way out. Karma brushed past Audrie so hard, she nearly knocked her off balance.

Audrie set a packet of two Aleve on my desk. "What the hell is wrong with her now?" she asked, rubbing her shoulder.

I grabbed the packet, opened it then threw the pills to the back of my throat and swallowed. I opened the bottle of water that was sitting on my desk and took a sip before responding to Audrie. "Why are you looking at me like that?" I set the bottle down.

"What happened now? That heifer almost tore off my arm when she was leaving out of here."

"She asked me what I thought she ought to do with the baby. I told her to abort it."

"Cole," Audrie screamed. She seemed surprised by my response.

"What?"

"Well . . . well, first of all . . . do we even know it's your baby? You could've just told her to kill someone else's child."

"Whoever the brotha is, I'm sure he thanks me."

"Cole," she screamed again.

"What, Audrie? Do you not agree that girl doesn't need to be anybody's momma?" Audrie looked like she was at a loss for words. "God forgive me, but I gave her the money to do what she needs to do."

Audrie shook her head. "I don't know what to say. But, I do know I wouldn't have told you to tell her to kill the baby."

"Audrie, for all we know she isn't even pregnant. I don't know how she made that second test show positive, but either way, pregnant or not, she just got paid to leave me the hell alone."

I put my head down on the desk. "Are you gonna be okay?" Audrie began rubbing the back of my neck.

"Yeah. Hopefully it won't take long for this medicine to kick in. Give me about half an hour then come back. I could use your help on the project I'm working on. It's finally almost done, but I'd like to know your opinion."

"Sure. I'll come back, baby. In the meantime, try not to stress, okay?"

Audrie left, then it took me exactly half an hour to feel better. Several thoughts ran through my mind while I tried to collect myself. One of them being how glad I was Karma wasn't going to be having a child by me. Another thought was of how close it was to the anniversary of Glenda's murder. I didn't know if I wanted to be in town to remember that I wouldn't be celebrating an anniversary with my wife because some idiots had snatched her life away.

I shook off my trance then went back to work. Audrie returned to assist me with the biggest account of my career. It had been a while since I first began working with Best Tronics, and I was too happy to be nearly done with the largest account in Essential Software Development history. Luther and the other teams would definitely deem me the man after the completion of this project.

Audrie and I decided to leave early for lunch and cut our break a half hour early as well because we wanted to get back to the project so we could finish without having to stay over. When we returned from lunch, everyone was on their break. The office was totally quiet.

"I bet we can get something done without interruptions now," Audrie stated.

"Yeah. I bet," I said, opening my door, which was partially cracked.

"You didn't lock your office before we left?"

I went into deep thought. "I don't remember. I thought I did, but on occasion, I've left it unlocked before."

We entered the office and turned on the lights. "I guess neither of us thought about it since we were in a hurry, and nothing really is in here."

I got comfortable in my chair. "You got that right. I don't leave money or anything like that in here anyway."

"Why is the monitor off?" Audrie asked, taking a seat next to me.

"What are you talking about?" I moved the mouse, but there was no response on the screen.

We both looked down at the power button and saw that the computer was off. "We left this thing on before leaving, right?" Audrie asked.

"Yeah." I began to panic. "Let me calm down. I saved everything to disc before leaving."

I rebooted the computer, but the monitor was still blank. After noticing the power light on, I called for the company's technician to check things out. In the meantime, Audrie and I took my disc and relocated to her desk.

"I tell you . . . it's always something, huh?" Audrie stated.

"You can say that again." I sighed then sat down in front of her computer and loaded the CD.

"I'm just glad you got that disc."

"Me, too, but I can still feel another headache coming on."

After loading the CD, I couldn't get it to pull up anything. I ejected it then inserted it again—nothing. I could see Audrie beginning to panic.

"What's going on, Cole?"

"I don't know. It should be opening up by now. It's not doing anything."

Audrie reached across her desk for another disc. "Here . . . try this one. Let's see if your CD is the problem."

As soon as Audrie put in her disc, its content began to open up. Audrie and I looked at each other. My stomach dropped hard, and I had a lump in my throat.

"Audrie, please tell me this is not happening."

"This is not happening, Cole. That disc is not defective."

I glanced at the backside of the CD. "Yes, it is, Audrie. Somebody has put deep scratches on it. Look," I said, breathing harder.

Audrie's jaw dropped. "Oh no, Cole. Let's check with the tech. He might've gotten your hard drive out."

Audrie and I practically ran back to my office. The tech was on his way out with parts in his hand. "What is all that?"

"I'm going to see if I can retrieve all your files on disc for you," the young man said.

"So you think it's likely I'll get my information?" I asked him.

"Yeah, it's very likely. Give me a few hours though."

I began to pace. "Okay . . . okay . . . I really don't have a choice. I'll be in my office when you're done."

Audrie went inside my office with me. I sat down at my desk to lay down my head. Audrie began massaging my shoulders. I just wanted some peace and quiet. I could feel myself losing control as the notions came that Karma was guilty of sabotaging me.

"You thinking what I'm thinking?" Audrie asked.

"Mm-hmm."

"She won't quit, Cole. She just won't quit."

"Audrie, please. Let's not talk about it. My head is starting to hurt again. This time I fear bursting a vessel or something."

She kept massaging me. "Okay, Cole, but just let me ask one more question: Did you save any of your work on a jump drive? You know one of those little external gigs?" I kept silent. "I take it you didn't." Still, I said nothing. "Cole, do you know what year it is? Why don't you have a jump drive? It doesn't take much to conceal and take that thing with you everywhere you go."

I sat up. "Audrie! Please . . . I think I'm doing a good enough job of beating myself up without your help."

"I'm sorry, baby."

"Yeah. Me, too. Do me a favor. I need some privacy right now. I just want to sit here alone for a while."

I could see the hurt in her eyes, but I couldn't change the way I felt. "Okay. Just let me know as soon as you find out something."

I waved at her then placed my head back down on the desk. An hour went by, and I'd had all I could stand of sitting still. I went into the technician's office to see if he had news for me. He looked up as soon as I entered.

"Mr. Patterson, I have a couple of discs for you. I'm not sure what's on them, but I'm still retrieving other files now," he said.

A sense of relief came over me. I looked at the vacant computer on the other desk in his office. "Do you mind if I sit there to see what's on this one?" I said, pointing.

"No. Go right ahead."

I couldn't wait to open the first CD. "C'mon . . . c'mon," I said, talking to the computer. "Oh hell yeah! Here's the folder I'm looking for." The tech glanced over at me then went back to doing what he was doing. "Wait. Where's the project?"

"What project?" he asked.

"Best Tronics . . . the one I'm looking for."

223

"I don't know, Mr. Patterson. You must not have saved it. I grabbed all the files I saw."

"No . . . no . . . no . . . I saved it. I saved it." My voice had elevated a bit.

"Well, don't holler at me. If that's the folder you saved it in, it should be there."

I went into a daze. *That bitch deleted it,* I thought. "I'm sorry, man. Thanks for your help." I darted out the door, very much in a hurry.

I went into Nick's office and found Karma sitting next to him. *Stay calm, Cole.* Karma had a sinister expression, but Nick seemed puzzled by my silence.

"Something wrong, Colby?" he asked.

I looked at Karma. "Um, no. Um . . . I need to speak to Karma for a moment, if you don't mind," I stated.

Nick looked at Karma then she glanced back at him before responding. "You can talk to me in front of my boo. What's up?"

I took a deep breath to keep from clicking. "Well, I'd really rather speak to you in private," I said as sweetly as I could. "I promise not to take up too much of your time."

She kissed Nick on the lips. "I'll be right back, baby. Don't start the project without me."

"No problem. I'll wait for you," he said.

"Nick, I promise this won't take long," I assured him.

Karma stepped outside the office then closed the door behind her. "Is everything okay, Colby?" she asked with an innocent tone.

"No. Let's take a walk outside for a second." Karma hesitated. "What's wrong?" I asked. "I just want to clear the air between us."

Audrie came walking down the hall. She slowed down, looking upside Karma's head as she approached us. "Is everything okay, baby?" Audrie asked.

224

"I'm fine, sweetie. Karma and I were just about to go for a walk, but we're good though. I'll come see you when we get back."

Audrie looked confused, but she went ahead and walked away. I reached for Karma's hand. She still seemed reluctant, but took my hand anyway. We headed outside near the smokers area. There was no one out there, so privacy wasn't an issue.

"Would you like to have a seat?" I asked, pointing toward the benches.

"No. Why're you being so nice, Colby?"

"You can call me Cole. That's what you've been calling me. . . no need in changing."

"Yes, there is. I have a man now, remember?"

"Cut the bullshit. You're only with him because you think it'll make me jealous. Well, I'm not, so you're only fooling Nick. Besides, you were just in my office earlier professing your love for me."

"That was before you told me to kill our baby."

I was stomped for words for a minute. Nothing had changed about the way I felt, I only wanted to trick her into giving me back my file. She turned to walk away.

"Karma," I called, "what do I need to do?"

"Excuse me? I'm not quite following you." I could detect a grin in her voice. She knew she had me where she wanted me—eating out of the palm of her hand.

"I'm not going to tell you I want you to have the baby, but the final say is yours. That project is important to me," I said, softly gripping her hands. "I'd love to have it back. You wanna keep that baby, I'll take back the check. Just tell me what I need to do to get my project back."

She smiled and squeezed my hands. "I love you, Colby Pat—" she cut herself off. "Cole, I love you."

I nodded. "I know. Karma, I know." I spoke in a ginger tone, hoping she'd soften.

She seemed to be melting. "Will you let me come over and spend time with you tonight?"

I sighed then shook my head. "I'll come to your place. That'll be the safest way to keep Audrie from blowing up our spot. Are you afraid of Nick showing up at your place?"

"No. Nick will do anything I tell him. I'm sure you know he's a sucker."

I let out a fake laugh. "I wouldn't know anything about that. I've never dated him." Karma laughed, too. "Well, let me get back inside before Audrie comes out here. I'll see you tonight around nine, after I put the kids to bed."

"Oh? Who's going to watch them?"

"Don't worry about all that. I'll be over to see you, okay?"

She smiled. "Okay."

We didn't let each other's hands go until we got inside. Audrie was standing near the break room, apparently waiting for me. She clearly looked disturbed. I took her hand and led her into my office.

"Baby, I'm going to ask for your trust and understanding on something," I whispered just after closing the door. She didn't say anything. "I'm going over to Karma's tonight—" Audrie gasped, interrupting me. "Let me finish. I have a plan to get my project back. Just trust me on this one, okay?"

I continued to fill Audrie in on my plans and asked her to watch the children. She reluctantly agreed to my scheme then hugged me. I held her tight thinking, *Karma Jolley has met her match. I can be sneaky, too. It's on tonight!*

Karma 28

I straightened up my place, lit some jasmine incense then dimmed the lights as I waited for Cole. Although I didn't have his new cell number, I knew he'd show because I had something that was very important to him. In truth, that was the only reason he was coming to my place, but I'd take him however I could have him. He could be drunk, blind, cripple, or crazy—it didn't matter. I just wanted him.

Whew, that Nick was so dumb. He didn't know when to stop talking. He told me what he and Cole would do to back up their files in case of an emergency, so I took invaluable notes as he rambled each day. I knew the information would come in handy at the right time.

All Nick could talk about was how much money and recognition Cole would get for completing the Best Tronics project, and what it meant to Cole, considering he'd never been acknowledged with the company before. I had been waiting on the perfect day to snatch all he'd done from under him, and it came soon enough.

Once I held the only key to him getting his work back, I knew he was mine. His work was secured on a jump drive. I planned to give it back, but only after he gave me what he thought I already had—his seed in my womb. My plan was to get him drunk, and then seduce him. I wanted to have Cole's child so we could be bonded forever.

I put the satin sheets on my bed, and then sprinkled a hint of baby powder on them. I had it all figured out how to get him into bed this once, but whether I'd get pregnant was the question. After carefully thinking about it, I knew I'd have to screw him then send him on his way without the jump drive so he'd have a reason to come back.

I decided to take a hot bubble bath so my skin would have a soft, irresistible touch. When I got out, I soothed my pores with the sensual scent of my Victoria's Secret Pear Glacé lotion. It was about to be on.

I put on a black-and-white, lace baby doll teddie that cupped my breasts right nicely, making them sit up and appear a full size larger. Just after adjusting my straps then glossing over my lips once more, the doorbell rang. Princess immediately ran to the door, scratching at it.

I anxiously skipped to the door. "Move, Princess. I know how to answer it," I yelled to her.

When Princess backed away, I looked through the peephole just to make certain it was Cole. It was, so I stepped back and let him in. He closed the door behind him then let his eyes wander all over my body.

"You like?" I asked, posing with my hands on my hips.

He licked his lips and rubbed his hands together. "I had forgotten how fine you are," he said.

He made me blush. I took his hand. "Are you hungry?"

"No. I've eaten already, but thanks for offering." He sniffed. He looked down at Princess. "What's up, girl?" She jumped up and down on his leg. "I miss you, too." He patted her on the head then redirected his attention to me. "Is that jasmine incense I smell?"

"Yep. What you know about that?"

"I think I've been around a lot longer than you have, young lady. Are you sure Nick won't be over tonight?" he asked.

"Positive. I told him I needed some space so I could study. He promised me he wouldn't interrupt me."

"Okay. Cool. So are you gonna offer me a seat?"

I couldn't believe he was actually standing in my living room. I had completely forgotten to offer him a seat. He looked damned good in his jeans and his long-sleeved Sean John T-shirt. I continued to sop him up with my eyes for a minute then I snapped out of my daze.

"Oh . . . I'm sorry. Yes, please have a seat on the couch," I said, motioning toward the sofa. "I can fix us some drinks if you'd like—"

He pulled me to the couch with him, taking my breath away. "I don't need anything to drink, Karma. I just want to spend time with you," he said, pulling me down on his lap.

Cole was definitely running game on me, but his game was tight. I liked how he made me feel, and it didn't matter that his words were fake. What mattered was that he was there with me, holding me, running his hand up and down my thigh. I looked into his eyes thinking he'd blink or look away, but he didn't. Instead, he gazed right back.

"You're so beautiful. Do you know that?" he said, stroking my hair.

"I'd like to think so." I smiled.

"Well, you are, and don't let anyone tell you anything differently. You hear me?"

I nodded. "Yes. I hear you."

He stared into my eyes for a while then attempted to get what he came for. "Have you decided what you're going to do about the baby?" he asked.

The check was already deposited. I stuttered for a second. "I . . . um . . . well, that situation has already been handled?"

He raised his eyebrows. "Really? That was quick."

"Yeah, I got it over with."

"Then we probably shouldn't be fooling around tonight then, huh?"

Again, I stuttered. "Oh . . . um, well . . . see . . . the truth is, I had the abortion the same day I saw you at the drugstore," I lied. "I only came in your office today to taunt you. It worked. I got my money back, and I got you over here."

Surprisingly Cole's expression didn't change. He still looked calm about what he'd just heard. "Okay, Karma, I guess there isn't anything else to discuss in the baby department then." He paused. "Karma, you know that project is important to me, right?"

"I know, Cole. What are you getting at? Can I skip my plan of seduction and just take you straight to my bedroom?"

He chuckled. "I have no objections to sleeping with you. Look at you. You're sexy as hell, and we've already done it, so I know you're the bomb."

"And? I'm listening." I batted my eyes.

"I don't want you to think I'm only here to sleep with you so I'd get my project back. I care for you whether you know it or not."

Cole wasn't a very good liar. I knew because he looked everywhere except in my eyes when he'd lie to me. This was one of those times. I played it cool though.

"Okay, Cole. I believe you."

"But, just for my peace of mind, will you show me the project?"

I rolled my eyes, stood then beckoned him with my finger. He followed me into the extra bedroom where I kept my office. Princess was fast on our heels. Once we entered the room, I instructed Cole to have a seat and boot up the computer while I retrieved his goody. He did as told.

I came back with the jump drive then placed it in the computer. He sat patiently waiting for the contents to open. I watched him nervously glance down at the drive a few times, so I knew I had better stay on guard in case he was thinking of doing something stupid like snatching it.

He saw his project and was quite pleased. "Are you sure you didn't alter it any?"

"I'm positive. The only thing I know how to do is delete it." I smiled.

"Very funny, Karma," he replied calmly.

"I'm not trying to be funny. I'm just telling the truth."

He looked down at the drive again. I knew I needed to do something to distract him, so I sat on his lap. If he had been thinking about grabbing the jump drive, I made his task go from easy to hard. I looped my arms around his neck. He wasn't going anywhere.

Cole planted a soft kiss on my lips then buried his head in my breasts. "Damn, Karma. You smell good. C'mere," he said, pulling my leg around so I'd have to straddle him.

He gripped my ass and kissed my chest. I couldn't feel his hardness through his jeans. I wanted to feel his hardness—bad. I opened my mouth to ask him to get out of his pants, but then there was a knock at the door. I sat up and looked toward the hallway out of reflex. That's when Cole tossed me off his lap then grabbed the jump drive.

I sprang from the floor then attacked him, scratching, kicking, and biting. I sank my teeth into his hand, trying to force him to let go of the drive. We ended up on the floor with him pressing my nose down as hard as he could until I released his hand from the clutch of my teeth, but not without me tasting his blood first.

The scene probably only lasted a minute, but it felt like it went in slow motion. Cole backed away from me. "That's Nick," he said, examining his hand, holding it away from himself to avoid staining his shirt with blood.

"How the fuck do you know?" I said, panting.

The second knock came harder. "I talked to him earlier today and told him you and I had discussed ideas of how to be more spontaneous in your relationship. I encouraged him to copy your key then sneak over tonight."

"You're a damn liar," I yelled. Another knock came.

"Look. You don't have to believe me, but he should be turning the key in just a minute. He doesn't know I'm here. My car isn't outside, but yours is."

I was furious. "I told him I was studying."

"He told me that, but I assured him you'd love to see him tonight, and that if you didn't answer the door by the third knock to just come on in—you'd be waiting for him."

"Why'd you do that? I thought you didn't want people at Essential Company to know your business. You want to be caught here?"

Nick apparently was inside because I could clearly hear him calling my name. "Karma? Baby, are you asleep?"

I bit my bottom lip, giving Cole a look of hatred then turned to meet Nick in the living room. He was heading down the hall as I stepped out the room.

"Nick? What are you doing here, and how did you get into my apartment?"

He smiled, sizing me up. "What've you got on? I like it."

"I asked you a question, Nick."

"Colby called me into his office today and told me about the conversation you and he had outside." Nick grabbed me around the waist. "Baby, I can't tell you enough how happy I was to hear him suggest we do one of your favorite things tonight—role play." I gasped, feeling disgusted. "So, if you don't mind," he said, "let's start over. I was hoping you'd be asleep so I could surprise you. I've got some champagne and everything. How about we play One-Night Stand? What do you think?"

I turned and looked toward my office. "Um . . . well, um—"

Nick looked toward the office door. "What's wrong? Oh, you were studying. Okay. How about you go back in here," he said, leading me into my office, "and sit at the desk. I'll play the horny man who won't leave you alone."

I tried to protest, but Nick had practically dragged me into the room. I saw Princess sniffing under the dust ruffle, apparently looking for Cole. I knew that as much as I didn't want my cover blown with Nick, neither did Cole want him in his business. Cole had worked his plan perfectly of getting Nick to distract me, but I had no clue of how he planned to get out without being noticed. I called Princess over to me then attempted to get Nick out of the room.

"How about we go into the kitchen to open that bottle of champagne first?" I asked.

Nick smiled then nodded. I picked up Princess then took Nick by the hand. Once we were in the kitchen, I took my time getting the glasses out of the cabinet, but Nick popped open the champagne so quickly, he began rushing me to give him the glasses. He filled both of them then proposed a toast.

"To a lovely one-night stand with a lovely woman," he said, raising his glass. We clanked our glasses. Shortly afterwards, we heard the front door shut. "What was that?" Nick asked.

I noticed Princess was no longer in the kitchen with us. "Oh that Princess is something else . . . she's bumping into things again."

"That sounded like the front door," he said, heading toward the living room.

I followed him. He made it to the door faster than I could say anything. He opened it then stepped out onto the front porch. I stood back in a bit of a panic. I didn't feel like explaining why Cole had just left my apartment. Nick came back in after a few seconds.

"The door was unlocked, but I didn't see anyone out there," he said.

"You probably didn't lock the door once you came in. Anyway, I told you it was probably Princess." I sighed.

He stepped over to me then pulled me close. "Sorry, baby. You're right. What do you say we get this show on the road, huh?" He leaned over me and kissed my neck.

I wanted to gag. I looked over at the front door and imagined I could see Cole standing there. *I'll get you for this, Colby Patterson. You can bet your ass on it.*

$\mathcal{M}$y hand was severely bruised and ached so bad I could hardly drive. I decided to make a detour to the emergency room. Audrie began calling my cell shortly after I arrived, but I was asked by security to turn off my phone after only one ring, and the nurse called me to the back shortly afterward. I figured I'd just give Audrie a shout once I left the hospital, but the only problem was I forgot how slow emergency rooms could be.

The nurse escorted me to a room where she examined my hand then had me wait on a doctor for nearly an hour. The doctor was a medium-build white man with exhaustion written all over his face.

"Mr. Patterson," he said, opening the door.

"That's me, sir," I responded.

He stepped inside then closed the door behind him. "Mr. Patterson, I'm Dr. Henry, and I'll be checking you out. I hear you've got quite a nasty wound on your hand," he said, reading my chart.

"Yes, sir. I was attacked by my ex-girlfriend. She bit the crap out of me, trying to keep me from leaving her."

"Oh, no." He frowned. "Have you or are you going to press charges? We can help you do that from here."

"I'm going to press charges, but I'd like to wait and go to the police precinct during the daylight hours."

The doctor shrugged. "Okay. Let's take a look at that hand." I held out my hand. "Wow. That is nasty," he said, examining the puncture. "It's a good thing you came in, you know?"

I shook my head. "Why do you say that?"

"Well, in case you hadn't heard, a human bite is much worse than a dog bite."

I couldn't believe my ears. "Are you serious?"

"Very. I know it sounds odd, but the fact is human oral flora harbors more pathogens than that of animals, and such viruses as HIV and hepatitis can be transmitted just by what this woman has done to your hand here," he said, pointing.

My eyes bucked. "No . . . no . . . please don't say that. I had no clue a dog's mouth could be cleaner than a human's. Now I'm really pissed."

"Well, don't go out and buy a gun, and if you already have one, don't consider using it. No need to panic right now. Let's run some tests and take some preventive measures that will help at the moment. You can get further testing later on."

The doctor accessed the wound for possible infections, treated it with peroxide, and gave me a Tetanus shot to be on the safe side against other growing bacteria. I learned a lot from that emergency room visit. I also wanted to go back over and choke the hell out of Karma for putting me through the pain. She was probably busy with Nick anyway. I had set her up to be occupied long enough so I could get away.

When I got home, it was one o'clock in the morning. I found Audrie covered up and asleep on my couch in the den. I tiptoed into my home office and made a couple of copies of the Best Tronics project then went upstairs to get some rest. I didn't sleep too well, so by four o'clock in the morning, I was back downstairs to wake Audrie. She looked as if she had been tossing and turning, too. Her cover was on the floor, and she had one leg sprawled over on the floor. I shook her to see if she'd respond. Audrie sat straight up and gasped. "What time is it?" She looked around as if she didn't know where she was. "Cole?" she asked, looking at me. "Are you okay? How long have I been asleep?"

"I'm okay, baby," I whispered, rubbing her shoulder.

"Cole, what time is it?"

"It's just after four o'clock, I think."

"Four o'clock? In the morning?"

I nodded. "Come in the kitchen and have some coffee with me. We need to talk."

Audrie followed me and began verbally attacking me soon after entering the kitchen. "You screwed her again, didn't you?"

I had just picked up the coffee pot to get it started, but I set it down and turned to her. "Say what?" I frowned.

"You heard me, Cole. Admit it because I know you did."

"What happened to asking how things went before making accusations?" I shook my head then began filling the coffee pot with water.

"It's four o'clock in the gotdamn morning, and you step up in here like everything is fine. You told me you'd only be a couple of hours max. I'm a grown woman, Cole. You can't play me."

I tried my best to act like I wasn't hearing the words that were coming out of her mouth. I turned off the water in the kitchen sink. "Audrie, I've got the project. It's fine, too. She didn't even touch it."

"Yeah, but how'd you get it?" She crossed her arms over her chest and twisted her lips.

I had a mind to cuss her out for what I believed she was thinking. "I didn't screw her because I know that's how you feel. I could have, but you'd be happy to know that I didn't."

"So how'd you get it?"

I started to walk away. "You know what—"

Audrie grabbed my arm. "Why are you walking away? I just asked a question."

"You're not just asking a question. You're insinuating things. I asked you to trust what I'd do. You said you would. I'm frustrated with you right now, Audrie."

"Cole, it's four o'clock in the morning. I've called and called, but you never bothered to call me back. I just don't see why—"

I held up my hand then unraveled the gauze the doctor had placed on it. "Does this look like I fucked her?" Audrie gasped. I opened my robe to show her the deep scratch on my collarbone. "And you don't get scratches like these from making love. Only a stupid-ass psycho bitch would lash out and do something like this," I stated, still holding my robe open.

Audrie reached out to touch my shoulder, but I jerked away from her. "What happened to you?" she asked.

It took everything in me not to cuss her out because I was angry enough to do it. "Oh, now you wanna ask me what happened?"

"I'm sorry, baby. Please tell me what happened," she said with a milder attitude. She put her arm around my waist and lifted my hand to her eyes.

I took a deep breath then sighed. I pulled away from her and began rewrapping the gauze. "The perfect opportunity came to grab the drive. Karma wasn't having it. We fought like dogs, scrambling about on the floor . . . her on top of me, me on top of her, until she couldn't catch her breath. She let me go, but not by her will."

"So nothing went as planned? Did Nick show up?"

"Everything went on schedule. And for your peace of mind, I only had to give her a peck on the lips. I'm sorry about that, but I feared she was reading me. Nick showed up on cue, just like I thought he would. That's when I made my move."

"So that bitch attacked you?"

"It was a hard struggle, but once Nick was in the apartment, I knew I was gonna get away. I didn't realize he could be so gullible. It's like she's got him whipped or something."

"That's the power of what we women have between our legs, baby. I thought you knew," Audrie said, smiling.

"I know, but still . . . you don't see me running over there to be with her crazy ass, do you?" Audrie stared at me. "So my point is ain't that much power in the universe."

Audrie laughed. "I don't mean to laugh, especially since I'm not totally over the fact that Karma's had my man, but you're just tougher than Nick is, baby. Anyway, I'm extremely grateful for him being naïve when we needed him to be. Judging by your battle wounds, she might've killed you if he hadn't shown up."

I nodded and had to laugh as well. "It's really not funny, but yes. I'd always heard that psychos are strong people. As little as that woman is, she put up a good fight." A flash of our vacation in Costa Rica came to me. "I need to check on that woman," I said, staring off into space.

"Excuse me? Now you want to know how Karma's doing?"

I shook my head. "No . . . no . . . I was just thinking of something."

"What's on your mind?"

"Karma almost killed someone while we were in Costa Rica."

Audrie took a step back. "Are you serious?"

"Yes. In fact, I'm willing to bet the accident was intentional like the woman said. I need to get in touch with her. Now I'm sure Karma tried to kill her, but what I don't know is why."

"You sound as if you have the woman's contact information." Audrie stood with her hand on her hip.

"It's not like that . . . please don't start again. I've got her husband's business card. The police were the ones saying she was accusing Karma of trying to kill her. I never spoke with her after the incident. I need to hear from her what happened because now that I think about it, Karma probably tried to kill Gavin, too."

Audrie gasped. "What? How? When were you gonna fill me in on all of this?"

"It's all just dawning on me. Karma made everything look like an accident."

"Yeah. Just like my fall at the skating rink, remember?"

I leaned against the wall. "Audrie, we really are dealing with a madwoman. There's no telling what else she's done or capable of."

"Did you do a background check on her before hiring her?"

I dropped my head. "I . . . I—"

"That's okay, Cole." I looked up at Audrie. Her eyes said they understood my embarrassment. "You were only doing what you thought was best at the time, and we have to admit, she was there for you and the kids."

"I just feel so foolish. Glenda wouldn't have ever let someone into our home without doing all of the proper research. My son could've been killed, Audrie. I don't think I would've been able to handle that."

Audrie put her arms around my waist. "Let's see if we can get a background check on Karma. If we can prove she has some kind of negative history or a criminal record, I'm sure Luther will relinquish her position at Essential Software."

"Well, let's pray. I'm not going to continue working there with her lurking."

Somebody better do something before I'm forced to kill Karma, and Lord knows I will.

---

*T*hanks to that damn Colby Patterson, I had to spend the night and early morning having sex with Mr. Scrawny Man. He banged his sack of bones into me as if he had it going on. I faked all the moans Nick loved to hear while thinking of all the different ways I could pay back Cole.

Nick had to hit it one more time before getting up. I let him have his way then jumped up to take a shower before him. I was pissed that Cole had gotten his project back. That wasn't supposed to happen. He was supposed to make love to me then plead for the jump drive. What was I thinking? I knew Cole would try something stupid, and I was on guard until Nick popped up.

Since Cole wanted to play hardball, I wasn't backing down. I didn't go through having his wife killed for nothing. Cole was mine, but since he just couldn't seem to grasp that, I was forced to show my bad side. He thought I'd been rude up to the point of him putting me out, but he hadn't seen anything yet. The more I thought about how he schemed against me to get his project back, the angrier I became. *He's got to suffer for not being obedient,* I thought as the water drenched my face. Nick began to pound on the door, breaking my daze.

"Karma," he called. "Karma, hurry up and come out here. I need to talk to you."

Nigga, what the— "A'ight. Hold on."

I hurriedly bathed then got out of the shower. After drying off then slipping on my bathrobe, I opened the door. I was startled as I nearly ran into Nick's chest. I looked up at him like he was crazy.

"Did you do it?" he asked, holding up one of the newspaper clippings of my parents' death.

I pushed him out of my way then turned around to face him. "I told you to stay out of my shit," I yelled. "Why were you in my closet—again?"

"They say the house was drenched with gasoline—"

"Who is they?" I snapped.

"The police . . . according to this article . . . and it says you were sentenced to serve time in a psychiatric ward—"

I walked away. "Shut up," I screamed as I headed for my panty drawer.

"Tell me. Did you do it?"

I didn't answer him at first. I put on my panties then my bra before sliding into a pair of jeans. I looked up to notice him standing naked with his third leg dangling as he appeared dazed. The sight of him made me sick.

"What if I did do it?" I walked around him then went into my closet for a blouse. "I've served all the time I could've done for the crime. Ain't shit else anyone can do to me."

"If you did it then I have only one other question."

"What's that?" I asked, snapping my head around toward him.

"How long had you stalked Colby before you approached him for work?"

We stood staring at each other for what seemed like several minutes, but it could've possibly only been seconds. I smirked then turned around to pick up my stiletto boots. Apparently Nick felt like jumping bad, so he grabbed my arm. That's when his eye met the pointed heel of my boot. He fell backward on the bed, screaming in pain. I jumped onto the bed, removed the boot from his eye, and then clocked him several times in the head with it. He finally stopped screaming and breathing all together.

When I climbed down off the bed, I noticed Princess trembling at my feet. I reached to pick her up, but noticed my hands were a bloody mess. "Hold on, girl. Mama can't pick you up like this," I said to her. I went into the bathroom to wash my hands. When I returned, I reached for Princess, but she backed away. "What's d'matter?" I asked her. She turned then ran out of the room.

"Fine," I yelled to her. "See if I care."

I looked over at the human beanpole lying on my bed then wondered how I was going to get rid of him. "Damn. Look what you made me do," I said out loud. "Now how am I gonna get rid of your ass without getting caught?"

I began to pace the floor, hoping to come up with a solution. I even stopped here and there to fuss at Nick's corpse some more. "Damn, damn, damn you. And I liked Memphis, too, but I don't think I'm going to be able to stay here now that you've made me kill you in my apartment. Everyone's gonna know I did it."

I paused and stopped walking. "I know . . . I could say it was self-defense." I began to pace again. "No . . . no . . . that won't work. They'll still jail me first, and it'll take a long time to prove my innocence. Not to mention people seem to think I have some type of mental problem."

I damn near burned a hole in the carpet before coming to the conclusion there was no way to cover up Nick's death. "Fuck it. I'm bailing out. I won't let the authorities find me. I'll stay hidden for a while, or at least until Colby comes to his senses . . . then we'll leave town together. We'll be one big happy family." I stared at Nick for a moment. "Thanks for listening. Oh . . . and sorry about the eye thing. I didn't mean for it to go in your eye, but you understand shit happens, right?" I shrugged then got out of my bloody jeans.

Once I had my clothes on and had finished packing, I realized it was after ten o'clock in the morning. I knew Colby and others would begin to miss Nick and me at work, especially since we were a no-call no-show, so I wanted to be out of my place before anyone came looking for us. Princess gave me somewhat of a chase before I caught her and carried her out the door with me.

I drove over to Cole's house to see if I could collect my remaining things and any pictures he might've had of me. Just as I had suspected, he had gone through with his threat of changing the locks. I was forced to call a locksmith so I could get in. I went back to my car to make the phone call.

"Do you have your ID stating your address with you?" the man on the other line asked.

"No. I told you I lost my purse with my house keys in it."

"Is it your house, ma'am?" he asked, sounding frustrated.

"Yes. Why would someone call you if it wasn't their house?"

"Oh, you'd be surprised, ma'am."

"Well, forget I asked that. Anyway, what do I need to do to get you to let me in my house?"

"Do you have a utility bill or a phone bill addressed to you at that address?"

"The mail is on the inside. Stop asking so many questions. I'm in a hurry, and I've got to be somewhere. Look . . . I'll tip you."

The man sighed then asked one other question. "Can your neighbors verify you live there?"

I looked around and saw Ms. Willis's old, nosy ass peeping at me through her curtain. "Yeah. I see one of my neighbors now. She'll be happy to come out to verify I live here."

"Okay. I'm on my way."

I hung up the phone then walked across the street. Ms. Willis closed her curtain then opened her front door. She stepped out onto the porch, pulling her housecoat together, tightly at the neck and in the middle. I walked up on her porch, carrying Princess.

"Ms. Willis, how are you today?"

"I'm fine. Is there a problem over yonder?" she asked, pointing.

"No, ma'am. I mean . . . I seem to have locked myself out."

"Oh, my," the old woman said.

"Well, I think I'm going to be okay. The locksmith is on his way, but he says he needs for a neighbor to verify that I live there before he can open the door for me. Do you mind speaking to him when he comes?"

"Of course not. I don't mind at all."

"Thank you, Ms. Willis. I'm going to head back over and sit in my car. I'll direct him over when he gets here."

"Okay, baby. I'll keep an eye out for him, too."

I started back across the street to my car. *Poor woman, I* thought. *Colby is going to blow a gasket when he finds out she had something to do with me being able to get into his house.* I was ready and a bit nervous about going inside because there could possibly be another obstacle in my way. Cole said he would change the locks, but he never mentioned changing the alarm code.

I began to rehearse in my mind my movements once I was in the house. I needed to be swift, so I could get in and out before the police came in case I wouldn't be able to shut off the alarm. As I continued to calculate what I needed to do, I noticed a white van and two police cars pulling up behind me. *Oh, shit, I* thought.

I got out of my car, playing as cool as possible. A man got out of the van then started toward me. I nervously rubbed Princess's coat as he approached. "Are you Karma Jolley?" he asked.

I was afraid to answer, but I took my chances. "Yes," I responded. "Are you the locksmith?"

"Yes, I am."

My fear turned into anger. "You called the police on me?" I snapped.

"It was for both your safety and mine, ma'am. Where's your neighbor who can identify you?"

I looked around him and noticed Ms. Willis heading across the street. The policemen got out of their cars and met her before she could get all the way to the sidewalk. I could see her pointing and bobbing toward me. The policemen nodded then turned to give the locksmith the okay to open the door for me. *Whew! That was close.* I waved at Ms. Willis and thanked her just before she started back to her house.

The policemen got into their cars and left. It didn't take the man long to open the door. I ran inside to shut off the alarm, and to my surprise, it hadn't been changed. I went back to close the front door and found the locksmith still standing there.

"Oh . . . I need to pay you, right?"

"That would help," he said, laughing, causing his belly to move up and down like Santa Claus.

I went into my pocket to get his fee. He rambled about how long he'd been in business for himself and how much money he made as if he could impress me. I put the money into his hand, thanked him then opened the door.

"I could make you another set of keys for the low-low," he said as he made his exit.

"No. I'm sure you have a great price, but that's okay. I have keys upstairs. Thank you though."

I shut the door in his face then went about my business. I went upstairs to my old room then searched all over the house for anything belonging to me that I might've wanted to take with me. I found nothing incriminating or of any value. Just when I started out the door, Princess began to act silly again. She backed up and barked at me every time I reached for her.

"Oh, so you wanna stay here, huh?" She just looked at me. "You wanna chose someone else over me, too. Is that how it's gonna be, Princess?" She barked at me. "Well, in that case, I'm just gonna give Cole some of his payback right here."

I reached down and caught her just before she could dart off. She began barking loudly, but that didn't stop my rage. I snapped her neck with one twist, instantly shutting her up. I threw her lifeless body down on the hardwood floor near the living room then went into the kitchen. I wasn't done with Princess yet. I wanted Cole to be shocked and even more upset than he'd made me when he snatched his project from me.

I took care of business then started toward the door. I turned around to look at my creation. I was tickled pink. I couldn't help but laugh. *Cole, you can't deny that this is a work of art—simply a masterpiece.*

*A*n hour after we'd come back from lunch, Audrie barged into my office in a panic. "Cole, we can't find him."

"Huh?"

"Nick. He's missing. Luther says he's not answering his cell or his home phone."

"I imagine neither is Karma, right?"

"Luther says he only had Karma's cell number, and you're right. She's not answering either. Cole, I'm worried. What if Karma has done something stupid?"

"Let's not think like that, Audrie." I was worried, too, but since Audrie looked as if she was about to pass out, I tried to play confident that everything was alright.

"But it's not like Nick to just not show for work. And you said yourself how crazy Karma is."

"C'mere," I said, beckoning her to me. I pulled her down on my lap. "I know what I said, baby, but we're going to be optimistic about this situation, okay? Nick is fine. He's probably had a late night with Karma, and now they're both tired."

"Cole, it's after one o'clock—"

"Optimistic, Audrie. We're not going to think the worst, remember?"

She nodded then placed her arms tightly around my neck. "I love you, Cole. I don't know what I'd do without you."

"Love you, too, sweetie. Everything will turn out fine. In the meantime, let's just focus on completing the Best Tronics account so I can get paid and take you on a fabulous vacation. How about that?" I asked, kissing her on the cheek.

Truth was, I wasn't convinced everything was alright. Nick hadn't answered any of my calls either—not like him at all. I couldn't wait for the day to end, so I could run by his house to check on him. I prayed he'd be there.

Audrie and I finished up the day without another word about Nick. The project was complete and on Luther's desk by four o'clock. Audrie said she was heading home and asked me to give her a shout if I heard from Nick. I agreed that I would then left the office to get the children. Since having to fire Karma, Audrie had been helpful with picking up the children on the days I had to work late.

After picking up Shawna and Gavin, I took a detour over to Nick's house. His place appeared quiet and untouched, but the most disturbing thing for me was that his car wasn't in the driveway. I tried his cell phone only to get his voice mail once again. I began to feel sick. *Nick, where are you?*

The children were in the backseat, singing and talking, basically racking my nerves when normally they wouldn't be. "Please, kids. Quiet. Daddy's not feeling well," I said to them.

"What's wrong, Daddy?" Shawna asked.

"I'm . . . I'm just not having a good day, honey. Do me a favor and try to hold down the noise, okay?"

"Okay," she answered. Gavin agreed also.

I drove over to Audrie's and blew the horn as I pulled up. She peeped out and saw me getting out of the car. She came outside. "What's going on?" she asked.

"I need a favor."

"Okay. What is it? You don't look so good."

"Audrie, to tell the truth, I haven't felt like this since nearly this time last year."

"When Glenda was killed?" She sounded sympathetic.

I nodded. "I can't explain the feeling, but it's not something I care to have happening with me. I'm going over to Karma's to see if I see Nick's car."

Audrie gasped and grabbed my arm. "Baby, please don't go over there."

"I just have to know if his car is there, Audrie. Something's telling me things aren't right."

She sighed. "Okay. So, what do you need from me?"

"I need you to come over and watch the kids while I drive over there. I think the kids will be more comfortable with doing their schoolwork at home." I placed my hand on her shoulder. "I promise not to go into Karma's place without the authorities if I sense danger, okay?"

"Cole, I don't like this, but okay. I'll keep the kids. You want me to drive over?"

"No, you can ride with us."

Audrie ran back into her place to get her purse and lock up. When she got into the car, I explained to the children that she would only be sitting with them for a little while. They seemed fine with it. They had seen Audrie enough times to be comfortable with her.

I pulled into the driveway then helped the kids out of the car. After unlocking the door, I noticed the alarm didn't buzz. I turned around to look at Audrie.

"What?" she asked.

"The alarm isn't buzzing. I must've forgotten to set it before I left this morning."

I allowed Audrie and the kids to go inside ahead of me. Shawna did her usual thing—drop everything in the middle of the floor to head for the kitchen, looking for a snack. Every evening they'd act as if they were starving and couldn't wait for dinner.

250

Audrie took Gavin by the hand and went behind Shawna. I bent over to pick up Shawna's backpack then I was startled by loud shrills. Shawna, Audrie, and Gavin were all screaming.

I ran to see what was going on. By then, Audrie had the children's hands and was backing up. They were all still screaming. I went around her and stumbled upon Princess in the middle of a pool of blood, gutted inside out with her head nearly severed. I turned around and looked at how terrified my children were as they clutched each of Audrie's legs. They were screaming, uncontrollably and Audrie couldn't seem to move. She was frozen in place with a steady flow of tears streaming down her face.

I couldn't help it. A tear fell from my eyes. "I'm so sorry you all had to see this," I said, backing them up. "Audrie, please. Take them upstairs while I call the police."

Audrie turned then inched toward the stairs with the hysterical children attached to her legs. I turned back and looked at Princess again, shaking my head. "God," I screamed, "in front of my children? What kind of person is she?"

I called the police from my cell phone. As I sat on the steps waiting for them to come, I could hear my wailing children upstairs. I felt like I had failed to protect them once again. I couldn't understand why so many traumas had entered my life in one year. I didn't deserve to lose my wife, and I didn't deserve a nutcase like Karma to come into the picture. The woman was evil for whatever reason, but I just didn't pick up on it from the beginning.

The police were at my door sooner than I expected. When I opened the door, they jumped, questioning the foul odor, which I didn't notice upon my entrance. I had so much on my mind that I just didn't have a sense of reality. I took them to Princess. One of them took out a handkerchief and covered his nose. The other immediately walked away, stating over his shoulder he was going to the car for a camera.

Several pictures were taken before they finally raked up Princess's remains. The police found a note from Karma stating, TO THE PATTERSON FAMILY . . . YOU WANTED HER, SO YOU CAN HAVE HER . . . FROM KARMA WITH LOVE. The police questioned Karma's connection to my family and how she'd entered the house. I had no idea, but I encouraged them to speak with my neighbor across the street because I knew Ms. Willis didn't miss much.

The children had finally quieted down. Audrie came over and sat next to me when I was sitting on the steps waiting for the police to come back and let me know what Ms. Willis had to say. I stared at the stairs, unable to speak.

"You're blaming yourself again, aren't you?" Audrie said, rubbing my back. I kept looking at the stairs. "The children don't blame you for anything, Cole. They don't quite know why we stumbled upon Princess that way, but I can tell they know you didn't have anything to do with it."

"Those are my babies, Audrie," I whispered with a shaking voice. "How am I supposed to explain what Karma did? I'm going to have to take those kids back to counseling all over again."

"If that's what needs to be done, Cole, then so be it. Your children are going to be fine, and so are you." She continued to rub my back.

A policeman stepped back into the house. "Mr. Patterson," he called.

"Over here, officer." I waved at him then got up to meet him at the door.

"Mr. Patterson, your neighbor Ms. Willis says she thought Karma still lived here. Apparently Karma called a locksmith to let her in, and Ms. Willis was the person who verified her residency."

I threw my head back. "I can't believe so much bad shit keeps happening," I said.

"Did you change your alarm code and password?" the officer asked.

I shook my head. "I didn't think I needed to because the locks were replaced. Stupid . . . stupid . . . stupid me," I yelled. Audrie grabbed my hand. "It's done, Cole. Just call up and have the codes altered right now. Call a locksmith back over to change the locks again, too."

I nodded then turned to the policeman. "I still need your help, sir." The man looked at me intently. "I have a friend who's missing. He didn't show up for work. He's been dating this woman for the last few weeks."

"You mean this Karma woman?"

"Yes, sir, and I'm afraid something terrible has happened to him. I know where she lives. Could I get you all to follow me over to see if his car is there?"

"Sure. Just let me call this in. If she's there, we'll arrest her, too."

"Thank you. Thank you so much."

The officer got on his radio. I looked at Audrie. She grabbed my hand then squeezed it. "I'll clean up the mess while you're gone," she said.

"Oh, Audrie, I hate for you to have to do that. Let me take you and the kids over to your place. I don't know if you should stay here until I get the locks replaced."

"Don't worry about it. The kids are watching television. I'm just going to clean up the remaining mess then fix them something to eat. We'll be fine. Karma's not that big of a fool to come back here this evening, Cole."

I stared at Audrie, trying to convince myself she was right. "Okay," I finally answered then kissed her lips.

The officer told me he and one other patrol car would follow me to Karma's place. I met Ms. Willis coming up my driveway. She was very apologetic, but I assured her it wasn't her fault and that I wasn't angry with her. She headed back home then I got in my car and drove over to Karma's apartment.

My heart sank when I saw Nick's car parked outside while Karma's was absent. I got out of my car, pointing at Karma's door. The officers got out of their cars then started toward me.

"Do you see your friend's car?" one of them asked.

Again, I pointed. "Right there, but I don't see Karma's car."

He nodded then instructed the other officers to follow him to Karma's door. They knocked several times then stepped over to speak to me.

"How long did you say your friend has been missing?" one of the officers asked.

"Two days," I lied. I knew they would only walk away if I told the truth. "We work together, and he hasn't reported to work or anything."

They stepped away from me to converse a bit then I noticed them heading toward the leasing office. I waited in my car for nearly ten minutes before they returned with a man wearing a maintenance uniform. He walked up to Karma's door, unlocked it then stepped back to let the officers in.

Five minutes later, an officer stepped outside, holding his stomach as he spoke into his radio. He paced in front of Karma's window. I got out of my car to see if I could hear what he was saying, but I couldn't. I started toward him, but he held up his hand, stopping me. That's when I knew my worst fears would be confirmed.

"He's in there, isn't he?" I asked.

"There is a crime scene in there, so I can't let you go in."

I darted past the officer anyway. He caught me in the living room. "Sir, you've got to come out of here," he said, holding me around my waist.

"Let me go. I wanna see if it's Nick. I just want to see if it's him."

The other two officers came out of the bedroom. "We can't let you go in there, but you can help us with a description of your friend."

I stopped fighting and stood still. "He's tall, thin, about my complexion, low haircut—"

My train of thought was interrupted when the two officers who'd been in the room looked at each other. They looked back at me. "Sorry, Mr. Patterson, but we're pretty sure the deceased man in that room is your friend," one of them said.

My heart fell—again. "What did she do to him?"

The same officer spoke up. "It's difficult to talk about at this time. We'll get you all the information you want soon. In the meantime, do you have contact information for relatives of the deceased?"

I stared off into space. I couldn't land back into reality, nor did I want to. One of the officers began shaking me. I came out of my trance then offered them Luther's cell phone number. I figured he'd be able to give them emergency contact numbers.

I started out of the apartment, but stopped when I stepped on a newspaper clipping that had obviously been dropped as Karma was on her way out. I kneeled to pick it up. It headlined, PATTERSON FUNERAL TOPS 1000. I took a closer look at the large photo and noticed the procession of family and friends entering the church. Then, I couldn't believe my eyes. There was a close-up of the mysterious woman dressed in black with the big, floppy hat in the middle of the line. I recognized the black dress from Karma's closet, and although the picture of the woman was a side profile, her jaw-line and silhouette clearly depicted Karma.

My hands began to shake. *This bitch killed my wife. She killed my wife!*

*A*fter leaving Cole's house, I drove over to Dixie Homes to look for Boo-bay and Hercules. Once again, I needed their help. I asked them to find me someone who would be willing to charge a hotel room and a rental car for me on their credit card and let me give them the cash. I didn't want my whereabouts to be traced. Boo-bay and Hercules only made ten dollars each for their services because they didn't have to do much. I assured them there was a bigger payday coming.

I checked into my hotel room then cut my hair as low as I could. I used water and lotion to slick it down on my head. I changed into the baggy male clothes I'd bought then put on a cap. I was sure that if anyone noticed me to be a girl, they'd think I was butch because I didn't put on makeup or carry a purse, and I changed my walk into a more masculine one.

I decided to drive past my apartment to see if there was any commotion going on. There were police cars and people every-where. I saw Cole's car pulling out of the parking lot, so I trailed him. He drove home. When I saw that bitch Audrie opening the door for him, I was pissed. She reached to hug him. They stood in the doorway hugging for a while then went inside the house. I drove away because I knew it wouldn't be long before Ms. Willis came to her window.

I was certain Cole thought I had a key to his place and would be changing his locks again soon. That would leave me out in the cold. I needed to speak to him. I had retrieved his new numbers from Nick's cell phone a couple of weeks before, but I decided to wait until the best time to use them. There was no better time than now. I needed Cole. I don't know why he couldn't see that. I pulled over to a payphone then dialed his home number first. The phone rang several times, and I began to fear he wasn't going to answer since he didn't recognize the number. Just when the answering machine should've picked up, I heard Cole's voice, live and in color.

"Hello," he answered.

I almost lost my confidence to speak, but I collected myself after he repeated his hello. "Cole, it's me. Please don't hang up."

At first there was silence. "You're in a lot of trouble, Karma."

"I know. That's why I'm calling. I need your help."

"Oh, you need some help alright, but I'm not the one to give it to you. Remember Patsy from Costa Rica?"

"No, but I do remember Patsy from Humboldt, Tennessee," I said, getting smart.

"Well, I just got off the phone with her, and now I know more about you than I care to know, Karma. You're a murderer. You killed your parents, tried to kill Patsy and my son—"

"Now hold on. I just wanted your attention. I knew Gavin wouldn't die."

"Oh, believe me . . . you've got my attention now. I've already reported everything I've learned about you to the police, and after what you did to Nick, you shouldn't even be calling me right now."

"I need you, Cole. You've always known I needed you."

"I don't want to talk about that. Karma, my friend is lying dead in your apartment. Why did you do it?"

I wasn't sure if I should answer him. I feared he could be recording our conversation. "Nick's dead?" I threw on an innocent tone.

"I'm going to hang up if you're going to play games, Karma." I sighed into the phone. "Is your girlfriend near you?"

Cole paused before answering. "No. Why?"

"Because I don't want her in on our conversation."

"She's upstairs with the kids," he said, still unable to tell a convincing lie. "Answer my question, Karma. Why did you kill Nick?"

"He was in my apartment, wasn't he?"

"Why did you do it? Did it have something to do with me setting him up to come over there, Karma?"

"Why do you keep calling my name like that? Are you recording me or something?"

"No. I just want to know what happened to Nick."

I wasn't ready for Cole to hang up, so I decided to tell him what he wanted to know. "What happened to Nick was unfortunate."

"Would you just tell me?"

"He went snooping around my apartment while I was in the shower. I'd warned him about that before."

"What did he find?"

"Nothing," I answered shortly.

"It had to be something. You killed him for something."

"I didn't mean to kill him. He grabbed my arm, and I hit him with my boot out of reflex." There was silence between us. "Do you forgive me, Cole? I still love you. I can't help it."

"Why did you have Glenda killed?"

I couldn't believe he was asking me that question. I could tell Cole had been busy discovering what I was all about. The only thing I hoped was that he could understand how much I loved him. My silence made him very angry.

"Answer me, damnit," he yelled. "After all you've put me through, the least you can do is give me an explanation."

I cleared my throat. "I don't know where you could've heard that."

"You did it, Karma. Let's not play any more games, okay? I just wanna know why."

I let the phone rest by my side as I took a few deep breaths. I could hear Cole calling me. I put the phone back to my ear. "I'm here."

"What did my wife ever do to you? She was a good woman. . . a great mother . . . and a wonderful wife. What did she ever do to you?"

"She had my man and my family," I yelled. "I'd seen you a few times before in Swig's. You were so professional and poised during your business meetings. I couldn't help my attraction for you. The only thing stopping me from approaching you was your wedding band, so I tried to create some drama between you and Glenda with the prank phone calls. When that didn't run her ass out, I got impatient. I needed you, Cole. I could look at you and tell there was no other man for me. I still need you."

I could hear Cole taking deep breaths. "You had my wife murdered . . . the mother of my children . . . because you wanted me—a stranger whom you'd only seen in the distance?"

"It must've been God telling me we should—"

"Now I believe what the authorities just told me about your mental disorder and your stay in the ward. I'll do my best to forgive you, but you need to turn yourself in for your own good. Not only am I suffering, but my children are hurting because of your psychotic foolishness."

"Other people can call me crazy, Cole, but I don't like it when you do it. I love you, and what you really need to do is make things work between us. Glenda was killed so we could be together. We can't let her death be in vain."

"Fuck you, Karma. Do you hear me? Fuck you and the banana tree you fell off!"

Cole hung up on me. After several failed tries of getting him to pick up the phone again, I headed back to my hotel room crushed. I couldn't focus. Cole needed to come around and see things my way. I did everything possible to prove I was suited to be his wife.

I pondered my next move for getting Cole back into my life. I ordered room service then watched the news. My apartment door seemed to be on every station until I flipped to the cable channels. Just as I had expected, my name was all over the television. I knew it was a smart move to have someone else rent me a room and a car. Thanks to Cole's abortion check, I would be okay for a brief minute, until I figured out some other way to get money.

After finishing up my dinner, I'd had enough of trying to be good. I decided I should try calling Cole again. It was around eight o'clock that night. I went to a different payphone then dialed his cell number. He picked up after three rings.

"Hello," he answered.

"Cole, it's Karma . . . and don't hang up," I rambled. "I need for you to listen." When he didn't say anything, I thought he had hung up. "Hello?"

"What do you want, Karma?" he asked abruptly.

"I . . . I . . . wanna say I'm sorry."

"Oh yeah? Well, tell it to the judge before he sentences you. Your ass is going to jail this time, Karma. I'm going to see to it. You can't mess with people's lives the way you have mine. You snatched my life right from under me when you killed Glenda."

"I wish you wouldn't say that. I didn't kill her. I never pulled a trigger."

"You might as well have. You're still guilty of murder, and I'm going to see that you pay."

"Cole, don't you think you're being oversensitive here? You've moved on since Glenda. You didn't seem to have any problems poking in and out of Audrie and me. You weren't thinking of poor little Glenda then, were you? The bitch is dead . . . where she needs to be. Get over it, and let me back in, Cole!"

Cole hung up on me. I tried to reach him again, but he wouldn't answer me. Furious, I drove over to his house in record time. I sped into the driveway, barely missing his car when I came to a stop. I jumped out then began pounding on the door. I saw someone spy through the peephole, but the door didn't open. I pounded on the door again and again. Cole flung the door open then began yelling at me.

"Karma, I will seriously hurt you," he said with Audrie mean-mugging me from behind him. "My children are in here, and they're terrified. I've already called the police, but if you beat on my door one more time, I won't need them to get rid of your ass. I've got a good mind to put you out of your misery right now."

He slammed the door in my face. I went down to the edge of the yard then picked up one of the large rocks that lined the grass. I found the heaviest one then walked back toward the house and swung it through the front window like I was the legendary baseball pitcher, Satchel Paige. The glass crashed with such a force that I even frightened myself.

I darted to my car, cranked it up then backed out the drive-way. By the time I put the car in drive, I noticed Cole jumping into his car. I figured he was coming behind me, so I stepped on the gas.

I drove about ninety miles per hour and even ran red lights, but Cole was fast on me. When I stared into my rearview mirror to see how close he was, I could see he was on his cell phone. I didn't know if he was talking with Audrie or to the police. Either way, I didn't intend on stopping or letting him catch me. I gave the road my attention and floored it even more.

Seconds after placing my eyes back on the road, my car hit the tail of a sports utility vehicle when I ran a red light. My car spun out of control, sending me into the brick wall of a Payless Shoe Source.

The impact was fierce as the airbag exploded into my face and chest. My mind said to get out of the car and run—run for dear life because surrender was not a part of my vocabulary—but

I was too weak to move a muscle. I fought hard to catch my breath. Then a feeling of claustrophobia began to take over me. I wanted to get out of the car badly.

I looked through the driver side window and noticed Cole running up toward the car with several panicked-looking people behind him. He opened my door and called my name twice. The best I could do was to answer him in my mind. I couldn't seem to make my lips move, then I could feel myself gradually losing consciousness as I watched Cole continue to try to speak to me. His words and face soon faded.

I'm not going back to the mental hospital. I've got to fight. I just can't go back—

Epilogue

One year later

The minute I stepped back into the house from getting the mail, Audrie, my new wife of six months, grabbed half of it then went to the kitchen table and began sorting it. I sat down at the table with her, moping and acting on the depression that wouldn't seem to go away. Audrie took notice then set all of the mail aside. "What's wrong, baby? I'm doing everything I can to keep you happy and preoccupied, but I suppose I'm not doing a good job, huh?"

"It's not you, Audrie. You know that. It's that time of year. I know I should be happy that I'm alive and around for my family. I'm really trying. I failed to cherish Glenda. She made me and the kids her world, but I'm not sure that I gave her enough love. I'm blessed to have you as my new wife, and I just don't want to make the same mistakes I did with Glenda."

"But, baby, I can see you're trying. I know you're still hurt about Glenda—that's to be expected. I get sad and depressed every year in June because that's the month my father died, and not to mention Father's Day is in that month. Still, I try to think on the things I have around me, and baby, we have a lot to be grateful for. Do you agree?"

I nodded, but the ill feeling in the pit of my stomach wouldn't settle. "I've been trying, Audrie. I don't want you to think you're bringing me down because you're not."

"Then what is it, Cole? When Karma got out of the hospital last year, she was sentenced straight to the mental institution where she should be, and she won't be bothering us for years to come. Hopefully she'll be on medication and have a little bit of sense by then, too."

I shook my head. "Something's not right, Audrie," I responded.

Audrie's expression let me know I'd caused her stomach to turn. "Cole, I hate it when you say that because you're always right. Why are you saying that?"

"I can't put my finger on it. Maybe you're right. Maybe subconsciously my mind is taking me back to the period when Glenda was killed. Don't worry about me. I'll shake it."

Audrie leaned over to kiss me. We gave each other two short pecks then smiled at each other. I loved Audrie dearly, and I knew she loved me, too. She had several qualities like Glenda, including making me and the children her world after all of the drama ceased. She could liberally do so considering Karma and the two men she conspired with to kill Glenda were all locked up. Karma was given leniency for giving up the names and whereabouts of her accomplices, and I was cleared of all allegations of having something to do with Glenda's murder. Audrie and I were free to live our lives happily ever after.

I took a few of the letters from Audrie then began opening them. Audrie continued reading mail as well.

"Cole, this looks like some type of card or an invitation to something," she said, holding up a pink, square envelope. "You think Shawna is being invited to a party or something?"

"Probably. Set it aside for last. We need to find out which bills came in already so we can prioritize the payments."

"Okay," she replied, sliding the envelope aside.

After about five minutes of reading mail and jotting down bills, I came across a letter from the mental institution that housed Karma Jolley.

"What the—" I said, cutting myself off as I read the letter. In my peripheral, I could see Audrie look up at me. She questioned my confused expression. "Is everything okay?" she asked. When I looked at her, she reached for the last piece of mail—the pink envelope and began to tear it opened. "What's that you're reading, baby?" she asked me.

I didn't immediately respond because I redirected my attention to the letter. My eyes were fixated on various words, which stated COURT APPEARANCE TO PROVE POSSIBLE PATERNITY.

Though I was speechless, I looked up at Audrie again. She had pulled out a card from the pink envelope and held it close to her face. I could see the front of it stated CONGRATULATIONS! IT'S A GIRL! As soon as she lowered the card, her eyes were bucked.

"Cole," Audrie screamed, handing me the card. My eyes bucked as well. "I thought you said she had an abortion."

I felt a lump in my throat and a churn in my stomach. "That's what Karma told me, Audrie."

She handed me the card which held a picture of a gorgeous, chocolate-colored, curly-haired infant, approximately three months old. Karma had signed the card, with love, Karma and colbya. I took a closer look at the baby and realized that even as an infant, she bore a strong resemblance to me, having eyes and a mouth like mine.

Lawd, naw! This can't be happening. Noooooo.

265

Discussion Questions

1. What did you think of Karma Jolley in the beginning? Did your feelings toward her ever change throughout the story? Why or why not?

2. How realistic or common do you feel Karma's situation with Melvin Jolley can be?

3. What did you think of Colby (Cole) Patterson in the beginning? Did your thoughts of him ever change? Why or Why not?

4. Did Colby grieve too much or not enough for Glenda before getting involved with another woman?

5. At what point did you guess why Glenda was killed and who all had involvement?

6. Which of Karma's actions were to the extreme or done out of desperation?

7. Was Nick a true friend? Why or why not?

8. Was Audrie crazy for sticking by Cole through the aggravating times?

9. What were some of Cole's biggest mistakes and what should he have done differently to protect his family?

10. Was the ending surprising and/or justified?

About the Author

Playwright, Screenwriter, and National Bestselling Novelist, Alisha Yvonne is a native Memphian. She is the Essence ® Bestselling Author of *Lovin' You Is Wrong* and *I Don't Wanna Be Right*. She is also nationally known for *Naughty Girls* and having contributed to the bestseller, *Around the Way Girls-3*.

Alisha continues to be prolific as she ventures into the nonfiction and young adult arenas. She is currently working on her next book.

Visit Alisha online at <u>www.alishayvonneonline.com</u> or email to: <u>alisha@ebonyliterarygrace.com</u>